THE PRODIGAL ONES

The One Who Shot Away

JOANNA ALONZO

Published by: Hineni Publishing
Cover Designer: Joanna Alonzo

CONTENTS

THE ONE WHO NEEDS TO THANK SOME PEOPLE

Thank you to Ikule, Lynn, and Joy for the friendship and encouragement. You give me courage.

Thank you to Nhof, Kurin, and Anne for being my Miraculous May sisters.

Thanks to this book's beta readers for their invaluable feedback:
Kelly, Christyle, Rachel, Anna, Kristi, Deborah, Sheelah, and Angela.

Thanks to the One Who keeps giving me another shot and refuses to write me off completely.

△.F.T.L.

To the ones who have
ever carried the burden
of second-guessing their identity,
may You be everything God
intended for you to be.
And remember: you can be light.

THE ONE WHO IS GIVING YOU A WARNING

[POSSIBLE SPOILER: READ WITH CAUTION]

I often refer to myself as an author who writes Christian Fiction with grit, grace, and wonder. This collection of books, in particular, has been described by multiple readers as both gritty and full of grace. That should be expected, I presume, given the title of the collection — *The Prodigal Ones* — because the parable of *The Prodigal Son* is definitely one of grit and of grace.

When I set out to write *The Prodigal Ones*, I wanted to address real-life struggles and challenges encountered by people who grow up in church. I couldn't possibly write this collection of books without exploring — even in some minor way — one of the most prevalent issues we encounter as Christians in this day and age: gender identity and same-sex attraction.

I struggled for quite some time on whether or not to include this subplot, but I cannot in good conscience write this collection without including a topic so relevant.

The story of Rachel is by no means an exhaustive look into LGBTQ+ issues; in fact, her struggle barely grazes the subject. Her story, however, draws from a lot of my own experiences — both being around women who have struggled with this and having briefly experienced same-sex attraction myself.

I will share a bit of my testimony at the end of this book, but for now, let this short note serve as a warning that as joyous as I would like to keep this story, it has a subplot that includes same-sex attraction.

It also has a subplot including drug use/abuse/addiction, which has already been touched upon in a previous book, *The One Who Danced Away*.

I can only pray that you find God's grace, hope, and love weaved within the pages of this book and in the story of Jeremy and Rachel. If you choose to bow out and read something lighter, however, I can not fault you for that.

Whether you continue reading or decide to back out, may you continue to be blessed!

Shalom and Mabuhay,

joanna alonzo

T H E **O** N E
W H O **S** H O T
△ W A Y

This is a story
    about leaving comfort zones
    and trying to be courageous.
About facing unknowns
    and braving the dangerous.
About embracing the different
    and loving the audacious.
About dying to self
    and serving the rebellious.

This is the story
    of the rebel and the righteous,
Jeremy and Princess Rachel,
    who, while growing up, never imagined,
    they would reach the ends of the earth,
    and there, learn to love each other.

part one

PRESENT DAY

CIRCA
LATE 2010'S

one

THE ONE
WHO SHOULD
HURRY

Neither the turbulence nor the bumpy landing was to blame for Jeremy Sinclair's hankering to get out of the plane. Even before the seatbelt sign turned off, Jeremy already took out his phone and turned off airplane mode. No signal, still. Neither mobile data nor Wi-Fi. Dead. Kind of like what would happen to Jeremy should he show up late for the wedding he should have been around to plan. He was, after all, the best man, though he wasn't feeling particularly best at anything, at the moment.

Why was this plane meandering along the tarmac like it had all the time in the world? Jeremy sure didn't.

He grunted as he ground the back of his teeth. He then quirked his jaw to the side. Speaking of teeth, he needed to squeeze a dentist appointment into his schedule before flying back out of the country a week from then. He scrolled through his contacts for his dentist's name. He stopped and rolled his eyes. Right. There was no signal. And what was he doing making a dentist's appointment when he should be laser-focused on getting to his best friend's wedding to no other than their friendly childhood dinosaur, Jenna Marquez?

Despite his building impatience, Jeremy smiled. Max was marrying Jenna! He had seen it coming way before everyone else had — even before Max!

Jeremy should be a matchmaker. The world would be a better place. More romantic.

After breaking up with Rachel Petersen, Max had eyes only for Jenna, even if he had insisted multiple times that she had been just a friend. Jeremy had tried his best not to roll his eyes at Max's denial when it came to his attraction to Jenna. Then again, could Jeremy blame his best friend? Rachel was his ex, and her looks proved to be a worthy distraction to many a man. Now, she was their maid-of-honor. How ironic.

Not as ironic was how much trouble Jeremy had gotten himself into when he had agreed to be their best man. It made sense for him to be the best man. He and Max had been best friends since childhood, but the wedding had been on such short notice, he was perhaps the most absentee best man to ever exist on planet earth. Thank God Rachel had covered for him countless times by fulfilling not only her maid-of-honor responsibilities but also his best-man obligations. He needed to make it up to her and beg her for forgiveness, while hoping her mother wouldn't join in on the piling on him. After all, he did travel halfway across the world to get to this wedding. That counted for something, no?

Ugh. Jeremy stretched his neck to peek outside the window, which was an aisle and three seats away from where he sat — a middle seat in the center row of four seats, where it was impossible for him to see anything outside. The plane's digital clock up front ticked six o'clock. The wedding was at ten, and the venue was at least two and a half hours away. Why was this plane so slow?

He already owed Rachel a leg, an arm, and at least one postcard from every country he had been to and planned to go to in the future. Jeremy couldn't afford to be late on the day of the wedding. Rachel must be going nuts by now, not having heard from him since he had boarded the plane. After all, he had told her his plane would land at four o'clock, not six. Jeremy shrugged. Was it his fault he had already been on the plane and without a network connection when the captain had announced the delay?

The airplane slowed down, and the sign to remove their seatbelts turned on with a ding. Jeremy's brain raced to figure out a way to get out of there quickly, but he had gone through this process countless times before. There was simply no way to get out. Not until the woman to his left and the old couple to his right stood up to give him space to get his backpack out of the luggage compartment and get out of there. Neither of his seatmates were budging. In fact, the woman beside him was still snoring. How she could sleep through all that turbulence was worthy of Jeremy's envy and admiration. It was a talent he didn't have. Then again, he wouldn't want to sleep through most of life. No way. He preferred to keep his eyes wide open, so he wouldn't miss anything. Like the way this old man was looking at his wife — wide-eyed and almost mystified — as she listed down all the belongings they needed to check before deplaning.

"Where are my glasses? I can't find them, Cody. I've looked everywhere." She stirred next to Jeremy and spread her knees to check if she had dropped them on the floor. "What if I crushed them while we were sleeping?"

He stretched his neck to check the top of her head and brushed her silver hair, the corners of his eyes wrinkling as he chuckled. "Are you sure you didn't leave them on your head like you always do, Lena?"

"Don't be silly, Cody." A double chin formed as she bowed her head and rubbed her neck. "They're not hanging on me. I should have brought that other eyeglass leash. The one that doesn't make my neck itchy."

Jeremy started looking too. Might as well help the old woman. He stood up to better check their surroundings. Ah, there her glasses were. Out of the pocket of her beige cardigan, hanging on the arm rest between them, a pair of glasses peeked out. Jeremy frowned at the cardigan in disapproval, because all the lady's shimmying to try and get it off herself had woken him up in the middle of the night. He would have to catch up on sleep on the taxi ride to the venue. He cringed. That would be an expensive taxi ride! He shook his head. Whatever. It was Max's wedding today. All of this was worth it.

Jeremy gently tapped the old lady's shoulder. "Excuse me, Ma'am." Jeremy pointed at the glasses. "Is that what you're looking for?"

The old lady jolted at the sound of his voice and looked up at him as if it was the first time she realized he was even there. She then glanced at her cardigan and saw what she was looking for. "Oh! Wonderful! They're right here. Thank you, sweetheart."

"You're welcome." Jeremy sat back down.

"They're right in my cardigan's pocket, Cody. This young man found them."

"Good, good." Cody nodded in approval as he stroked his wife's back. "We wouldn't want you walking around the airport, bumping into things without those glasses of yours, Lena." He smiled at Jeremy. "Thank you for the help."

"No problem."

People were lining up in the aisle to disembark. Jeremy needed to get out of there and give Rachel a call lest the poor woman lose her mind. He wrinkled his nose at the woman who was still sleeping in the seat beside him. His bag was in the compartment on her side of the aisle. He scratched his head.

The old man grinned at his predicament and signaled for a flight attendant to approach. Once Cody had caught one attendant's attention, he pointed at the sleeping passenger. Unfortunately, the stewardess couldn't get to them, given all the passengers crowding the aisle.

Lena must have gotten impatient, because she reached across Jeremy and tapped the sleeping woman's shoulder. "Wake up, honey. It's time to go. This young man has places to go and shouldn't be stuck inside this flying tin can."

Jeremy laughed. "Flying tin can. I like that."

"Oh, that's what it is." Lena's brows met as this incredulous expression covered her face, like that's what airplanes should have been called in the first place — flying tin cans.

"Where are you off to?" Cody asked.

"My best friend is getting married," Jeremy said, even if in the back of his mind, something was demanding for him to get out of the plane and get himself to Max's wedding. That something was Rachel yelling at him — in that sweet way only she could pull off — to hurry up. Jeremy winced. "I'm the best man, and I'm running late."

"Oh!" Lena clapped her hands before shooting her husband an affectionate gaze. "Do you remember our wedding day, Cody?"

Cody smiled, his eyes glazing over, like a memory had somehow pulled him out of that moment. He then patted the back of his wife's hand. "It was a beautiful day, wasn't it, Lena?"

She nodded slowly.

Both their eyes moistened. The man's grip on the woman's hand tightened, and a bittersweet smile appeared on both their faces.

"I wouldn't trade a single day spent with you for anything, Lena," Cody said, his voice choked up.

Something about the scene unfolding in front of him told Jeremy this was a story he couldn't afford to miss, and the urge to find out more about Cody and Lena overpowered the voice of Rachel in his head, urging him to "Please, Jeremy. Please, please, please don't be late."

"God, help me," he whispered as he cleared his throat and extended his hand toward Cody. "I'm Jeremy Sinclair."

"Cody de Leon. This is my wife, Lena."

The woman who had been sleeping was now fully awake and attentive to what was going on around her. She was even giving Jeremy and the couple curious looks as she stood up to retrieve her bags. That meant Jeremy could make his way out of there now, but the world today rarely made couples like Cody and Lena anymore. Not in his generation, and something about the two reminded him so much of his own father and mother. Sam and Aida

Sinclair could have ended up this way if only— Jeremy choked up. It took him a moment to recover from the sudden bout of melancholy. He had to get it together. This was a beautiful day. No need to dwell on heart aches.

"Seeing you interact, I can't help but be curious about your story," Jeremy said to the couple. "I have what is called a vlog, which basically means I post videos online, usually about stories of people I discover in my travels. Do you mind sharing your story with me for one of my vlogs? Something tells me it's going to be interesting."

The couple's faces lit up.

"God really does hear our prayers, doesn't he, Cody?" Lena squeezed her husband's arm.

That was enough to confirm to Jeremy he had an interview and a prayer that God would somehow extend the time or take him to the wedding venue faster than was humanly possible. After leaving the plane, Jeremy spent an extra thirty minutes taking a video of Cody and Lena. As the old couple's story unfolded, Jeremy pushed away any regret or doubt over his decision to stop and take a moment to listen, because it would have been a shame to miss out on hearing about the powerful lives of Cody and Lena de Leon. By the time they finished, Jeremy had brand-new, possibly viral, content for his channel, an idea for his best man's speech, and a ton of missed calls from Rachel and whoever else. Mostly Rachel.

Jeremy definitely had a lot of making up to do, and he couldn't have been any more aware of this, as he rushed out of the airport, hoping that by some miracle, he would find a ride soon. He was about to pray for a helicopter to miraculously swoop in and take him to the wedding, but all he got instead was a familiar face waiting for him at the arrival area.

Knox Cartier was waiting outside the airport, leaning on the classic Ducati Jeremy used to drool all over as a teenager.

"Knox!" Jeremy jogged toward his friend to give him a bro hug. "What are you doing here?"

"Rachel begged my wife to send me here to fetch you, because one, Rachel is a hundred percent sure you'll find a way to be late."

Both men shrugged.

"Accurate." Jeremy nodded.

"Two, we'll get there faster by motorcycle."

"I can't believe you brought the Ducati!" Jeremy exclaimed as he secured his backpack on his shoulders. "Haven't seen this beauty in years!"

Knox grinned. "Thought you might appreciate me taking this baby out of hiding. I've been riding it lately just for nostalgia and to keep it travel-ready." He tossed Jeremy a helmet. "Get on."

"I'm so up for this." Jeremy secured the protective gear on his head before getting on the back of the motorcycle behind Knox.

Before driving off, Knox said, "Rachel says you owe her a lot more than one, and she plans to collect."

"You have no idea." Jeremy chuckled. He had no objections to owing Rachel anything. Whatever she asked for, he would have to give her, after how much she had covered for him in preparation for the wedding. He could worry about that later, though.

For now, Jeremy leaned back and drank in the exhilaration of the speed and the scenery, all the while wondering if he would ever find someone who would love him the way his mother loved his father, the way Lena loved Cody. What did it matter? Jeremy had love right where he was — it was alive and bustling all around him, and he longed to revel in every minute of God's extravagant love.

So, blessed by what he believed to be a divine encounter at the airport and relieved to be on the fastest possible way for him to get to his best friend's wedding, Jeremy enjoyed the motorcycle ride and trusted that, late or not, he would get to his best friend's wedding at just the right time.

two

THE ONE
WHO NEEDS
AN ESCAPE

This was no time to be late, and Jeremy Sinclair was undoubtedly the most inconsiderate person on earth for not bothering to call her to let her know where he was. Had his plane already even landed?

Rachel Petersen shut the door of the bridal room, where the photographer was taking a series of stylistic shots of Jenna. As maid-of-honor, Rachel should be inside, taking care of the bride, but no. Here she was, trying to track down the best man. She should have expected complications like this when she had taken on the role of being her best friend's de facto wedding planner, but who would have expected the best man to be this late?

Rachel took her phone out of her silken pink clutch with crystal studding. It was already nine, and she still hadn't heard from either Knox or Jeremy. She started calling Jeremy. No answer. Same with Knox.

What was with these men and a complete lack of communication? Guests were already filling the venue, and they still didn't have a best man! Max and Jenna should have hired a wedding planner for this. Rachel paced the carpeted floor as she widened her eyes at nothing. How could they hire a wedding planner? They got engaged less than three months ago! A professional wedding planner wouldn't take the job on without charging Max and Jenna a fortune they didn't have. Her poor friends. So, here she was, to the rescue, volunteering her time and services mostly because she didn't have anything better going on. She had brought this upon herself, all this stress she was experiencing over the absence of Jeremy Sinclair.

How was Jeremy even related to Pastor Sam, even more so to Mama Aida? The members of his family were upstanding models of society, but somehow, Jeremy managed to end up tardy, carefree, and infuriatingly inconsiderate! How?! She paused. Was she being too hard on the man? To be fair, Jeremy's niece, Lily Red, was supposed to be the flower girl, but would most likely not be able to make it in time. At least Serene had the decency to let them know days in advance! Why couldn't Jeremy be more like his sister?

Rachel hurried past the long hallway to get to the log-house-turned-hotel's lobby. She reached the elevator and gathered her wits about her as she checked her appearance in the mirror. She smiled. Not a hair out of place. Perfect.

If only the rest of the world was as orderly and responsible as she was and Jeremy's shenanigans weren't throwing every wrench variety into her perfectly planned wedding, this day would be perfect too. Rachel caught her own hubris and reprimanded herself for it, as the elevator dinged and its doors slid open. The first person that caught her eye was her mother entering the lobby from the back entrance. Mom must have entered the main resort building from the wedding venue. Out of pure panic reflex, Rachel stepped right back into the elevator and hit the close button multiple times in quick succession.

Thankfully, the elevator slid shut before Mom could catch sight of her. Rachel had enough to stress about without her mother scolding her for giving so much of her time to this wedding, but now what? Where should she go? She pressed the button back to the third floor and took in a deep breath. Again, she perused her reflection in the elevator mirror and smiled in approval. She was good at that. Smiling. "Never leave the house without a smile," her mother had told her many times while growing up, and it had served her well all these years. Her smile had always made people feel good about their day, about themselves. Why then couldn't it do the same for Rachel? What was it about today that was shaking her peace so much? Why did she have a lump in her throat and a weight in her chest? Was it really just Jeremy's tardiness? Was it the fact that she was planning to escape with him to the ends of the earth after this wedding? Or was it something deeper?

Rachel winced. The mere thought of her secret plan was making her feel guilty. Running off to the other side of the world with a male friend was not becoming of a good Christian girl, and that was what Rachel was. In fact, she wasn't just a good Christian girl. She was Connect Church's Little Miss Perfect!

The elevator dinged open once again, revealing an empty hallway. Rachel stepped into the carpeted floor, the soft thud of her heel somehow comforting her, as she pressed her palms down the blush pink, tulle-covered halter gown with white floral lace trimming cinching her dress around her waist. She stopped pacing to admire her dress. Simple, but elegant. What a blessing to Jenna to have her as a maid-of-honor. Rachel rolled her eyes at herself. She should stop congratulating herself and figure out where on earth the best man was. It was a wonder Max wasn't losing his mind over how his best friend hadn't shown up yet. Then again, Rachel had been doing a good job covering for Jeremy and pulling his share of the workload. What a blessing she was to Jeremy, as well!

She was about to call Jeremy again when the elevator door slid open and the chatter of women filled the hallway. Rachel immediately flashed her smile, bracing herself for whomever would appear.

"Rachel!" Hannah Cartier and her sister-in-law, Nova Grant, gave her some company.

Rachel forced a wider smile. "Hannah! Nova! You both look so beautiful!"

"So do you, sweetie!" Hannah hugged Rachel.

Nova was more reserved with the affection and brushed her palm up and down Rachel's arm to acknowledge her. "You look lovely, Rachel. As usual."

"Thank you." She straightened her dress, even if it didn't have a single wrinkle on it. "Where are the twins?"

"With my cousin. They're most likely on their phones." Nova rolled her eyes. "Pre-teens."

"I'm not so sure about them being hooked on their phones," Hannah said. "Last time I saw them, they were going somewhere with my kids. Nate mentioned something about wanting to see the waterfalls."

All the talk of their children and what their children were up to got completely lost on Rachel. She had her own kid to worry about: Jeremy.

"Have you heard from Knox?" Hannah asked. "He should be on the way back here by now."

Rachel shook her head. "I haven't, no."

"Oh dear. Let me give him a call." Hannah opened her purse to search for her phone.

"No need for that." Rachel took hold of Hannah's arm. "I'm sure they're already on their way here. Don't worry about it."

"I hope they get here on time." Hannah frowned. "The wedding is about to start."

"Whether they make it or not—" Rachel tried to suppress the worry and irritation from her tone; it was her job to keep everyone calm, after all "—Knox has done this wedding a huge favor."

"It's not a big deal, really. My husband will be happy to have any excuse to ride that motorcycle of his. Also, it's not as big a favor as the one you have given Max and Jenna, putting this wedding together, Rachel." Hannah raised a brow. "Don't think it has gone unnoticed."

"You did an amazing job, Rachel," Nova said. "Especially on such short notice, this is incredible. The only other couple I know who pulled off something like this was Knox and this lady here."

"Only reason we were able to pull it off was Knox's grandfather," Hannah said.

Nova nodded slowly. "It pays to marry into a rich family."

"Or to have a friend like Rachel." Hannah gushed as she took hold of Rachel's wrist. "Praise God for your talent at organizing events like this. I don't know what Max and Jenna would have done without you." She took pause. "Since Nova mentioned family, that reminds me. I bumped into your mother, right as we arrived. She's looking for you at the lobby."

Rachel squared her shoulders. The last thing she wanted was to talk to her mother, but Hannah and Nova didn't need to know that. "Yeah? I must excuse myself then." She pointed at the elevator behind her with her thumb. "Probably best if I go find her now."

"Go, go." Hannah waved her off, but Nova's stare lingered on her enough for Rachel to bristle and let out a sigh of relief the moment the elevator hid her from their view. Rachel needed to be careful around Nova, who was sharper than most when it came to observing people and seeing past their defenses. Besides, Rachel didn't want to end up as inspiration for a character in one of Nova's novels. Or maybe that wasn't so bad. Only if Nova would paint her as a hero and not a villain, of course.

Rachel reached the ground floor, exiting the elevator and walking into the open-space lobby. Thankfully, there was no sight of her mother. Unfortunately, there was no sight of Jeremy or Knox, either. Her phone buzzed inside her clutch. She pulled it out and almost jumped in victory upon seeing Jeremy's name on call register. He was starting to feel like one of her accomplishments. She answered before he could have any chance to drop the call. "Jeremy! Where are you? The wedding is starting in less than an hour. You're not even dressed yet, and I doubt you've already showered."

"Hello to you too, Rachel. My flight was fine, thank you very much."

"This is no time for jokes. Where are you? Are you with Knox?"

"Yeah, I am. Relax. We should be there in ten minutes. We just had to stop for gas. Thanks for sending him to get me. The motorcycle ride has been epic."

"I'm glad you're having a grand time, Jeremy, but your enjoyment is not the top priority right now."

"True, but it's always good to be thankful for the little, joyful things in life, Rachel."

His positivity was grating at her nerves. "How are you acting so chill right now? It's not normal, considering how late you are to your best friend's wedding. You should have already been here three weeks ago."

"You have a point, but we're here now. I can panic about being late or I can recognize what a beautiful morning this has been. Despite the rough landing and the delayed flight, my day started out awesome with this amazing story by the most adorable elderly couple ever and a ride on Knox's Ducati — again, thanks to you. I'm telling you, Rach, God can make any day beautiful, if you let Him. Also, I'm learning it helps to stay on your good side."

"What makes you think you're on my good side?"

"Faith." Jeremy chuckled. "I'm about to get on the motorcycle now. See you soon. Until then, inhale and exhale, chill, and find something beautiful to gaze at. Take a few seconds to appreciate the beauty you helped create."

"Spare me the motivational speech and get here, Jeremy." Rachel reached the doors leading outside to the main garden venue.

"I will! Max is marrying the dragon at your princess party! If that's not proof of miracles, I don't know what is."

Rachel laughed, said goodbye to Jeremy, hung up, and did exactly what he asked her to do. She paused and drank in the scene before her. Guests were already milling around the garden where they were holding the ceremony. Chatter filled the place as people enjoyed the hors d'œuvres at the refreshments table, while their church's worship team played an upbeat reggae tune. With a stunning natural waterfall as a backdrop and a variety of colorful hydrangeas lining the aisle, Rachel had to admit how right Jeremy was. This was beautiful.

Mingling with the crowd was the groom himself. Warmth spread over Rachel's chest at the sight of him. Max Owens would always hold a special place in her heart. He was, after all, her first boyfriend — the only one she had ever had so far. As happy as she was for him, a tinge of the heartbreak he had caused her when he had broken up with her still surfaced whenever she was around him. He had done her a favor by breaking up with her, of course, but still, there had been far too many times growing up, when she had dreamed of eventually becoming his wife. Max was a reminder that hard as she tried to follow after God with all her heart, she wasn't immune to mistakes. She wasn't quite as pristine as Little Miss Perfect should be.

Before she could dwell on her shortcomings too much, Rachel twirled the ends of her hair and marched confidently toward Max, who was standing alone, checking his watch, looking more than a little lost. He turned around to check the crowd as if looking for someone. Most likely Jeremy. Rachel huffed. Normal for the groom to be looking for his best man half an hour before the scheduled start of the wedding. Once she got close to him, she forced a grin and said, "You're marrying the dancing dragon. Can you believe it?"

Max turned around, and the huge beam he gave her made her heart ache. He brought her in for a hug. "Rachel, you make a lovely maid-of-honor." He took a step back to give her a good look.

Rachel blushed as she continued twirling the ends of her blonde hair before striking a pose. "I have to agree. Thanks for noticing, groom. I must say you're rather dashing, though slightly frazzled. Can't blame you. I would be nervous too if I were marrying a dragon."

Max squinted an eye and shook his head at her. "If I remember right, Jenna was a dinosaur."

"That's what she says!" Rachel threw her arms in the air and dropped them quickly, her shoulders sagging as she let out a practiced pout — the kind that still made her appear cute. "But she was definitely a dragon."

"We'll agree to disagree." Max chuckled.

Rachel found his amusement comforting. There really was something about Max that made people at ease around him. That's what made him a good youth pastor. He would make a great leader for their church someday. Rachel pushed the thought away. That topic was another thing she couldn't dwell on, because it brought with it too many concerns she could do nothing about.

Something caught Max's eye behind her, so Rachel turned to find out what or who he was looking at. Had Jeremy finally arrived? Either that or Jenna somehow emerged in her wedding gown when she should be chilling in her room, making sure she remained stunning for the big reveal. Speaking of which, Rachel was the maid-of-honor. She should be getting back to Jenna soon, not babysitting the groom and searching for the missing best man. A cool breeze caressed Rachel's skin. The fragrance of lavender, jasmine, and rose made her smile. She had really done a fantastic job with the setting. She should make a career out of this. Gah! Yet another thing in her life unsettled. How had her mind become a land mine of issues she shouldn't dwell on, because there was nothing she could do to control much of anything? She should just focus on the person in front of her and hopefully be of help, even when she couldn't help herself.

Not quite figuring out who or what had caught Max's eye, Rachel was about to tell him she needed to go see the bride, but Max wrung his fingers and took a deep breath like he was anxious about something.

"Relax, Max." Rachel waved a hand in the air. "If it helps, I'll agree that Jenna is a dinosaur."

"It's not that." Max shook his head while doing that thing with his lips where one side would curl up to signal his uncertainty or nervousness "Jeremy's not here yet."

"Don't worry." Rachel lowered her gaze and gave herself an inward pat on the back for being such a good person that she would still cover for Jeremy right up to the eleventh hour. "He will be." She should figure out where the absentee best man was and then do what she was actually supposed to do: check on Jenna. "I have to get back to the bride. I'm sure Jeremy is on his way." She gave Max a deadpan look before grabbing hold of his arms and shaking him. "I still can't believe it! You and Jenna are about to get married. It's crazy!" She forced another smile, collected herself, and waved Max goodbye before sauntering away.

Right as she got back inside the log cabin serving as the main entrance of the lake house resort, she let out a breath of relief when Jeremy emerged from upstairs wearing his best man suit. Nothing about him looked out of place. His brown hair was brushed back, sleek and kempt, his jaw was freshly shaved, and his tux looked perfect on him. Rachel drew a breath at how handsome he was. If only he didn't have that SLR camera hanging by its strap on his neck, he would've been the picture-perfect best man.

"Finally! What are you doing with a camera? You're the best man. We have a camera crew in charge of taking all the official wedding photos."

"Good morning to you too, Rachel." He bent his head to remove the camera strap from around his neck. "It's great to see you after all this time. You are stunning, as usual." He lifted his camera and pointed it at her.

Despite her building irritation with this man, Rachel paused and posed for the shot.

"Gorgeous!"

She opened her mouth to start scolding him, but he already had his hands in the air and a sincere expression of apology on his face.

He laid one hand over his chest, while the other dropped to his side, his camera secure in his grip. "I am so sorry, Rachel. I truly am. Like I've promised you—" he lifted his hand as if to swear an oath to her "—I'll do anything to make it up to you."

"Yeah, yeah." Rachel shrugged. What else could she do? "Just get to Max." She pointed back to the garden outside. "He's worried sick you won't show up. Go assure the man."

"You're the best, Rachel." He gave her a side hug and a peck on the forehead.

"I know I am."

Jeremy let go of her and headed for the glass doors.

"Jeremy." Rachel snapped her fingers to get his attention right as he was about to step outside. "Camera."

He frowned. This was the only time he had shown any sign of distress, like Rachel was punishing him for confiscating his camera.

"Come on. Give it. You'll get it back after the ceremony."

Jeremy dragged himself back to her and handed her the gadget.

"How long will you be around?" she asked.

"I leave for the Philippines in a week." He shrugged and winked at her, seemingly over losing his camera for a few hours. "I'll go see my best friend now." He didn't wait for her to say anything and just took off.

Meanwhile, his response to her question had left Rachel's head in a spin. Did he just say Philippines? All her preparations had been to get herself ready to go with him to China! That was where he had been for the past year. Why was he going to the Philippines? Rachel gulped. He was leaving in a week. She had to adjust her plans.

Rachel blew out a long breath to calm her nerves. She couldn't lose her cool here. People were looking. Right now, she had to focus on Jenna and the wedding. At least Jeremy Sinclair was already here. That meant her escape plan was in motion. He was leaving the country in a week, and there was no way she could let him go without her.

Rachel needed an escape, not necessarily away from something, but mostly in search of something. What that something was, she didn't know, but she had long ago convinced herself that Jeremy Sinclair was the safest way for her to find whatever it was she was looking for.

three

THE **O**NE
WHO HAD A
SECRET

The first thing that caught Jeremy's attention when he stepped out of the cabin into the garden venue was the sound of gushing waters. His jaw dropped at the single waterfall dropping from a high wooded cliff down to an otherwise quiet lake. He reached for his camera, only to find it missing. A strangled groan came out of his mouth. He shouldn't have let Rachel confiscate his camera. There must be a way for him to get it back later. For now, though, what a magnificent setting! The woman had certainly outdone herself with all the work she put into this wedding.

Jeremy caught sight of Max strolling along the classically elegant setting, its overall aesthetic like something out of a Pinterest board pasted into reality. He jogged his way toward his best friend. "Max!"

Relief washed over the groom's face upon seeing him. They exchanged a quick hug.

"I thought you might not make it," Max said.

"Are you kidding? I told you I'd come."

"You cut it close."

"Give me a break. Came here straight from the airport."

"Thanks for flying back for the wedding, man."

Jeremy clapped him on the shoulder. "Wouldn't have missed it. Still shocked, though. You're marrying

Jenna Marquez. You haven't even told me how this happened!"

"Not my fault. You're hard to get a hold of."

"I deserve that." Jeremy scratched his head. "Sorry for shirking all my best man responsibilities."

"You can apologize to Rachel for that, but I have to say I can't blame you. The wedding was short notice."

"Exactly!" Jeremy threw his arms in the air. "Not all my fault. Please remind Rachel of that." Max's vote of confidence might get her to return his camera. She might also go easy on him once she somehow finds the time to list all her demands for him to make up for his delinquency.

After all, Max was right. This whole thing had been on short notice. Jeremy had found out Max and Jenna were getting married even before anyone told him they had become an official couple. It was like the two had decided to skip the dating stage and jumped right into engagement, and now, here they all were. "Why the rush, though?"

Max shrugged. "When you know, you know."

Jeremy chuckled. "I don't remember you knowing back then."

"She wasn't the woman I wanted to marry back then, and I wasn't the man for her either. Now, she is. I am. We are."

"Hey." Jeremy lifted his palms up in mock surrender. "If you say so. You know what you're doing."

The grin on his best friend's face spoke volumes to Jeremy. Between the two of them, Max had always been the straight arrow, and Jeremy had been the one always getting them both in trouble. A lot of people used to refer to Max as Jeremy's shadow, but that was so far from the truth. Max was his own man, and Jeremy was the one living in his shadow. He was the one trying to walk the straight and narrow road like Max had managed to do, despite everything he had been through. Despite even Jeremy.

Someone caught Max's eye, and he nodded.

Jeremy's father, who was officiating the wedding, was signaling to start the ceremony. Everyone there knew him as Pastor Sam, but he had always been just Dad to Jeremy. Dad waved at him, the fondness in his eyes mixed with what Jeremy had always interpreted as disappointment. Was there a part of his father that wished Max had been his son and not Jeremy? He shook his shoulders to banish the thought. No point in dwelling on things he could not change. It wasn't like Jeremy could redo the past. He could only reform the future, and Rachel certainly wasn't the only one on his list of people he had a lot of things to make up for. In fact, it would be easy to make up for his faults toward Rachel. Toward his father? It would take a lifetime. Even then, Jeremy doubted he could ever get enough time to make up for his father losing his mother because of him.

Rachel marched down the aisle with her cheeks aching from the smile — great in photos and perfected over time — plastered on her face. That smile was the fruit of hours upon hours snapping selfie after selfie on her phone to get the best angle or the correct upturn of her lips, so her appearance would dazzle without appearing forced. Even if she really was forcing it more times than she cared to admit.

Among the audience, she caught a glimpse of her mother, who also had a smile on her face just like Rachel and everyone else. Rhoda Petersen, however, might be fooling everyone else with that show of mirth, but her sharp look existed to remind Rachel how much trouble she was in. Rachel's grip on the bouquet of roses tightened as she tried to keep her expression and her gait as leisurely as possible. Not too rushed. Elegant. She wouldn't want people to think she was rushing to get this over with.

She reached the end of her walk and took her place across the aisle from Max and Jeremy, who, for reasons she could only guess at, were snickering at her.

Jenna emerged from the back end of the aisle, and her loveliness gripped Rachel's chest, spreading joy all over her soul. How far her best friend had gone from the bitter and faithless person she had been back in college! Jenna was a testament of God's goodness and a reminder of His grace. Rachel certainly understood the beautiful unfairness of God's grace because of how she had seen it at work in Jenna's life.

As happy as Rachel was for Jenna, the glare her mother was shooting her way shot slivers of shame into Rachel's system. The unexpected and unwelcome awareness of being under Mom's scrutiny blocked air from entering her lungs, and she struggled to breathe as Jenna floated along the aisle.

Her heart outpaced the rhythm of the drum and the acoustic beat flowed right along with the tear threatening to ruin Rachel's pristine makeup. Good thing she had enough forethought to make sure everything on her face that day was waterproof. It didn't help to see the tears in Max's eyes as he watched his bride walk to him.

They were perfect together.

Rachel carried no doubt God had put this marriage together, so why? Why didn't she have the fullness of joy over this Godly match, one she had many times encouraged?

Her mother's cold stare reminded her why.

Jenna reached the end of the aisle. Rachel immediately went into motion, making sure the train of Jenna's dress was in its proper place. Jenna handed the bridal bouquet over to her before Max took his bride's hand and led her up the stage to Pastor Sam, who instructed them to face each other.

Rachel took her seat next to Jeremy, who had his arms crossed over his stomach, looking as relaxed as ever. Was he even aware of all his responsibilities? She would have to remind him, because nobody should have the right to be this cool about everything.

He leaned closer to her, his breath warm on her jawline and neck. "What did you do to your mother?" he asked in a low voice, just loud enough for only her to hear. "I know what a genuine smile of approval from Mrs. P looks like. The way she was staring at you when you were walking down the aisle, that ain't it. You're in trouble for something, aren't you?"

"Shhh..." Rachel struggled to retain her brilliant smile. Apparently, her mother wasn't fooling Jeremy Sinclair, either. Could Jeremy also detect Rachel's fake smiles? "Pay attention."

Pastor Sam laid his hands on Max's and Jenna's shoulders as they bowed their heads in prayer. Rachel shut her eyes. It took two seconds before she opened them again to check if Jeremy had done the same. He had. Good. Rachel closed her eyes again.

"Our Father in heaven," Pastor Sam said, "we all have come together today to celebrate the uniting of the hearts of your two wonderful children, Max Owens and Jenna Marquez. We bless them today, Lord, and pray for the accomplishment of Your will for their lives and their future family. We thank You for Your presence with us this morning. In Christ's Name, Amen."

"Amen," Rachel whispered, as she lifted her head to find Jenna giggling. Max, on the other hand, had this almost adorable looke of confusion on his face.

"What?" Max mouthed at his bride.

"Ready to dance now, Pastor Max?" Jenna asked.

It was Rachel's turn to mouth, "What?"

"What do you mean dance?" Max asked Jenna.

"I added it to the program." Jenna shrugged. "Hope you don't mind." She grinned at her groom before glancing over at Rachel, who had no clue if she should be doing something at that moment. Did the band know about this? Should Rachel get them to play music? What dance did Jenna plan to do, and what type of music would go with it?

"What are you talking about?" Max thankfully asked. "What kind of dance?"

Exactly! Rachel fidgeted in her seat, unsure of what to do.

"The spontaneous kind." Jenna winked at Max.

The band began to play music, to Rachel's relief. The crowd cheered before clapping to the beat. For the first time since she had helped plan this wedding, she had no clue what would happen next. Apart from Jeremy's absence, everything had gone according to plan. Then again, it wasn't like Rachel had expected Jeremy to be involved and present, so this definitely was the first time in this wedding she had been left in the dark.

Jeremy snickered beside her.

Forgetting to keep her smile as she tried to process the commotion, Rachel asked, "Will they really dance before going on with the ceremony? Isn't that out of order?"

"Well, that's what happens when you marry Crazy Jenna. What has my man gotten himself into?" Jeremy's snickers turned into guffaws as he stood up and watched the groom try to follow the bride's lead. Max was no dancer, but Jenna's skill made up for where he was lacking. Jeremy was having the time of his life, clapping his hands over his head, as Max and Jenna danced in the aisle before the ceremony even began.

Rachel fought the urge to facepalm, as she stood up and watched what was going on. This wasn't how weddings were supposed to work. They weren't even married yet! What were they celebrating? For all they know, a volcano could erupt, ash could fall, and the wedding would be canceled! Rachel caught her wild train of thought and blamed it on Jenna's influence on her. This was the result of spending too much time with Crazy Jenna. Cray-cray was contagious.

The upbeat tune by some contemporary Christian band singing about dancing for Jesus wasn't doing anything to lift Rachel's mood. Somehow, the unexpected reminded her of all the reasons her heart was weighing her down. Jenna slid to the side and circled her groom. The image of the bride and the light in her eyes brought about memories of Jenna coming to Rachel's eighth birthday party dressed as a dragon — or a dinosaur, depending on who was telling the story. It brought about all the nights at their dorm room when Jenna had managed to make the most stressful of moments seem bearable. Jenna had been Rachel's window into a world her Christian upbringing had never allowed her to venture into. The gamut of emotions wreaking havoc on her soul at the moment was inescapable, and Rachel's saving grace was Jenna's spontaneous dancing, because it was distracting everyone from the lack of a smile on Rachel's face. She and melancholy had never gotten along well.

They were already halfway through the song when it happened. Rachel couldn't stop herself. It started with one deep breath. When she tried to exhale, it came out as a sob. Jeremy stopped all his merry-making to glance at Rachel. To her horror, tears were already trailing from her eyes and down her cheeks. Another sob escaped her when she tried to smile and explain away her tears.

Jeremy's face crumpled as he angled his head sideways. "Rachel?"

"They're tears of joy, I swear," she said.

His eyes narrowed at her as he nudged her shoulder with his. "You're not jealous, are you?"

Rachel opened her clutch and brought out a pack of tissue. "That's nonsense."

"I mean, it's okay if you are." Jeremy shrugged. "My man, Maximus, is pretty awesome. You never should have let him go, but yeah. Here we are. I kind of just assumed this wedding had your blessing, you know. Pfft. You practically planned the wedding, and you're the maid-of-honor, so—"

What was this man going on about? "I'm not jealous over Max, Jeremy." Rachel gently dabbed her cheeks with the tissue, trying her best to avoid spoiling her makeup. "Drop it."

"Hey. If you say so. I'm just saying there's no shame in it." He flicked his brows at her before rubbing her back just below her shoulder.

"I'm happy for them. I am."

Jeremy smiled, and out of nowhere, his smile turned from mirthful to thoughtful. He brushed his fingers against her shoulder blade and looked at her like he never had before. "They would not be as happy as they are if it hadn't been for you. You made this day possible, Rachel, so on behalf of everyone, thank you."

His words were kind, but Rachel already knew all of that. She just kind of wished Jeremy would stop staring at her so intently, because he was proving to be a lot more observant than anyone would give him credit for. If he looked closely enough, he might realize Rachel wasn't jealous over Max, even if he was her only ex-boyfriend, and she had once been truly in love with him. No. Only one person knew the truth other than Rachel, and that one person was shooting her glares she hoped to avoid.

Rachel swallowed hard, as she dared glance her mother's way. Sure enough, Rhoda was looking at her with this expression of disappointment that made Rachel pray to God for a volcano to erupt or for the ground to swallow her whole, because Max wasn't the reason for her tears. The reason she had been struggling with this wedding was the same reason she had volunteered to be the wedding planner, to begin with. It was Jenna. Her best friend. The woman she now so deeply loved and admired was the same girl she had looked down upon and bullied in the past. This was the woman she had once been so infatuated with, she had begun to question her identity.

Rachel cringed at the memory, which brought with it so much guilt, shame, and disgust.

She no longer had feelings for Jenna — of that, she was sure. Why then was her mother's stare making her feel like she was once again infatuated with Jenna? That wasn't the case, Rachel was sure of it. Far be it from her to question how God had helped her overcome the same-sex attraction she had once had for her best friend.

Why then was she so ashamed?

Rachel bit her lip as she recognized once again why she needed to escape. It wasn't to run from the secret that she had once held a deep, inexplicable, attraction to Jenna. It wasn't even to run from her mother or the pressure to choose a career or all the trouble brewing at Connect Church. Rachel needed to escape, because even she could no longer tell which of her smiles were authentic.

Rachel had never felt more lost than she did at that juncture of her life, and she could only pray that Jeremy would agree to be her escape. She needed to step away from the familiar and go into the unknown. Hopefully, she would find God out there, hear His voice, and draw life from His smile.

Maybe then, Rachel could smile truthfully again.

four

THE ONE WHO COULDN'T FIND HER WAY

Max and Jenna kissed each other for the first time as man and wife. Everyone clapped and cheered, including Rachel, who almost teared up with gratefulness at how happy she truly was for them, especially Jenna. Rachel was well aware of how much her friend had struggled with her previous relationships, so to see her married to a man like Max — someone who would cherish her and value her the way she deserved — brought joy to Rachel's soul.

Jeremy nudged her.

"Hmm?" She asked, her focus still on the newlyweds.

"Your mother is giving you that microscopic glare again."

Rachel's cheekbones twitched, threatening to erase her smile. "Stop paying attention to my mother, and it won't bother you so much."

"I can't help it. I've conditioned myself to be on high alert whenever Mrs. P is around."

At that, Rachel had to giggle. Did Mom really have that effect on Jeremy? Why did he even care?

"I'm usually the one she gives that glare to, so I'm beyond curious why you, of all people, are the one under her microscope today." Jeremy stroked his chin. "What did I miss? Why is Mrs. P targeting her little princess?"

Because Rachel was no longer doing everything she could to please her mother. She was no longer trying to do things the Rhoda Petersen way. "Maybe because I'm not little anymore," Rachel muttered under her breath.

"What did you say?"

"Nothing." Rachel sighed. She wanted to change the subject. She didn't need more reminders of how her mother was scrutinizing her, not when she was already so aware of her mother's disapproval. Also, was Jeremy so oblivious of what had been going on at church lately? Had his family not told him anything? "Leave her be. I'll get through this wedding, and Mom will find me, eventually."

"Don't want to be in your shoes right now, that's for sure." Jeremy winced. "What I do want, however, is my camera. Can I get it back now please? Life has been happening all around me, and you, Princess, have confiscated my primary means of capturing all this awesomeness. I need it back. This has been torture. I'm dying to take pictures."

A slight smirk appeared on Rachel's face. "That is so strange," she said. "It's like you have a codependent relationship with your camera."

"Heh. Not really. I doubt my camera cares if I'm around or not, assuming it's perfectly fine wherever you left it. It's okay, right?"

"Of course. Let's just get through the rest of this ceremony. I'll take you to it before the reception. Jenna's having a change of clothes, anyway, so I need to go to the bridal room, where I left your precious camera."

Jeremy let out a sigh of relief. "Okay, great. Bridal room. Before reception. I can't just run there now to take it, right?"

"No. You're not allowed in there." Rachel huffed before narrowing her eyes at him. "What do you plan to take pictures of anyway? I already told you. There are photographers."

"And they're amazing, I'm sure. I trained some of them myself. Were you aware of that?"

"No. None of them ever mentioned it."

"Ask them." Jeremy grinned. "Still, you've seen some of my work, Rachel. As great as these guys are, I'm sure you can agree my shots are unique."

"You do have an exquisite eye for what is worth taking pictures of. It's not something that can be learned, can it? To be honest, I would've hired you as a photographer, if you weren't the best man."

Jeremy let his gaze on her linger enough for Rachel to playfully shove him by the shoulder.

"What?" she asked.

One corner of his lips lifted as he kept his focus on her face. "I agree. I do have an eye for beauty."

Rachel didn't quite get what he was trying to say, at first, but when she finally did, all she could bring herself to say was, "Oh," before lowering her gaze. Jeremy wasn't still into her, was he? Had he ever been, though? She couldn't tell for sure. He had only asked her out once, and he had been delirious from drug withdrawal, so she wasn't sure if that counted.

"If only I had my camera to take a picture." Jeremy pried his eyes away from her and leaned back in his chair.

"You'll get it, Jeremy." Rachel smiled, hoping the awkwardness between them was all in her head. Surely, all the frustration throughout the entire process of planning this wedding was enough to show how incompatible they were. Incompatibility. That had been the reason behind Max breaking up with her. Rachel was beginning to think she wasn't compatible with anyone. There was a time when she had entertained the idea that this might be because she was attracted to women rather than men. Now, she could only shudder at how misguided she had been. She had long-established that couldn't be the case, because she had been genuinely attracted to Max. And it was that attraction that had served as a baseline for whatever she had once felt for Jenna.

Why then were these thoughts revisiting her now? Was it because the only two people Rachel had ever been infatuated with had just gotten married?

Or was it something more? Why were all of her comfort zones — her church, her family, her friends, her own smile — suddenly so uncomfortable?

Rachel said a quick, hushed prayer to fight against the stray musings clawing at her soul. *God, You are intentional in the way You make us. I know who I am in You. I live by faith and not by what I feel, nor by the discomforting thoughts assailing me right now. Rescue me from the lies the enemy is sending my way. Ground me in Your truth and the identity You have given me as a woman.*

She had already fought this battle before, and she had come out of it victorious. Today, she needed to stand her ground.

"Let's call in the best man and maid-of-honor! Kindly take your place next to the groom and bride, please!" The photographer directed Rachel to stand next to Jenna, and Jeremy to stand next to Max. They took their positions and got lost in a flurry of picture-taking, giving Rachel a much-needed reprieve from her introspection, before everyone headed toward the reception venue.

"Thank you so much for everything, Rachel." Jenna squeezed her hand as they prepared to go to the lake house where Jenna would change outfits in the bridal room. "You have outdone yourself. Everything is so beautiful."

"I'm glad you like it." Rachel linked arms with her best friend. "All of it pales in comparison to how stunning you are today." She lifted a brow. "Though you almost gave me a heart attack with that dance of yours. You couldn't have told me?"

"And spoil the surprise?" Jenna gave Rachel a goofy grin before shrugging. "I was trying to be spontaneous. Also, you never would have approved. I'm glad the music team caught on quickly."

"Not even they knew?" Rachel's mouth hung open. "Jenna!"

"Don't act so shocked. You know me."

Rachel did. All too well. Jenna had a freedom about her that Rachel had always craved, and at times, resented. Her best friend had a way of coming up with the unexpected, taking everyone by surprise. That was one of the many things Rachel adored about Jenna, one of the many things she wished she could have herself. Jenna was so free to be herself, and it reminded Rachel of why she needed to take a step back from her life and re-assess. Jeremy was her easiest way out, and she had no idea how to even broach the subject to him. How would she even explain when she herself didn't fully understand?

After walking Jenna to the bridal room for a change of outfits, Rachel was able to excuse herself and go to the bathroom, where she stared at her reflection in the mirror. There, in the privacy, she got rid of her smile. The restlessness caught up with her. Her world was closing in on her, suffocating what was left of her joy. This wasn't normal, was it? To be this cunning and two-faced. To have the world so fooled by her outward appearance. Little Miss Perfect. Princess Rachel. The one who had it all together.

Sometimes, Rachel wanted to shoot herself.

She tensed. What a horrible thought for her to allow to even graze her mind!

To fight back the dark spirits trying to take a foothold in her life, Rachel prayed. "God, what's going on within me? Why am I so restless, so lost? Why is the past haunting me today? I know I should be happy, and I am, but why isn't my heart aligning with what is in my head? Please, God. Guide me. If it's Your will for me to get myself out of the picture before everything around here blows up, let Jeremy be okay with me leaving with him. Whether it's to China or the Philippines or even a far-off planet, I don't care, as long as I get my escape."

The bathroom door swung open. Before even knowing who had come in, Rachel flashed a smile like it was her default setting in someone else's presence. She turned around, and the urge to drop the façade became almost unbearable. Her mother was standing there, tapping her foot like she had been waiting for Rachel to do something. Rachel didn't falter and stayed strong. She kept not only the smile, but her well-practiced composure. Her performance today was enough to convince Rachel she could pull off being actual royalty, considering how she could smile through almost any situation.

Whether the smile was fooling Rhoda Petersen was another question altogether.

Her mother shook her head while keeping that sternness in her eyes.

"What's with the glare, Mom?" Rachel asked, genuinely confused.

"I saw you with Jeremy. After all the trouble that man has put you through, being selfish enough not to show up at least a few days before the wedding, you still manage to flirt with him?"

Rachel's mouth dropped open. "Flirt with him? Mom! Where is this coming from? Jeremy and I were not doing anything close to flirting. How do you even—" She paused and shook her head. "I can't. How can you think that?"

"Don't talk to me like that, young lady. I have eyes. You have been ribbing about and joking around with him the entire time." Mom walked past her and toward one of the sinks to wash her hands. "It was unbecoming the way you two were snickering back there, where everyone could see you."

"That's because we're friends who haven't seen each other in a while. Of course we were trying to have a bit of fun." As if this day wasn't challenging enough, her mother had to throw this random issue at her? There was no way to smile through this conversation without looking like she should be sent to rehab. "Jeremy and I have been through a lot together, and our best friends just got married. Why color it a certain way when it's not at all like that?"

Mom took a deep breath, as she wiped her hands dry with tissue. "Okay, fine. Perhaps I'm overreacting. I believe you, Rachel. I trust you enough to know you wouldn't go after someone like Jeremy." She rolled her eyes, not bothering to hide her disdain.

That irked Rachel. As if her mother wasn't already causing enough trouble with the way she kept going off with that mouth of hers. "Why, Mom? Why not Jeremy? He's a decent guy who loves the Lord and is serving God in places neither of us could even imagine going to, much less living in."

"So are you saying you're interested in him?"

"No, Mom. Nothing like that is happening between us. I'm just defending Jeremy, because all things considered, he's quite a catch. He's had a rough past, sure, but it's amazing how he's done a one-eighty and is now serving the Lord with everything he's got. That counts for something."

"Oh, come on, Rachel." Her mother frowned. "You know I am coming from a place of love. I desire only what's best for my only daughter. You are well aware of the many reasons I wouldn't want you to end up with someone like Jeremy Sinclair, especially considering how easily influenced by your friends you are. Now, if you had held on to Max like I advised you to, maybe you would be the one in a wedding gown today."

"Mom, you're unbelievable. He just got married to my best friend!"

"Your best friend? Is that what you're calling Jenna now?"

The pointed look her mother was giving her made Rachel bristle. Was Mom throwing her past at her? Why? What would that even accomplish? Rachel didn't even have the will to address her mother's insinuations. She helped Jenna because she loved her best friend, nothing more. Her past attraction to Jenna had nothing to do with any of this.

To Rachel's relief, her mother didn't broach the topic further. Instead, Mom found another issue to bring up. "It's appalling how these two didn't even bother to pay you a single cent for all the work you did for their wedding. Really. Doesn't sound like much of a friend to me." Mom faced the mirror to touch up her lipstick. She side-eyed Rachel. "You're not retouching your makeup? You need to after all the crying you did. What were you tearing up for, anyway?"

"I don't know, Mom. Two of my dearest friends just got married. Can't I shed tears of joy on their behalf? Also, I volunteered to help them as my wedding gift to them. Besides—" Rachel hung her shoulders "—it's not like I have anything going on right now. I had time to help."

Her mother gave her that stern glare once again. "You only have yourself to blame if there's nothing going on in your life these days, Rachel."

"Please don't start."

"I'm just saying that you should take that job at your dad's firm, which was the right thing to do from the get go, instead of taking this gap year of yours. With a steady job, you can focus on something with substance and purpose, instead of—"

"Mom, please. Not today."

To her relief, her mother relented and focused on perfecting her makeup.

All Rachel had wanted was to drop her defenses and find time to collect herself before facing everyone again. This conversation was not letting her do that. Not with her mother being in such a combative mood. It wasn't like her mother was just gonna let go of whatever was bothering her. Rachel doubted it was Jeremy, her tears, her friends, or her lack of a career plan that was bothering her mother. Something else was grating at Rhoda Petersen, and right now, Rachel could only guess at what it was, considering all the issues surrounding her mother these days. Why wasn't she used to this by now? Her mother had been neck-deep in relational issues for most of Rachel's adolescence.

Her mother remained silent, so Rachel moved on and entered one of the bathroom stalls to relieve herself and get some peace and quiet for a few minutes. In a perfect world, by the time she stepped out of her stall, her mother wouldn't be there anymore, or at least someone else would have already entered. Another person present would be enough to keep her mom silent if only to keep up appearances. The Petersens were a perfect family, after all. Little Miss Perfect could only come from perfect parents, right?

When Rachel stepped out, however, her mother was still there. Alone.

"Rachel, please." Mom frowned as her eyes followed Rachel to the sink, where Rachel washed her hands. "I know you don't want to talk about it, but when will you stop wasting your time? This is foolish. A great, lucrative job is waiting for you at your father's firm. Executive assistant to the CEO? That's an amazing job offer — a blessing from God — and it's a job you will thrive in!" Mom threw her arms in the air. "Just look at what you did for this wedding! God has gifted you with the ability to turn chaos into order, and what did you do after earning your degree? You decide to spend an entire year doing what? Nothing. Your friends treat you like their lackey, and I don't understand it, Rachel."

"Can we have this conversation some other time, Mom? Please? This is neither the time nor place."

"When is the right time, Rachel? Where is the right place? Is it at home? Because you haven't dropped by the house in weeks, you have been avoiding my calls, and you haven't even been sitting with your father and me at church on Sundays. After services, you're immediately off to some other errand or appointment with your friends."

"That's because I've been planning this wedding."

"For free, let's not forget." Mom huffed. "Honey, just because you were able to save money from all your side jobs and that theater play you pulled off with Max, that doesn't mean you don't have to earn a living like a functioning adult anymore. Your volunteer work with Annette at that non-profit of hers doesn't count."

"She gives me an allowance. Why wouldn't that count?" Just the mention of the work she was doing with Max's mom at *Lady Lacey League* warmed Rachel's heart and helped lift the heaviness in her soul. It was the one thing that made her feel like she was making a difference in the world, helping under-aged girls choose better lives by staying pure and surrendering their lives to God.

"It's not a career, Rachel. Your father's boss has been so gracious in holding the job open for you, only because of your father's good standing with the firm, but your one year will soon be up, and you better make a decision soon. No one gets favors like this, Rachel. You should be grateful for how blessed you are."

"I am, Mom. I'm grateful, but—" The conversation was depleting her energy. Rachel was so used to meeting people's expectations, so she herself couldn't fully understand why this was one expectation she was struggling to meet. This career option was one of the biggest reasons she wanted to run off to the other side of the world with Jeremy. At this point, she just wanted to get her mother off her back and talk about something else, so she wouldn't be forced to make a commitment she wasn't ready to follow through on. "Mom, I've been hearing rumors going around." Rachel's jaw tightened, as she second-guessed whether it was worth broaching the subject just so she could deflect from the issue her mother was pressing.

Mom's disapproving scowl grew. "I raised you better than to listen to baseless rumors, Rachel."

Her lip curled. Was that true? Most of the baseless rumors Rachel had heard growing up had come directly from her mother's mouth. She gulped. "Nothing then."

"Oh, for crying out loud." Mom stomped her foot on the bathroom floor. "What is it?"

"Is it true you and Dad are planning to leave Connect Church?"

The indignation and horror in her mother's eyes added another ton to the weight already crushing Rachel's chest.

"Who told you that?" Mom asked.

"It's just rumors, right, Mom? Baseless ones?"

Mom's jaw twitched as she averted her gaze and shook her head. "Your Dad and I are praying about it."

One thing Rachel was sure about when it came to her mother was that she would never knowingly lie. If Rhoda Petersen was saying something, it was because she believed it to be true — and right — with all her heart. "Why? This is our church, Mom. Our family. Why would you leave it?"

Mom lowered her eyes. "This is neither the time nor the place to talk about that."

Now, she cared about the proper place to discuss matters? How long had they been standing in this bathroom?

"If you showed up at home once in a while to visit your father and me these past weeks, you would know our heart in this situation and why we feel this is necessary for us to do."

"Mom, what could justify dividing our church?"

"Come visit us and find out, Rachel. Then again, you don't seem to have time for that, even if you have all the time in the world to plan an entire wedding for your *best friend*, Jenna."

"Mom—"

The tears brimming her mother's eyes were difficult to see. The only consolation Rachel had was that they didn't actually fall down her cheeks. They stayed there, like a threat of sorrow that wouldn't deliver.

With one final look of disappointment cast Rachel's way, her mother twisted on her heel and walked out of the bathroom, leaving Rachel standing there, more hollow than ever.

That exchange with her mother was enough of an answer from the Lord for Rachel's request for guidance. The next few months could only get worse from here, and Rachel would rather not stay around to watch everything erupt. Not because she didn't care, but because she cared too much, and she knew she wouldn't be able to smile her way through it.

Today, however, she could still manage, so Rachel straightened her dress, gathered her composure, pushed back all the chaotic thoughts rumbling in her head, ignored the pain in her heart, and put a smile on her face.

Now, to get Jeremy his camera; hopefully, he would snap a photo of Rachel so exquisite, it would convince even her that she was as happy as she made herself look.

five

THE ONE WITH A BROKEN LEGACY

Jeremy smirked at the cliché circling his mind: what was it with women and taking forever to get dressed? He stood in the hallway outside the bridal room — or at least he hoped he was in the right place — after having been dispatched by his father to make sure Jenna would be ready to show up at the reception on time. Apparently, this was supposed to be Rachel's job, but nobody seemed to know where she was, which was strange to Jeremy, because usually, Rachel was the one on top of things and pestering people — like him — to be where they were supposed to be. This was so unlike Little Miss Perfect.

Not that he was complaining. This could work to his advantage. Being here, he could ask someone where his camera was, because if Rachel had it and she'd gone off wherever, it would be his turn to hunt her down. Also, her disappearance could help him convince Rachel to knock a few points off the long list of things he owed Rachel Petersen. Though, all things considered, he didn't mind owing Rachel if it meant she would let him take a picture of her with that gorgeous waterfall as a backdrop.

He would have to get his camera first. Where was everyone?

Tired of hanging around in the hallway like a creepy stalker, Jeremy stepped forward and knocked on the door to the bridal room. Almost immediately, it swung open. Jeremy held his breath. *Please be Rachel.* His shoulders sagged and his face fell when one of the bridesmaids stood before him instead.

"Wow." The pretty brunette shut the door behind her and narrowed her eyes at Jeremy. "Sorry to disappoint. Were you looking for someone else?"

Jeremy searched his mind for the girl's name. She was new to the church, and they had been introduced in passing before. Rachel and Jenna knew her from university. Ah, yes. "Candace, is it?"

She threw her head back, her chin pressing against her neck, and her brows flicking up. "You remember me?"

"Sure. Max introduced us once." He grinned, extended his hand toward her, and winced as they shook hands. "I'm sorry if it seemed like it disappointed me to see you. It's not like that at all. I was just hoping you would be Rachel."

"Oh! I was just about to go looking for her. She said she needed to go to the bathroom, so—" Candace pointed inside the bridal room "—we assumed she went to the one inside the room, but I guess not."

"Dad sent me over to make sure Jenna is ready in ten minutes, and that was ten minutes ago."

"You didn't think to knock then?"

"I did." Jeremy rubbed the side of his neck. "Ten minutes ago. It was Nova who answered the door. She told me to wait and that Jenna will be ready soon. Is she ready?"

"Oh, sure." Candace nodded as she grasped for the doorknob behind her. "Give us a few more minutes. I'll check, okay?"

Jeremy smiled, mostly at how unconvincing she sounded. "Since you're going in, can you check if my camera is there? Rachel told me she left it there for safe-keeping."

"Sure, but—" Candace pointed at the end of the hallway, where Rachel emerged from a door, with this rare, serious look on her face, like she was about to head off to battle, or she had come from one. At the sight of him and Candace, almost like instinct brought it out, that brilliant smile of hers made her seem like an entirely different person. In a split second, there Rachel was, gliding through the hall, with that flowy pink dress of hers sashaying from side-to-side like a gentle wave keeping her afloat.

Jeremy swallowed hard.

Candace laughed. "Interesting."

He pried his eyes away from Rachel and found Candace giving him this goofy grin before she raised a brow and glanced at Rachel.

"Of course it's her you're interested in," she said.

"Hmm?" Jeremy squinted an eye. "Nah. You got it all wrong. It's not like that. We grew up together. She's like a little sister to me."

Candace shrugged. "If you say so, but it's okay to admit it, if you are."

"There's nothing to admit. It's just that she's stunning. No one can deny that, can they?"

"Who's denying what?" Rachel asked.

Candace gave her a knowing smile. "Nothing. Jeremy was just telling me about how he felt about you."

"Annoyed, most likely." Rachel lifted a brow at Jeremy. "Did you get your camera?"

Jeremy shook his head. "I also need to get the bride to the reception."

Rachel squared her shoulders like she had just been caught off guard. She opened her little pink, sparkly, half-purse, half-wallet thing. How her phone could fit in there, Jeremy wasn't sure, but there it was now in her hand. "Oh no." Rachel frowned. "I was supposed to bring Jenna to the reception at least five minutes ago."

"Ten, actually. That's why Dad sent me on a man hunt for the bride and the maid-of-honor. Works for me, because it gave me an excuse to start looking for my camera."

This deadpan expression that Jeremy found adorable covered Rachel's face. "You and your camera." She walked toward the door while nudging Candace to follow her. It took another two minutes or so before she emerged from the room with his camera in hand and the entire bridal entourage in tow.

Jeremy grinned as he took his camera from Rachel, who didn't lose time marching all the ladies down the hall to get them to the reception area. He checked his camera first before jogging forward to get in step with everyone. He stopped when he was already beside Jenna, who was still wearing a white lace dress. It was shorter than the one she had worn during the wedding — still exquisite, but a lot more comfortable.

"Why the clothes change?" Jeremy asked. "Getting ready to dance again?"

Jenna laughed. "Maybe." She twirled around several times in this graceful manner one would expect to find in a professional performance.

Jeremy threw his head back. "Impressive," he said. "You've gone a long way from the random wild gestures you used to throw into the air and called dance when we were kids."

"People change. They improve in the things they are passionate about." Jenna shrugged. "You know all about that."

"Hundred percent." He nodded. "But today is not about me. Congratulations, Jenna. I gotta say I didn't see this coming. Never as a kid did I imagine you and my man, Maximus, would end up married."

"Oh, don't worry." Jenna swayed from side-to-side with every step she took forward. "Neither one of us saw it coming, as well. Actually, Max saw it coming before I did, but I'm sure you've already heard the story."

"I've been told a few versions of it via video chat. Genuinely, Jenna, I'm happy for both of you, but take care of Maximus, okay? He's quite the man."

The affection that appeared on Jenna's face at the mention of Max was enough assurance for Jeremy. "He really is, isn't he?" A soft blush covered her cheeks. "I'll do my best, Jeremy. Rest assured that I'm thankful beyond words that God brought us together."

"I have no doubt about it."

Rachel cleared her throat while still walking in front of them. She slowed down her march toward the reception area and spun around to face them both. "To be fair, Max is also blessed to have Jenna."

"I'm not questioning that."

Rachel shot him a sharp glare before huffing out and moving on.

What was her problem? Was she angry?

Jeremy shrugged it off as nothing but the pressure and stress Rachel was under. He would be irritated with everyone and everything too, if he had to plan an event like this on his own. It didn't take long before they reached the reception area which was basically just a giant white tent in the middle of the lake house's garden, opposite of where they held the ceremony. That meant it was far from the waterfall — disappointing to Jeremy, but he could find a way to escape the reception and get to the waterfall later.

Once at the reception, however, the beauty surrounding him was more than enough to make up for not having the natural beauty and wonder of creation nearby. The fairy lights hanging in the air, the fairy tale-like vibe of the indoor setting, and the strange standing tree-like lamps with perfect round bulbs on each branch made Jeremy wonder if some mythical creature would appear somewhere. He brought out his camera and grinned. It was the first time since he had arrived at the wedding that he felt like he was in his element — with that camera in his hand, recognizing beauty everywhere. The first thing he snapped a picture of was none other than Rachel herself.

As Jenna rejoined Max, and he led her to the dance floor, this unusual expression of somberness covered Rachel's face. She wrapped her arms around herself, like she was trying to comfort herself, before pressing her palms together in a praying motion and pressing the sides of her forefingers against her lower lip and chin. An almost unbearable melancholy covered her face.

Jeremy cocked his head to the side. He had only been joking earlier, but was Rachel Petersen still in love with his man, Maximus? He photographed the rare seriousness of Rachel's face as she watched Max and Jenna dance. Jeremy stared at the photo from the screen preview of his camera. It tugged at his heart, because of the knowledge that only he would ever know what — who — Rachel was looking at with sorrow in her green eyes. Jeremy strode over to Rachel and stood next to her to join her in watching the newlyweds. Standing where Rachel was, he saw what she was seeing, and it knocked his breath away.

Max and Jenna looked almost ethereal in the way they were gazing at each other as they danced. Jeremy had never seen Max this happy before. He had witnessed with his own eyes the way Max had been with his exes, Rachel included. It was nothing like this. Jeremy brought up his camera and snapped a photo to immortalize the moment. By the time he dropped his camera, he had tears in his eyes.

Beside him, Rachel snickered. "Tears of joy?" she asked. Her pensiveness was gone. In its place was her usual smile — one teasing him.

"I wouldn't be here right now if it wasn't for Max. He saved my life and reminded me of God's love when I needed it most. It's just overwhelming to see him this happy. He hasn't had an easy life."

"Awww..." Rachel squeezed his arm. "And here I thought you were jealous of him marrying Jenna, but you were never into Jenna, were you?"

"Jenna? Nah... She'll always be Crazy Jenna to me."

Rachel rolled her eyes. "Be thankful she has embraced that name, because I'd fight you for calling her that if she hadn't."

"You really care about her, don't you?"

Rachel's smile faltered and a muscle in her cheek twitched. "Of course. The same way you care about Max. She's my best friend, after all, and she hasn't had an easy life either."

Jeremy made a face. "What is this? My mama is better than your mama, but with best friends?"

"Pfft. We both know your mama is better than mine," she blurted out. "I miss Mama Aida so much."

The statement threw Jeremy off, and it seemed to have thrown Rachel off as well, because she suddenly gasped and covered her mouth with her hand.

"I'm so sorry," she said. "I shouldn't have said that. Things have been rough between Mom and me, but that doesn't excuse the statement. As for Mama Aida, I do miss your mother. Everyone does."

The mention of his mother got Jeremy all choked up. "She always liked you. Growing up, she often teased me about us becoming a thing once we're older. I told her your mother would never agree, so she shouldn't keep hoping."

Rachel didn't say anything, and Jeremy took that as acknowledgment of what they both knew to be true. Rhoda Petersen was the main reason neither of them could see each other as anything more than friends.

Jeremy had long ago accepted that, and from the look on Rachel's face, she had as well. He couldn't blame her or Mrs. P, could he? After all, what could he offer to Little Miss Perfect, when here he was, still struggling to stay on the straight and narrow — a road she had been treading her entire life?

Though a part of him wondered if his late mother had seen something no one else had, which is why she had always teased him about Rachel. Still, Jeremy couldn't see himself pursuing Rachel unless God Himself intervened, because how could he live with himself if he ever tainted Rachel's pristine legacy with his broken one?

No, Jeremy and Rachel was not a pairing that could ever come to be. His past would never allow it, and neither would he.

part two

THE PAST
TWENTY-TWO
YEARS AGO

six

THE ONE WHO GLOWED FROM THE INSIDE OUT

- JEREMY, 5 -

Hands folded over his lap, Jeremy swayed his legs back and forth in his seat at the front of their church sanctuary. His older sister, Serene, had told him to wait there until she got back, because she had to help her best friend, Nolan, set up for the worship service later. Jeremy had no idea where his parents were or who they were talking to. They were always busy during church events, and this was no exception. Jeremy heaved a huge sigh as he bemoaned his predicament. How long was he supposed to just sit here?

He fidgeted in his seat and scratched his nose. He twisted his torso from side-to-side to exercise while checking who had already arrived for whatever was going to happen that night. Were there any kids around to play with? Would Serene get mad if he left his seat to play with them? She didn't expect him to just sit there all night, did she?

He shifted his position in the cushioned chair to bend his knees over it and check whatever was behind him. He frowned. There weren't many people around yet. Only Mrs. P and Miss Hannah from Sunday School were there. They sat several rows behind him, whispering to each other.

What were they talking about? So focused on their conversation, they didn't notice Mrs. P's kid hobbling down the aisle toward Jeremy. Where was Rachel going? Jeremy hadn't even known she could already walk. He waved at her when she caught him staring. She giggled before shoving her fingers inside her mouth and chomping on them.

Jeremy snickered. She was funny and so darn cute! Rachel clapped her hands together when she saw him laughing and sped up in her quest to get to the front of the sanctuary. The speed must have knocked her off-balance, because she started to wobble. Without thinking about it, Jeremy hopped off his chair and rushed to catch her before she could fall. She didn't actually fall, but delight sparked in her eyes upon seeing him. She sure was happy to have some company. At least somebody understood what Jeremy felt whenever he had to go to church so much earlier than all the other kids. Why did his family always have to be extra early anyway?

"Ba-ba-ba-ba-ba!" Rachel blurted out, drool dripping down the side of her mouth, as she clapped her hands in rhythm with her babbling, like she was trying to give Jeremy an object lesson.

He pinched her cheek — not too hard, though. He didn't want to get in trouble with Mrs. P, who always found reason to scold him for anything he did. "I hope you don't grow up to be always mad at me like your momma is, Rachel."

"Ma-ma-ma?" Her green eyes widened, and it was undoubtedly the cutest thing Jeremy had ever seen in his life.

"Yes. Mamama." He nodded before turning her the other way to take her to Mrs. P.

"Mamama!" She started mumbling out a bunch of words that sounded to Jeremy like speaking in tongues.

At least she wasn't about to cry anymore. What a nightmare that would be! He walked Rachel up the aisle. Two rows away from where Mrs. P and Miss Hannah sat, something caught Rachel's eye in the row of seats by the aisle. She pointed the way she wanted to go and dragged Jeremy along with her, while she continued babbling out syllables in rapid-fire succession.

"Rachel, where are you going?"

"Lablooblashelasha!"

"Right. I don't know where that is, but I know where your momma is. Do you want to go to Mama?"

Rachel wriggled her hand out of his grip and got on her hands and knees on the carpeted floor. She crawled faster than she walked and took cover under one of the chairs.

"Rachel, don't do that," Jeremy said in a hushed voice, fearing that he might get blamed if Rachel got stuck under a seat or something. He was about to pull her out of there when she started giggling. Something was in her hand. What was it? Jeremy tilted his head to the side and pried her closed fist open. In her palm, he found a shiny pink marble. What was that doing there?

"Ball?" Rachel's eyes widened.

Jeremy nodded. "Ball."

She threw the marble at him, and it hit him on the forehead, most likely exactly where David's stone had hit Goliath. "Ahh!" Jeremy pretended to fall on the ground, playing dead.

Little Rachel must have thought it was the funniest thing, because she burst out in uncontrollable giggles. Jeremy grinned. He was about to get up when music started playing from the stage. It was beautiful music, so it must be Nolan tinkering with his guitar. Jeremy folded his hands over his stomach as he shut his eyes and listened. In his head, he imagined Serene painting as Nolan played his music. She made the prettiest pictures and always made Jeremy want to see what she was seeing in her mind, because she always came up with something beautiful. Mama Aida had told him once that when Serene was Jeremy's age, she could see the heavens. Jesus had blessed her with vision, and she often painted the things He showed her. Jeremy had tried hard to do the same thing and had prayed every night for Jesus to give him vision as well, but Jesus hadn't answered or given him anything yet. Jeremy had eyes, but no vision. Maybe he wasn't praying hard enough, or he was praying wrong.

As he lay there, he prayed again for God to give him vision, since God had already given him eyes anyhow. He squeezed his eyes shut. Tighter and tighter, but he still saw nothing. What God seemed to give him, however, were ears that could hear Mrs. P talking to Miss Hannah even through Nolan's guitar-plucking.

"I don't think he has it anymore," Mrs. P said. "Nolan has lost his anointing. It's just skill and talent at this point, not the Holy Spirit moving through his music. We need training for the worship team. Real, solid, Biblical discipleship that transforms hearts and minds — even lives — not this celebrity culture we're building up here, where we all ooh and ahh over natural-born talent, without doing the work of making sure these young ones become men and women after God's own heart."

"Do you truly believe the Holy Spirit isn't moving through Nolan's music anymore? It's beautiful music, Miss Rhoda," Miss Hannah replied.

"There's no denying that, Hannah. As I said, the boy is talented, but what is talent good for if not coupled with character that honors God? The boy is charismatic, but arrogant. He is dragging our pastor's daughter into his juvenile ways, and I don't understand how Sam and Aida have allowed their daughter to be so close to a boy. It was somewhat acceptable when they were children, but they're both teenagers now. At thirteen, how healthy is it for them to be around each other so much, especially when we all know the pitfalls of adolescence?"

"You're right," Miss Hannah agreed. "Have you talked to Pastor Sam and Mama Aida about this?"

"Oh, I plan to. I'm not just going to sit here and let this slide. I have a young daughter who needs to grow up in the ways of the Lord, and I don't want her to have ungodly role models."

Jeremy frowned. Mrs. P certainly sounded like she disliked Nolan and Serene.

"Mimi?"

Jeremy opened his eyes to find Rachel standing by the top of his head, bent over, her face hovering over his. "Mimi!" She patted his cheek, a big drop of her drool falling on his forehead.

"Ew!" Jeremy immediately hopped to his feet. Rachel must have thought it was a game, because she giggled and began hopping on her feet too.

Only then did Mrs. P and Miss Hannah notice them.

"Young man, what are you doing?" Mrs. P asked.

"Rachel drooled on my face!" Jeremy said, not sure whether to wipe it off, because that would only spread Rachel's germs all over him.

Mrs. P sighed. "Where is your mother?"

Jeremy shrugged.

She rolled her eyes. "How can they take care of the flock if they can't even look after their own son?" She brought out a pack of tissue from her giant pink bag and approached Jeremy to wipe Rachel's drool off his forehead.

Rachel was oblivious to the damage she had done. She was busy giggling and hopping around in circles like a bunny.

"What have you taught her now?" Mrs. P asked after she had finished wiping him off. Still, a smile appeared on her face at the sight of Rachel. She laughed.

It was the first time Jeremy could remember ever seeing Mrs. P laugh. She was always so serious or angry or upset over something or someone, but at that moment, she was looking at Rachel like Mama Aida looked at Serene and Jeremy. Even if Mrs. P had trouble loving everyone else, it seemed she had no struggle whatsoever when it came to loving Rachel.

Jeremy couldn't blame her. He grinned at Rachel, who was giggling at herself uncontrollably as she continued hopping around. It was funny and beautiful all at the same time, and Jeremy wished then — at five years old — that God would somehow give him a way to capture beautiful moments like this. The same way Serene used her paintings to capture the beautiful visions God kept showing her.

Jeremy grinned. On the topic of beauty, someday, he would make a movie, and it would be about a hopping rabbit with green eyes and golden hair called Rachel.

"She said what?"

Jeremy scrunched his nose as he tried to twist the legs of his new toy together. He shouldn't have told Serene about what Mrs. P had said about her and Nolan last night, because she sounded like someone would after falling and having a large, painful cut on the leg — like the one Jeremy had after he had fallen from the monkey bars at school. What was Serene so upset about? Who cared about stinking anointing, anyway? If Nolan could still play the guitar and Serene could still paint, then what was the anointing for? Jeremy wouldn't be surprised if Mrs. P made it all up, just to have a reason to scowl about one more thing. Why couldn't she be happy? All Jeremy had was this robot that had come with his meal, and he was happy.

"Jeremy, pay attention." Serene tapped the table at their favorite booth at their favorite fast food restaurant.

Jeremy blinked his eyes to look at her, as he tried to stop figuring out if his new toy could turn from a robot into anything else. "What?"

"You heard Mrs. P say Nolan and I don't have God's anointing anymore. Is that right?"

He nodded. How many times did he have to repeat himself?

Nolan's face darkened. "What else did she say, Jeremy?" he asked.

54

Was Nolan mad at him? What had he done now? "I don't remember, because Rachel dropped her drool on my forehead and distracted me." Jeremy giggled. "Then, she started hopping around like a bunny. She was so funny."

Nolan and Serene exchanged glances. No laughter there. Jeremy frowned. If only he had somehow captured what Rachel looked like! If they had seen her themselves, they would laugh too. But no. Nolan had now dipped his fries on the ketchup about seventy-nine bajillion times. Soggy ketchup fries. Ew. Why were people around him always getting upset over something? Only Dad and Mama were always happy. Even Nolan and Serene were now unhappy, and they used to always have a fun time, laughing or painting or making music together.

Jeremy popped a non-soggy fry into his mouth and fiddled with his new toy again. In his opinion, everyone should get a new toy, so they could all be happy about something.

Serene breathed out a long, long breath that made Jeremy look up to check if his sister was trying to lose all her air or if she would shrink like a deflated balloon. Was that why she could see the heavens? Because she was part-balloon and could sometimes fly?

"Is it true you saw heaven, Serene?" Jeremy asked. "Do you fly there?"

Again, Nolan and Serene exchanged glances. Were they still kids? When Jeremy became thirteen years old, would he stop being a kid? Would he be all grown up like Nolan and Serene? They were a lot more fun when they were twelve. Were they still kids then? Now, they were all sullen and somber and having secrets all to themselves that they never shared with him.

Nolan took a huge bite from his hamburger while Serene fixed her stare at Jeremy.

"I used to see the heavens," she said. "Or at least I think so. Now, I don't anymore."

"Why not?" Jeremy wrinkled his nose. "Did you do something to make God mad? Did He put you on time out?"

"No." Serene giggled. "I don't think so. God's not like that, Jeremy. He's kind."

"It all stopped when you were born, Jeremy," Nolan said.

"Nolan!" Serene slapped his shoulder. "Don't say that."

"What? It's true. It stopped when we turned eight. That's when Jeremy was born."

"That doesn't mean it had something to do with him. A lot happened that year. That was also when your older brother died."

The light left Nolan's face. "I remember. One of the worst years of my life."

Jeremy frowned. He couldn't complain about that year, because if he was born on that year, then it must have been a good year for him. What had made it so miserable for Nolan and Serene? Why did they seem so miserable now? "Why are you best friends? Mrs. P said it's not safe for you to always be around each other so much."

Nolan directed his glare at Serene. "What is it with Mrs. P and always saying bad stuff about us? It's like she's obsessed with you and me."

She shrugged. "You should stop listening to the things Mrs. P says, Jeremy. She says a lot of things that aren't true or noble or kind. The Bible says to think only of those types of things."

"But—" Jeremy squirmed in his seat "—Mrs. P is my teacher in Sunday School. She always tells me to listen to her and not disrupt everyone, or she'll send me to a corner. Is it bad for boys to be best friends with girls?"

"No." Serene shook her head. "Nolan and I have been friends since we were your age, and there's nothing wrong with that. God loves it, when we all get along."

"Don't you want a girl best friend, Serene? I want a boy best friend, but none of the other kids at school or at church are my best friend. They all aren't any fun after a while."

"God will give you a best friend someday, Jeremy." She reached forward and tapped the top of his head. "Whoever your best friend will be, it'll be an amazing friendship, like the one Nolan and I have."

The way Nolan was looking at Serene, though, it was how Dad looked at Mama sometimes. Yeah. Jeremy didn't want a girl best friend. Not even Rachel, who was both funny and cute. She was too small anyway. It was better for him to have a boy best friend, so Mrs. P would leave him alone. That way, he could go on more adventures without her trying to make him do something else. Like sit down and stay still, which was no fun for any boy anywhere. Right now, Jeremy was beginning to hate Sunday School, because all he was allowed to do was be quiet and listen to Bible stories, when he already knew all of them. Meanwhile, he could be out exploring inside their church, outside their church, everywhere! It was a big, huge, gigantic world, and Jeremy wanted to see every bit of it. Not just sit in that stuffy old classroom listening to Mrs. P talk on and on and on.

Nolan snapped his fingers in front of Jeremy's face. "You still with us, buddy?"

"Did you like Sunday School when you were five, Nolan?" Jeremy asked.

A grin appeared on Nolan's face, and his eyes glazed over. "I did, actually."

"Why?"

Nolan stared at Serene, and her cheeks went all red as she widened her eyes at him. He shrugged. "That's where I got to know Jesus, buddy. What's not to like? Don't you like Sunday School?"

Was he allowed to tell people he didn't? He couldn't remember Jesus ever coming to visit them at Sunday School. "Do you like Jesus, Nolan?"

Nolan didn't bat an eyelash. "Of course I like Jesus. I love Him. Don't you?"

"I don't know. Dad and Mama love Him a lot, so I think He's not bad at all, but is He anything like Mrs. P?"

"Not at all." Serene shook her head furiously. "Jesus is nothing like her. He is good and kind and patient with us. He loves us a lot."

"Doesn't Mrs. P love us? I know she loves Rachel, but she always finds stuff to be upset about."

"That's Mrs. P's problem, not ours." Serene nudged Nolan with her elbow. "Right, Nolan? Don't you agree?"

"Right." Nolan nodded.

Serene grabbed Jeremy's shoulder and shook him. "Come on. You know all this. Dad and Mama taught us."

Right then, Dad and Mama approached their booth with a bunch of shopping bags in their hands.

"We're done. Are you kids ready to go home?" Dad asked as Mama slid on the booth next to Jeremy's.

Serene pointed at Jeremy with her thumb. "Jeremy has been asking what Jesus is like."

Dad's and Mama's faces lit up, especially Mama's. "Is that true, Jeremy?"

He nodded. Why were they acting like this was a big deal? Had he done something wrong?

"You've accepted Jesus as your personal Lord and Savior, right, Jeremy?" Dad asked, his brows creasing.

"I think so." Jeremy smeared a piece of fry with ketchup. "I talk to Him a lot, like you taught me."

"But you know all about what Jesus did for us, right?" Serene asked.

Jeremy made a face. This story again? "He came down from heaven, became a baby, grew up, and died, so I don't have to be punished over and over and over again for all the times I mess up. And He became alive again, and He's alive forever and ever and will never die."

Dad chuckled. He pulled up a chair from an empty table nearby and sat at the head of the booth. There, Dad told him all about Jesus. Again. After the long story, they all stared at Jeremy with expectant faces, asking him if he wanted Jesus in his heart. Of course, he said yes.

That's when they led him to pray a prayer, and with all Jeremy's heart, he believed Jesus had somehow decided to live inside him. Why Jesus would want to do that was confusing to Jeremy, because if He had all the heavens to Himself, why would He want to live in anybody's heart? Then again, was this what had to happen for Jeremy to see the heavens like Serene used to?

Expectant, when Jeremy got back home, he climbed onto his bed, sat cross-legged on top of it, shut his eyes, and waited for something to happen. He waited and waited and waited. When he opened his eyes, a bright light greeted him, along with Serene shaking him awake. It was time to get ready for church. So much for the heavens. All God had decided to give him for letting Jesus live in his heart was more Bible stories and Sunday School class. Ah well, Jeremy smiled still. At least he could see cute and adorable little Rachel at Sunday School every week. Even if she couldn't be his best friend, that was okay. Jesus was Jeremy's best friend for now — at least until God would answer his prayers and give him a best friend of his own. Hopefully, a boy, and not a girl.

- FOUR YEARS LATER; JEREMY, 9 -

Max Owens was a strange, sullen kid whose wide, brown eyes made him look like he had seen a ghost somewhere. That's what drew Jeremy to him when he became the new kid at Jeremy's school. Everyone else was avoiding the strange new kid, and it didn't seem like he wanted to be friends with anyone anyway. He seemed perfectly all right sitting by himself during lunch break and recess. All the teachers were extra kind to him and told all the kids to be nice to him. No one was allowed to make fun of Max in any way.

Everyone tried to be polite to Max, but almost everyone avoided him, because they were afraid of getting in trouble with the teachers. Also, sometimes, he stunk, which was strange, because he always showed up to school with wet hair to show he had showered. Jeremy concluded the stink must come from his clothes.

By the second week of seeing this same pattern happen every day since Max had first shown up in the middle of the school year, Jeremy decided he would make Max his friend.

So, one Friday morning, during recess, Jeremy told his friends he didn't want to play dodgeball with them. He was going to the swing set, where Max always was, with his feet firmly planted on the ground, as he rocked himself back and forth on one of the swings. Did he not understand how swings worked?

Jeremy hopped on the swing next to Max's. "I'm Jeremy," he said.

"I know who you are."

"Do you want to play dodgeball?"

"I'd rather stay here. Thank you very much." Max had his eyes glued to his feet, which Jeremy didn't find all that interesting.

"Do you not like dodgeball?" Jeremy pushed.

Max shook his head.

"You're tall. We can play basketball instead."

"I don't play basketball either," Max said.

"What can you do then? Don't you ever play?"

He shrugged. "I used to like riding bikes, but not anymore. I don't like anything with wheels."

What a strange thing to say. "How do you get anywhere then?"

Max didn't respond, so an awkward silence followed. Didn't Max ever get tired of being so sulky? How could they be friends if he never wanted to do anything?

"That's fine." Jeremy nodded.

"What's fine?"

"You don't need to like wheels to be a Christian. Jesus didn't get to ride cars when He was on earth. He always walked everywhere He went with all His friends. One time, He even walked on water and got

His best friend, Peter, to walk on water too, but only for a while, because Peter was too chicken."

Max scrunched up his nose. "Did he die?"

"Who? Peter? No. Jesus saved him and brought him back to the boat with all their best friends. Jesus saved me too. He's just awesome that way. He likes saving people, so when he was on earth, He had twelve best friends. Today, anyone who wants Him as a best friend can just ask, so He's like best friends with millions of people everywhere. I don't even have one best friend."

"Isn't Jesus your best friend?"

"Well, yeah, but He doesn't count, because He's the best friend of everybody who knows Him. Do you have a best friend?"

Max shook his head.

"Me neither, and I can't be best friends with a girl. My sister was best friends with our neighbor, Nolan, and now, they're kissing all the time."

Max wrinkled his nose. "Ew."

"Right? That's why I can never be best friends with a girl. It gets disgusting at some point, because you can't just stay best friends forever."

"I don't want to be best friends with a girl either," Max said.

"You and me both then." This was perfect, Jeremy decided. They already had something in common. "What do you want to be someday?"

Max sighed. "Alive."

That's another thing they had in common. Who wouldn't want to be alive in the future? "I want to be a missionary like this guy from our church. Joshua Grant."

"Who is Joshua Grant?"

"I told you. He's a guy from our church. He flies all over the world in airplanes and goes on a lot of adventures."

"I don't know about that. People get in all sorts of danger when they travel too much."

"Yeah, but planes don't use their wheels as much as cars. It's only when they need to take off—" Jeremy made his hand zoom up in the air "—and when they need to land." He slid his hand down, like it was about to make a smooth landing. "Do you not like wings as well? You should be okay with planes, right?"

Max leaned his head on the chain the swing was hanging from. "I guess. I just don't want to die from an accident."

"My dad says that if we want to live forever and ever and not die, we need to believe in Jesus. Do you believe in Jesus?"

"I knew someone who believed in Jesus with all her heart. She isn't alive anymore, though."

"She's alive, but she's not alive here on earth. She's in heaven. If you believe in Jesus, you get to have eternal life in another place, even when you die. If we want to live in heaven forever, then maybe we shouldn't have a problem with flying."

"How do you believe in Jesus?"

"Oh, it's easy." Jeremy shrugged. "You have to pray a prayer. I'll show you how, but first, let me tell you about what Jesus did for us."

Word for word, Jeremy shared the Gospel to Max the same way his family had shared it to him. He led Max to accept Jesus as His Lord and Savior, and it amazed Jeremy, because after they said their prayer, Max looked different. There was this light on his face that wasn't there before.

Max creased his brows, looked up at Jeremy, and let out this huge smile. "I think I know now what she meant about Jesus changing people on the inside, so that they glowed on the outside."

"What who meant?"

He shook his head. "Someone I love. The one who loved me and Jesus. I want him to be my best friend as well."

"Great!" Jeremy exclaimed. "We can all be best friends. You, Jesus, and me."

Max grinned. "I like that."

That Sunday, Jeremy brought his new best friend to church. They had been best friends since. As for Jeremy's friendship with Jesus, that proved to be a lot more complicated, because the honest truth was that Max might have wanted Jesus as his best friend, but Jeremy wasn't sure he did. After all, Jesus didn't seem to like Jeremy at all, because if He did, why wouldn't He show him the heavens? Why didn't Jeremy know what it felt like to let Jesus change him on the inside, so he could glow on the outside? Was Jesus living in his heart at all?

If so, could Jeremy ever change? People like Mrs. P seemed to believe that he couldn't, and God liked her so much more than He liked Jeremy. Maybe that was why Jesus was not interested in being best friends with someone like Jeremy. Maybe that was why as Max's light grew brighter, Jeremy's fire began to look more like a dying ember, flickering desperately, hoping that someone could recognize his light.

seven

THE ONE WHO KNEW THE RIGHT WAY

- THREE YEARS LATER; RACHEL, 8 -

Barefoot and barely awake, Rachel blinked her eyes as she made her bed. The music from her alarm clock filled the room. She preferred to not turn it off immediately and leave her favorite song playing as she fixed her bedroom first thing in the morning. With everything in order, it was easier to face the day with a smile.

Her days started at six-thirty every morning, so she could read the Bible and be downstairs for breakfast by seven-thirty; her eighth birthday was no exception. Her princess party was happening today, and the thought of wearing her puffy, pink chiffon dress was enough to tug the corners of her lips upward. Today was going to be a beautiful day, and nothing could ruin it!

She ran her palms against the thick pink duvet covering her bed to make sure it was as smooth as possible before placing her pillows in their proper places. Having accomplished her first task of the day, Rachel dragged her feet across the polished hardwood floor and proceeded to her reading nook — a little cushioned alcove in one of her room's walls. Her Bible, prayer notebook, and sparkly pink pen were already waiting for her there.

Rachel switched on the overhead light in her nook, climbed the seat, and opened her Bible. She picked up from where she had left off the night before. She had finally finished the book of Job — hallelujah! That story was so confusing. Why did God let satan punish Job so much, and why was God so upset when Job kept asking Him why? Rachel would ask why too if all those things happened to her!

She removed the bookmark from the page and flipped her pink Bible to the book of Psalm. She grinned. Chapters in this book were much shorter. Also, she had already memorized the first chapter of Psalms.

Rachel recited the chapter out loud. "Blessed is the man that walketh not in the counsel of the ungodly..." She continued reciting the entire verse as she opened her notebook and started writing her entry for that morning. Her mother would check later that night, and the last thing she wanted was to upset Mom. "...But his delight is in the law of the Lord; and in his law doth he meditate day and night..." Rachel sighed as she tried to write faster about how the chapter meant she needed to love God's Word and choose good friends so her life would prosper like a tree by the river. She wrinkled her nose. That didn't work out for Job, did it? God was so hard to understand sometimes, but Rachel loved Him anyway, because how could she not? He was God, and He loved her. Rachel wanted to keep it that way, so she had to do everything she could to stay on God's good side. "...For the Lord knoweth the way of the righteous: but the way of the ungodly shall perish..." Rachel scribbled on her notebook as fast as her handwriting could go. Her parents had always told her that the consequences of sin were painful, so she felt bad for all the sinners out there who were perishing. Not Rachel, though. She was alive in Christ! And the proof of that was her birthday!

Rachel drew a heart instead of a dot to finish her final sentence before writing down at the bottom of the page: *Thank you for my birthday and my pretty dress, God! I love it!*

She shut her notebook and her Bible. All done! She checked the digital clock on top of her desk. It wasn't even seven yet! She still had time to braid her favorite doll's hair before her shower and still be able to make it on time for breakfast with Dad and Mom. She placed her stuff back in their proper places and skipped toward her doll to braid her doll's hair the way she wanted her hair braided. It took about ten minutes to finish. With every task she was accomplishing, Rachel's mood kept lifting, her awareness of being alive growing.

At exactly seven-thirty, Rachel showed up at their breakfast table, already wearing her birthday dress. She came just in time to find her mother laying a plate of toast, a jar of strawberry jam, and some butter on Rachel's side of the table. She licked her lips. Her favorite!

"Good morning, Mom. Good morning, Dad!" She threw her arms in the air and swiveled her hip to the side. She held that pose so her parents would notice. "It's my birthday!"

Her father, who was sitting at the head of the table, lowered the newspaper he was reading to get a good look at Rachel. "Good morning, sweetheart. Happy birthday!"

"Hello, Rachel," Mom said. "Come, sit down and eat. Sam and Aida will be here any minute now. It would be nice if we've already cleaned up by the time they arrive."

"Dad, do you love my dress?" Rachel twirled around on her tippy toes.

"Yes, of course." Dad folded his newspaper as he smiled at Rachel. "You're very pretty. Now, do what your mother says." He turned toward Mom. "What time did Aida say they were arriving?"

"She mentioned dropping the boys over at nine-ish." Mom huffed as she sat in her regular chair. "Whatever nine-ish means. So like Aida to not just say a specific time. She can be so flighty sometimes, that friend of mine."

Dad nodded slowly. Rachel doubted he agreed, though. Sometimes, he just wanted Mom to be quiet. Sometimes, Rachel did too.

"Jeremy and Max are coming?" Rachel asked.

"Yes. They're supposed to help prepare for your party, but how much help can those boys give? I'm the one who's helping Sam and Aida. They have to go somewhere, so Sam asked if they could drop the boys over a bit earlier. Something to do with that man who used to stalk Nova."

"Knox?"

"Yes. Him. I still can't believe they're letting him come to our church. I never feel safe whenever he's around. It's a good thing I can trust Hannah to be vigilant in keeping a close eye on the young women."

"Come on, Rhoda." Dad sighed. "I've had a few conversations with Knox. God is working on him. Let's give him a chance to show us how he has changed."

Mom widened her eyes. "I know God can change people, Robert. Don't you think I believe that? Still, the times are different, and it pays to be wise. Jesus has warned us, after all, that we are lambs among wolves, and that we need to be watchful in case the enemy sends us wolves disguised as sheep. We have a daughter — Lord, have mercy on us — and the man has gone to prison for terrorizing a woman. Since they were in high school, apparently!"

"From my understanding, he did leave Nova alone for years before returning to her life, and—"

"Rachel. What are you still doing standing there?" Mom pointed at Rachel's empty seat. "Sit down and eat."

Rachel climbed onto her chair. "I like Hannah," she said. "She's my favorite teacher in Sunday School."

"Yes." Mom nodded with approval. "Hannah is someone you can trust. She can be a good role model for you if she keeps following Christ like she is now."

There were only a few people in church who made Mom happy. Hannah was one of them. That's why Rachel wanted to be just like Hannah when she grew up.

"Shall we say grace?" Dad asked. "Rachel, do you want to pray? It's your birthday, after all. It'll be a good time to thank God for all your blessings."

Rachel nodded. She laid her elbows on top of the table, pressed her palms together in prayer, closed her eyes, and recited the words they had taught her to pray. "God, thank you for my dad and my mom. Bless our family. Bless the food we are about to eat and let it be nourishing to our bodies. In Jesus's— Oh wait! Thank you for my birthday too!" She clapped her hands and giggled. "I'm so happy to finally be eight years old. So many of my friends in school have turned eight, and no matter what I did, I was still stuck at seven. Until this day came! Thank you, Jesus! In Jesus's Name, I pray, amen!"

She opened her eyes to find her father's affectionate smile directed at her. "Thank you for that prayer, Rachel."

"That was a good prayer, honey." Mom smiled. "Now, eat. We have a long day ahead of us. Be careful not to get any food on your dress." She frowned. "Why are you wearing your dress this early, anyway? It'll get soiled by the time the party starts. Let's go to your room and get you changed. You can wear your dress later, right before the party."

"But Mom—" Rachel's lips quivered "—I'll be careful not to get it dirty, I promise."

"Now, Rachel. You know what the Bible says about promising. Don't make promises. Let your yes be yes, and your no be no." Mom stood from her seat and motioned for Rachel to follow. "Come on now. Let's get you changed. I'll give you a cupcake as a snack later. You don't want all that strawberry filling all over your pretty dress, do you?"

Rachel reluctantly gave in. There was no point in arguing with her mother, anyway. By the time they finished picking out an outfit for Rachel, their pastor and his family were already at their entryway, chatting with Dad. Would Mom get mad that they weren't done with breakfast yet before their guests arrived?

"Thanks for agreeing to have the boys over early," Mama Aida told Dad. "I hope it's not too much of an inconvenience."

"Of course not," Mom answered for Dad as she descended the last flight of stairs. "Hello, Aida." She nodded at their pastor's wife, then at their pastor. "Sam."

"Good morning, Rhoda." Pastor Sam smiled.

Meanwhile, Mama Aida was waving at Rachel. She had a gift bag in her other hand. Rachel grinned. It had to be for her! "Happy birthday, Rachel! Aren't you extra pretty today? More so than always, hmm?"

Rachel's grin grew. "And I'm not even wearing my birthday dress yet! It's pink and fluffy and shiny and it's the prettiest dress there ever was!"

"Now, Rachel—" Mom patted her head "—be careful. We don't want people thinking you're vain."

Mama Aida gave Mom a strange look.

Behind her, their son, Jeremy, was ribbing his best friend, Max. Her cheeks flushed red. Were they making fun of her? Should she be embarrassed? Her lips quivered, but Jeremy made a funny face at her. She giggled. He motioned for her to approach them.

Rachel skipped their way. She figured the adults could talk, and since there weren't any kids her age yet, she had to make do with the only other kids there with her. Hopefully, they would stop treating her like a kid now that she was already eight. They were only twelve, after all. They weren't much older than she was. She stopped in front of the boys, gave them her biggest smile, and waved.

Jeremy smiled back at her. "Hey, Rachel. That's a nice braid you have."

"Thank you! My doll has a braid just like it. Do you want to see the backyard? There are castles and everything! I get to be a princess today."

"Is that so? Should we call you Princess Rachel then?" Jeremy patted her head.

She shrugged. "If you want to, but—" she tapped her cheek with her finger "—I'm not sure if that makes me vain. You would have to ask Mom for permission."

"Permission?" Max asked. "To call you Princess?"

She bobbed her head up and down.

Jeremy shook his head. "Not a conversation I want to have with Mrs. P." He turned toward Max. "Want to volunteer?"

"No way. I plan to stay on Mrs. P's good side today. Only way to survive."

"We'll call you Princess Rachel in secret," Jeremy decided.

Rachel was about to tell him her mother didn't like her keeping secrets, but Pastor Sam and Mama Aida were already leaving, so Rachel had to be polite and say goodbye to the grown-ups.

When Mama Aida noticed her approaching, she gave Rachel a huge hug. "You are so precious to God, Rachel. Don't ever forget that. Happy birthday, sweetie."

Rachel beamed. "Thank you, Mama Aida! You're precious to God too!"

"That is true." Mama Aida laughed before standing up straight. "You both are raising her so well," Mama said to Dad and Mom. "She is such a lovely and kind girl."

"Only by God's grace." Mom pointed at the ceiling.

Why was she being so nice? Only a while ago, she was saying a bunch of stuff about Mama Aida in Rachel's bedroom. Rachel couldn't remember most of it, though. She had been too busy figuring out if Mom would agree to braid her hair the way she wanted it. She shrugged it off and led the boys to the backyard, convinced they would be mighty impressed with her shiny new kingdom of pink and lace. When her parents had shown her everything the night before, she had shrieked with delight.

Jeremy and Max, however, didn't shriek at all. They didn't seem too impressed, because after exchanging looks, both started snickering. Didn't they know they shouldn't be mockers? Rachel stomped her foot, planted her hands on her hips, and harrumphed at them.

They both tried to hold back their snickers, but it was Jeremy who managed to stop and say, "It's definitely fit for a princess like you, Rachel."

She smiled, hoping that meant something good. "Thank you!"

"Where are those kids?" The screen door leading to the backyard swung open, and Mom appeared from inside. "There you are!" Her eyes softened upon seeing them. "Have you boys eaten breakfast yet? We had to take care of Rachel's dress, so we haven't finished eating yet. Would you boys like to join us?"

Again, the boys exchanged looks like they were somehow communicating secret messages to each other to decide what to do. Rachel wished she had a friend like that. Her friend from school, Erika, never seemed to get what Rachel was saying — especially when she started talking about God. Maybe she should stop mentioning God to Erika, so they could become best friends like Jeremy and Max were. Would God be upset with her if she did that?

"Rachel!" Mom tugged on the sleeve of Rachel's blouse. "Come in and finish your food, honey."

"What about Jeremy and Max?" she asked as she pointed at the boys, who had both taken seats at one of the tables set up. Both took out their phones. Why did they get to play games? It was her birthday, not theirs.

"Weren't you listening, Rachel? They said they already ate breakfast, so we can go ahead." Her mother pulled her inside the house, shut the screen door to the backyard, peered at the boys through the screen, and huffed. "This is why I wanted to finish eating breakfast first. Who knows what those boys will be up to, if we just leave them there?"

"Can I just spend time with them, Mom? I'm not hungry anymore."

Her mother paused and curled her lip to give it a moment's thought. "I think you should at least finish some of your breakfast. I'll ask your dad to give them something to do anyway, so they won't have time to hang out with you."

As usual, Rachel gave in. It was better to be obedient. She was sure the Bible said something like that somewhere. Hannah always emphasized that at Sunday School. They all had to be obedient.

All the kids. Not just the younger ones. Even Jeremy and Max.

Rachel didn't think of it any further and complied with her mother's wishes. Back at the breakfast table, she sat down and bit on her slice of cold, stiff toast with clumpy butter and strawberry jam. It wasn't much of a birthday meal, but it wasn't her party yet. She wasn't even wearing her birthday dress yet!

"Can you give the boys something to do while I make sure Rachel is fed and taken care of?" Mom asked Dad.

"Sure, Rhoda. There's a lot they can do to help set up. They're good kids."

"Ha! Good? Please." Mom scoffed. "I can say that about the Owens boy. Considering what kind of mother he has, it's amazing how well-mannered and put-together that boy is. He always has been polite and cooperative when he's on his own, but when he's with Sam and Aida's boy—" Mom shook her head. "I'm telling you, Robert. Keep an eye out for Jeremy. If anything untoward happens this afternoon, it will most likely be his fault."

Dad sighed and rubbed his palm up and down Mom's arm. The way his shoulders sagged and his eyes drooped made Rachel worry. Was he tired? Did he ever sleep at all, or did he work all the time?

Mom's expression softened. "I'm sorry, Robert. It's just that people put Sam and Aida on a pedestal all the time. No one ever calls them out on their imperfections. Those two have brought me so much hurt! The gall of Aida to talk about the way we're raising Rachel, like we need her seal of approval. Meanwhile, her daughter is out there chasing a worldly music career with that punk boyfriend of hers, and her son — don't even get me started! Jeremy is a menace."

Behind Mom, Jeremy cleared his throat. Upon seeing him, Rachel tilted her head before taking a huge bite of her toast. How long had he been standing there? Had he heard Mom call him a menace? Rachel scrunched her nose. What was a menace, anyway?

"Mrs. P, I was wondering if you had some water. Max and I are both thirsty."

Mom didn't move a muscle. From where she sat, Rachel couldn't see her mother's face. Why wasn't she moving? Had she not heard Jeremy?

"Sure." Dad stepped in. "I'll get you some."

"Thanks, Mr. P." Jeremy nodded toward Dad, then to Mom, then to Rachel, who grinned at him and popped the last of her toast into her mouth.

"I'm done eating!" she exclaimed as she hopped off her chair. "I'm going outside with Jeremy!"

To her surprise, Mom didn't object. Good. Who knew how long her freedom would last? She had to savor every moment of it. She skipped toward Jeremy and held his hand before tugging him toward the backyard.

She wanted to show them the bouncy castle, even if she wasn't sure if they were allowed to bounce inside, considering how big they were. Especially Max, who was taller than Jeremy.

"Watch me bounce!" She leaped into the castle, hoping her mother wouldn't suddenly come out to stop her.

"Way to go, Princess Rachel!" Jeremy cheered.

"We can be her bodyguards," Max said.

Rachel stopped bouncing. "What are those?"

"You know." Max shrugged. "They guard the princess, so no one will harm her."

Rachel wrinkled her nose. "You mean like from dragons?"

"Sure," Max said. "Dragons."

"I think we should be called knights instead." Jeremy began checking the walls of the bouncy castle.

"Are those the same as bodyguards?" Rachel asked.

"Uh-huh. Only more epic." Jeremy winked. "Princess Rachel has her own castle, her knights, and a dragon."

It sounded great to Rachel, though there was no way a dragon would show up. Mom asked all the party guests to come looking like princes and princesses. Who would want to be a dragon? She shouldn't give it too much thought. They could be her knights if they wanted. Rachel bounced a bit more but decided she should get out before her mother showed up.

Max and Jeremy, like the good knights they were, helped steady her on her feet.

Rachel didn't know why Mom didn't like Pastor Sam or Mama Aida or Jeremy. They all seemed like perfectly nice people to her, not at all like the ungodly people her Bible told her not to walk with. It was hard to figure out how to please her mother, but Rachel would rather be on her mother's good side than on her bad side, so between Max and Jeremy, she needed to pay attention to how Max behaved. He was the one who had Mom's approval.

So, until her party could begin, Rachel did just that. She observed everything Max did as opposed to what Jeremy didn't. While Jeremy sat down and checked his phone every time he finished a task, waiting for someone to tell him what to do, Max would ask what else he could do once done with a task. Max always stood from his seat whenever Mom showed up. He always opened the door for Mom whenever there was an opportunity to. Jeremy hadn't done any of those. Not even once.

All morning, Rachel played her quiet game of comparison between the two boys to find out what types of behavior irked her mother and which ones pleased her. By the time the party started and finally, Rachel was wearing her pretty pink dress and the beautiful-est tiara her father had given her as a gift, she already had a long mental list of ways to please her mother.

Everything was perfect.

And then Jenna came in.

While everyone else was wearing costumes fit for royalty, Jenna showed up as a red, fire-breathing dragon. Rachel couldn't believe her eyes. Where were her knights when she needed them? "Jenna, why are you a dragon?!"

"I'm not a dragon." Jenna frowned. "I'm a Tyrannosaurus Rex. Haven't you seen *Jurassic Kingdom*?"

Rachel frowned. She had heard about the movie, because everyone in school was talking about it. "My parents don't let me watch scary movies."

Jenna's face twisted in confusion. "What's so scary about *Jurassic Kingdom*?"

What did she mean what was so scary about it? "Don't people get eaten by dinosaurs?"

"Yeah. So?"

Rachel couldn't keep herself from looking at Jenna funny. "You're weird."

Jenna stuck her tongue out at Rachel. "So are you."

"You can't say that to me! It's my birthday!"

Jenna roared at Rachel, who shrieked in surprise. Meanwhile, beside her, Jeremy and Max were doubling over in laughter. Why weren't they doing anything to save her from this weird little girl? Her eyes grew wet. It was her birthday. They weren't supposed to treat her this way. She ran off to find her mother to tell on Jenna, and once she told Mom everything that happened, she realized who her real knight was. It was her mom — not Max or Jeremy — who would always defend her.

A sneer appeared on Rachel's face. She knew now who was definitely not walking on the right path. It was Jenna. She was about to promise herself to stay as far away from Jenna as possible, but she remembered she shouldn't make promises, so she stomped her foot and decided Jenna would never be her friend. That way, Rachel would always stay on her mother's good side, where she belonged.

eight

THE ONE
WHO WAS
DISAPPOINTED

- ONE YEAR LATER; RACHEL, 9 -

Since the day dragon-clad Jenna danced in the rain instead of running inside the house for cover like everyone else, all the kids at Sunday School and later, at school, had been calling her Crazy Jenna.

Rachel often instigated the name-calling, only because she wholeheartedly believed it to be true. Jenna was crazy, and she certainly proved that when one morning, while they were all preparing for Sunday School, Jenna punched Tyler Price right on the nose.

"Stop calling me that!" Jenna yelled right as her fist connected with Tyler's face.

"She's crazy!" Rachel shrieked after seeing her friend, Tyler, topple down to the ground. "She's crazy!" she repeated before rushing toward Tyler to check if he was okay. He wasn't. Not with all that blood on his nose.

Meanwhile, Jenna stood over him, legs wide apart and fists clenched, scowling at him like the menace she was.

Max showed up at the door.

Jeremy followed soon after. He turned to his best friend. "Did she just—"

Max nodded. "I think so."

"What's going on here?" Mom walked past the boys and gasped when she saw Tyler.

"She hit me!" Tyler blurted out, half-yelling, half-whimpering. His face crumpled in pain, like he had just realized the hurt Jenna had caused him. A loud wail blared out of his lips.

Rachel squirmed. Would everyone hear him all the way to the sanctuary?

"Jenna!" Mom planted a hand on her hip and wagged her finger at the girl. "It is not good to hit people!"

To Rachel's shock, Jenna didn't even say sorry. She rubbed her fist like she was ready to fight even Rachel's mom. "He asked for it!" She stomped her foot on the floor. "He threw a cockroach at me, and he keeps calling me Crazy Jenna, and I'm not crazy! I'm not!"

What was she going on about? She was crazy. Did she not know that? Even Max, who never said anything about anyone, called her Crazy Jenna. That was saying something, as far as Rachel was concerned.

Feeling sorry for Tyler, who was still bawling, Rachel decided to stand up for the boy who, only minutes before Jenna had punched him, had been trying to throw a plastic cockroach at Rachel. "That cockroach isn't even real," Rachel said. "Tyler was just having fun."

"I'm not crazy!" Jenna said again.

Jeremy snickered, making Max glare at him. Jeremy whispered something in his defense, and Rachel lost interest in them. She was too curious about what punishment Jenna's actions would meet. Her mother tsk-tsked at Jenna, whose appearance was a lot more defiant than repentant. Mom ignored her and went to Tyler to help the boy up. "Oh honey, it looks like she broke your nose." She turned to Max and Jeremy. "Boys, please find Tyler's and Jenna's parents."

Mom watched as the boys raced outside the room before checking further on Tyler. Rachel glared at Jenna before crouching down next to her mother. "Is he going to be okay? Why is she so strange?"

"Tyler will be fine, honey. We'll get him some help once his mother gets here," Mom said. "As for Jenna, we just have to forgive her, because her parents have all sorts of problems. Paolo never should have married Eden. We told him over and over again that he should choose a woman who loves the Lord; instead, he chose someone who doesn't believe in God. Now, all they do is fight, and this poor little girl is acting out because of it. Go to Jenna, and calm her down, Rachel."

That was the last thing she wanted to do, because Jenna was always shooting her glares at school and acting like Rachel had been mean to her, when Rachel had been nothing but nice. Still, Rachel had to obey her mother, so she squared her shoulders, put on a smile, and approached the crazy kid.

"Jenna, why don't you take a seat while we wait for your daddy to get here? Max and Jeremy called him." Rachel tried to brush her fingers against Jenna's arm, but she flinched away from Rachel's touch.

"Don't touch me." Jenna growled at her.

Rachel stepped back. Why was Jenna always acting like an animal with all this growling and walking around like a dragon hunting down bugs? "Don't be so angry, Jenna. It's why all the kids think you're crazy, because you act so strange all the time."

"Leave me alone, Little Miss Perfect," Jenna said through gritted teeth. She stomped out of the room.

Rachel certainly wasn't going to follow her outside. "Mom, Jenna's leaving!"

"Please check on her, Rachel." Mom sounded tired as she dabbed cotton on Tyler's bloody nose. "Her father might not be able to find her."

Rachel hesitated. Why couldn't Jenna be someone else's problem instead of hers? She just wanted to hear a story from Sunday School, color some pages, and have a snack. Still, she had to obey. She reached the lobby and got distracted when she saw Serene crying on Jeremy's shoulders. What was she upset about? Meanwhile, Max was giving Jenna, who was crying to her father, a sad look.

Rachel's shoulders sagged at all the sadness surrounding her. Where was everybody's joy? They were in the house of God! They should smile and be happy, because God gives joy to anyone who asks for it. Mom would, for sure, say something about it, if they kept skulking around like this. Not knowing what to do, Rachel twisted on her heel and returned to the Sunday School room to report on her findings. She discovered Tyler's mother was already there, so Mom had diverted her attention to gathering the children to start Sunday School.

"Jenna is with her dad," Rachel reported.

"Good." Mom patted the top of her head in approval. "Thank you, Rachel. Take a seat now."

Rachel took her seat, but Jenna's words lingered in her mind. Little Miss Perfect. That was what Jenna had called her. Did Jenna think she would be upset at being called that? Why? What was wrong with being perfect? It was certainly better than being Crazy Jenna.

- JEREMY, 13 -

The breakup of Nolan and Serene followed Jeremy everywhere. All week in school, his classmates kept asking him what had happened, and it was beginning to irk him. Why would they assume he would know? It wasn't like anyone at home bothered to explain why his older sister was crying all the time, and it wasn't like it was his priority to stay updated on pop culture drama. At thirteen years old, it had made him roll his eyes over and over again, the way people tried to get close to him, hoping he would become somewhat of a bridge for them to befriend Serene.

Jeremy shied away from the spotlight. He had long discovered he was better able to get away with whatever he wanted when he wasn't under the scrutiny of people around him — more specifically, the scrutiny of Mrs. P, whom he was almost about to declare his personal archenemy. Especially one Sunday, as she openly spoke out her opinion about Serene.

"Have you seen Serene around?" she asked someone.

Max cast Jeremy a worried glance as they sank into the velvet couches of their church lobby, where they had snuck off to in the middle of the service.

Jeremy scowled, his ears prickling over the things he was hearing from the women, unaware of the boys' presence as they slumped further down on the couch to avoid detection.

"I can't believe Sam and Aida are allowing their daughter not to come to church. Sure, she has a broken heart. I understand that, but she needs God now more than ever." Mrs. P huffed, her heels clacking against the marble floor.

Who she was speaking to, Jeremy could only guess, but she was somewhere close, most likely pouring herself a cup of coffee at the refreshments table. What was she doing in the lobby while the sermon was ongoing? One could ask the same about Jeremy and Max, of course, but that was different. They were thirteen. Mrs. P was old. She was supposed to be the example, not them.

"It's sad how she turned out," another female voice responded. "She and Nolan used to be so anointed, so blessed, so passionate about the Lord. Still, let's pray about her and give her time. God isn't finished with her yet, I'm certain."

It sounded like Miss Hannah to Jeremy.

"I'm praying for both of them, because I do love Nolan and Serene. It is sad how everything turned out." The compassion was evident in Miss Hannah's voice.

"Of course it is!" Mrs. P exclaimed. "The saddest part, however, is it could have all been prevented. Look at you and your siblings. There are six of you, and your parents have raised you so well. Meanwhile, our very own pastor has one daughter who barely believes in God and almost sold her soul to the world, and a son who is one of the most rebellious, obnoxious, and belligerent teenagers I've ever met."

He exchanged glances with Max and rolled his eyes. Max winced before coughing out loud and jumping to his feet. "Mrs. P!" He walked around the sofa before the women could check to find Jeremy there. "Mrs. Price." Max's voice was softer now. "Miss Hannah."

So there were three of them. Jeremy rolled his eyes. Of course, Miss Hannah and Mrs. Price were with their ring leader. What was it about Mrs. P that made them follow her so devotedly?

"Max." Mrs. P sounded a little choked. "How long have you been there?"

"Too long," Max responded. "I was about to go back to the hall to listen to Pastor Sam preach. Shall we go?"

Mrs. P coughed. "Of course, of course. Come on, ladies. We should listen."

To stifle the snicker begging to escape, Jeremy clamped his palm over his mouth. Thank God for his best friend! When the lobby was once again silent, Jeremy rose from the couch and frowned at the idea of having to finish the rest of the service, but there were worse things to experience on earth than another half hour of repetitive Biblical sermons. He snuck back in and found Max, who seemed to be intently listening to what Jeremy's father was saying on the pulpit. Something about forgiveness or grace or having countless chances here on earth. Nothing Jeremy hadn't heard before.

While Max listened, Jeremy retreated into his mind and went on an adventure. As he did, an idea formed in his head — one he couldn't shake until he could get it done. Giddy with excitement by the time the service was over, he asked Max to go to the Sunday School room, which was usually empty once the service was over. They waited until Miss Kelly and Miss Olivia finished cleaning up before going in.

"What?" Max asked.

"I have an idea." Jeremy grinned. "I can't stand Mrs. P anymore, and I think I know how to get revenge."

Max scratched his brow. "Revenge?"

"Yeah. We need to avenge Serene from all the things Mrs. P has been saying."

"Didn't you listen to your father's teaching this morning? He said vengeance is the Lord's."

"Yeah, but this is a fun kind of revenge. Once we pull it off, everyone will think it's funny. Come on, Max. Back me up here. It will be so fun."

Max wrinkled his nose and shifted his weight to the other foot. He sighed. "Fine. Not like I could ever say no to adventures with you, anyway. What did you have in mind?"

Jeremy laid out his plans, and the week that followed involved a bit of work trying to execute the plan. Sunday came, and it was time to put everything into motion. Jeremy told a few lies here and there — like telling Serene to drive five humongous bags of popcorn to the church parking lot for Sunday School. He also spent quite a bit of his savings to buy all that popcorn, but meh. All in good fun. It would be worth it. While the service proceeded, Max and Jeremy snuck out to get the popcorn from Serene, who was looking at them funny.

"What is this really for, Jeremy?" she asked.

Jeremy refused to flinch or show any signs of weakness. "I told you. It's for Sunday School."

"Why would they need this much popcorn?"

"I don't know. I think they plan to have a movie night. Do you want to ask Mrs. P?"

"Ugh." Serene frowned. The hurt in her green eyes as she shook her head reminded Jeremy why he was doing this. "I can't stand her right now. The last thing I want is to talk to that woman."

"I know." Jeremy nodded. "Thanks for doing this anyway, Serene. And for all it's worth, a lot of people here still love you. Miss Hannah and Nova keep asking about you."

Serene sighed. "Yeah. They invited me out for coffee this week."

"Will you go?"

"We'll see." Serene shrugged. "I just need space right now."

"You sure you don't want to come in?"

"Next week," she said. "Maybe."

Jeremy didn't push. He opened her car door for her and stayed in the parking lot until she drove off. Once her car was out of sight, Jeremy and Max hauled five bags of popcorn toward Mrs. P's brand new SUV.

"Now, how do we get it in?" Max asked.

Jeremy grinned, fished the keys out of his pocket, and dangled it in the air.

Max's eyes shot open. "Jeremy! How did you get those? Dude, you're scaring me. This is borderline criminal."

Jeremy shrugged. "Mrs. P doesn't pay attention to her purse when she's in church. It was easy to pick it off of her unattended bag."

"Aren't we going a little overboard?" Max was clinging to three unopened bags of popcorn as he eyed the key in Jeremy's hand. The concern on Max's face was enough for Jeremy to hesitate.

"Do you think we should back down? It's just a prank, Max. It's not like we're stealing their car."

Max stared at his feet, reminding Jeremy of the shell-shocked version of Max in their school playground. How had Jeremy gone from leading Max to a relationship with Jesus to leading him to some good ol' juvenile delinquency? Jeremy bristled. His jaw tightened. Should they stop? But they were already here! What were they going to do with all this popcorn? Donate it to the youth group or the children's ministry for their next movie night, maybe?

Jeremy heaved a sigh before giving in to the heavenly tug in his heart. For now, they could leave it to God to take vengeance on their behalf. He owed Max that much.

"So? What do we do? I honestly don't think this is a good idea, Jeremy. Also, their car is new."

Jeremy lifted a bag of popcorn. "And this is buttered popcorn."

Max's stoic expression was enough to tell him what Max thought about this whole thing.

"Fine, Jiminy Cricket," Jeremy said. "Let's get these bags inside."

It was actually harder than they had anticipated to drag five giant plastic bags of popcorn across the parking lot to the church lobby. They were both sweat-drenched by the time they reached the lobby, where they sighed with relief at the wisps of cold coming from the air conditioner. Their relief, however, was short-lived, because they had barely caught their breaths when Mrs. P and Rachel emerged from the hallway connecting the sanctuary and the lobby.

"Rachel, are you sure?" Mrs. P tugged Rachel's arm. "You shouldn't make up stories."

"I'm not making things up, Mommy. I saw Jeremy take it."

His heart sank.

"Oh no," Max whispered beside him.

"Don't say anything," Jeremy instructed. "I'll handle this." Before Mrs. P could breathe a word, Jeremy handed her the car keys. "I'm sorry," he said. "I shouldn't have taken your keys."

"What has gotten into your head?" Mrs. P tapped her temple with her forefinger before pointing the key at Jeremy, like she was about to stab him in the eye with it. "Did you drive it? You don't have a license yet. You better believe your father will hear all about this after the service. I can't believe you would do something like this. Why would you steal from us? In church nonetheless! Don't you have any fear of the Lord left in you, child?"

Was this what Jesus felt like when he stood before Pilate and the Sanhedrin?

Mrs. P didn't seem to want answers, so Jeremy remained silent and listened to her ask one question after another. There was no reasoning with this woman. Or her daughter. He fought the urge to smirk at Rachel, who was standing next to her mother, arms crossed over her chest, scowling at him. Why was this kid so cute, even when she was trying to be a mini version of her mother? Her face was so stinking adorable.

"Are you even listening to me?" Mrs. P poked Jeremy's shoulder.

It wasn't like he was thinking about retaliating, but his knee-jerk physical reaction to her touching him was to ball his fists.

Mrs. P noticed. She tsk-tsked and shook her head. "Unbelievable." She took her daughter's hand in hers, turned toward the sanctuary, and dragged her daughter forward. "Come on, Rachel. I don't want to stay here and do something I'll regret later. And don't even get me started on why these boys have all that popcorn. Did they steal those from somewhere, too?"

Rachel turned to smile at Max, then stuck her tongue out at Jeremy, who grinned and waved at her. She pulled back her tongue and stared at him in confusion.

"Now what?" Max asked once they were alone in the lobby again.

Jeremy shrugged. "Let's take these to the storage room. Dad can figure out what to do with them later."

"That's it? Aren't you scared?"

"Nah. What can they do to me? The worst that can happen is I'll get grounded. Mrs. P will probably demand my crucifixion no matter what, but if Jesus survived a crucifixion, I can too."

"Not funny."

"Look. I'll come clean and tell them I was planning a prank, but you talked me out of it. It'll be fine."

It wasn't fine. Mrs. P was livid — more livid than Jeremy thought the crime he committed deserved. What would have happened if he had gone through with the prank? Would she have demanded he be sent to a juvenile detention center?

Inside his father's office, Mrs. P berated her own pastor about the dismal job he was doing raising his kids. Jeremy squirmed in his seat. Max was white as a sheet beside him, like all his trauma had somehow returned. Guilt came over Jeremy for being the one who introduced God and the church to Max. So much for the Gospel being good news. How good was it if it led people to situations like this?

It took at least a full ten minutes before Mrs. P calmed down — after having mentioned how much the car was and the damage that could have been done if Jeremy had driven it. Because Jeremy hadn't even been given the opportunity to speak yet, he still wasn't able to clarify that he never even touched the car! All he wanted was to pour popcorn in it, not drive it. Mrs. P and her hypotheticals.

Dad sat behind his desk, unmoving. He neither looked at Mrs. P nor at Jeremy and Max. His focus was on the Bible on his desk. "Are you done, Rhoda?" His voice was deep and ominous, almost like it was carrying a threat with it.

"Yes." Mrs. P's response was breathless. Her spine relaxed and her shoulders lowered as she took the seat next to the desk, opposite from where Jeremy and Max sat. "I'm quite done."

"Do you have anything to say for yourself, Jeremy?"

He wanted to retaliate. He wanted to defend himself and explain. Didn't it count for something that this woman had been slandering his sister while she was at her lowest point — not to mention their entire family for years and years? Didn't it count that Jeremy and Max didn't even go through with the prank? Afraid the indignation would reflect in his voice and make it worse, Jeremy remained silent and shook his head in response.

"That's unacceptable." Dad's tone deepened. "You can at least apologize and own up to what you've done."

Jeremy winced before forcing himself to look Mrs. P in the eye. "I'm sorry. I shouldn't have stolen your key. Max knew nothing about it."

"Why did you do it, Jeremy?" his father pried. "Why did you steal the key?"

He sighed. What did he have to lose at this point? "I wanted to fill their car with popcorn. I never intended to drive it."

His father's eyes widened in surprise. His lip twitched — almost as if he was suppressing a smile.

Mrs. P, on the other hand, lifted her chin at Jeremy like she was some hoity-toity noble woman turning her nose up on a lowly peasant.

"Max talked me out of it," Jeremy said.

"Come on." Max bumped his arm with a fist. "Pastor Sam, it's not fair to let Jeremy take the—"

Jeremy elbowed Max's rib.

"Ow," Max mouthed as he clutched the assaulted area.

"Who helped you get all the popcorn here?" Mrs. P asked.

Jeremy half-expected her to rise to her feet and pace the floor with her hands behind her back, like she was a prosecutor in a court of law, ready to bang the gavel on Jeremy's head for no good reason. There was no way in planet earth he would let them know Serene had any involvement — not that she even knew what she had aided and abetted. Mrs. P was already using his family as target practice. Why would Jeremy give her more ammunition?

No matter what his father or Mrs. P said to convince him to tell them who else was involved, he kept his lips sealed. What did it matter? The crime hadn't even been committed. Part of him even regretted not going through with it, because he ended up getting punished anyway. At least if they had pushed through with it, Jeremy would have the satisfaction of knowing Mrs. P was driving around in a car that smelled like buttered popcorn.

Jeremy didn't apologize again, even when asked. One apology was enough. Mrs. P should get over herself and forgive him. That didn't seem like it would happen, because Mrs. P walked out in a huff after almost an hour of interrogating Jeremy.

With tired eyes and a heavy countenance, Dad shook his head — whether at his son or Mrs. P, Jeremy wasn't sure. Was Dad disappointed in him?

"Son," Dad said in a voice firm, but affectionate, "our family is going through a lot with what's been happening to Nolan and Serene. It's best not to rock the boat and give people more reason to criticize us. Do you hear me?"

The disappointment washed over Jeremy. That was what his father was concerned about? The optics? What his church members thought about their family? That was the most important consideration they had at the moment? Not the fact that Rhoda Petersen was being a horrid person to his own children?

Jeremy stayed silent, but he walked out of his father's office, shaken. What kind of religion was this? What kind of God would allow His children to act this way? They were supposed to be the light of the world and the salt of the earth. How could that happen when they continued to treat their own so horribly? That day watered the seed of doubt that had been planted in Jeremy when Serene had first started questioning God's existence. What if they had it all wrong? What if he had been raised to follow a false religion?

That evening, in the quiet of his bedroom, Jeremy booted up his laptop and began scouring the internet. If he was to be sure that his religion was the truth, he had to figure out what other religions had to offer, and so it started — Jeremy's journey down the prodigal path.

nine

THE ONE WHO GOT AWAY FROM COLLEGE

- FIVE YEARS LATER; JEREMY, 18 -

When the needle almost hit the bone on Jeremy's wrist, he almost shed a tear. Why had he subjected himself to this again? He couldn't remember. The buzz of the tattoo gun and the pain in his lower right arm were overwhelming his senses. The tattoo artist lifted the device and dabbed cloth on the blood oozing out of Jeremy's reddening skin, which didn't have a chance to recover before the tattooist traced another ray of the blazing blue sun, making the rays wrap around Jeremy's wrist. Again, the needle almost grazed bone. Jeremy hissed.

"You all right, man?" the tattooist asked.

Jeremy nodded. He wasn't about to speak, because he was pretty sure his voice would come out a squeak. On the tattoo station next to him, Max was wincing in pain just as much as he was. The look on his best friend's face made Jeremy smirk. As usual, he had been the one to convince Max to do something they might regret in the future. He hadn't expected Max to agree, but to his surprise, Max had pounced on it in an instant, so here they both were, trying to man up and not show too much weakness despite the voluntary agony they had subjected themselves to.

All in the name of art. Or freedom of expression.

His father would not approve of this. Not one bit. Nor would any of the ladies in church — especially one in particular. The horror in Mrs. P's face brought enough pleasure for Jeremy to momentarily forget the pain snaking around his arm.

The art on Max's upper left arm took form. Lilies. A piece Max had asked Serene to draw for him.

Jeremy hadn't yet asked why Max had chosen the image — mostly because Max had refused to show it to him until the last minute. "What's with the lilies?"

Max's eyes glazed over. He bowed his head and followed the movement of the needle on his skin with his eyes before he responded with, "They remind me of innocence and purity."

Despite the curiosity Max's words triggered, Jeremy snickered. "You're tattooing yourself with innocence and purity?"

Max just shrugged. His eyes darkened.

That was enough of a cue for Jeremy not to pry further. Max was rarely ever in these quiet, contemplative moods, but when he was, Jeremy knew better than to ask about things Max would rather be silent about. More often than not, it was better not to poke the ghosts from his past, especially those that were clearly still haunting Max.

Jeremy leaned back in his seat and tried to relax as the tattooist moved on from the sun and started on the calligraphy Jeremy himself had designed. The words, *I will be light*, would go from Jeremy's wrist up the side of his radius bone. He braced himself for the dull ache caused by needle inking over bone. He stared up at the ceiling as Max's words circled his mind. Innocence and purity.

So many times growing up, with all his pranks, shenanigans, and adventurous exploits, his parents' church had made him feel guilty and impure. Unacceptable in their midst. Now, right after settling down in their college dorm, the first thing Jeremy decided to do was to get a tattoo — something he never would have had the guts to get back home.

And after taking days to figure out what he wanted to permanently mark himself with, he decided, for some reason, to go with the blazing blue sun Serene had once sketched for him and the words, *I will be light.*

His mother's face after she had kissed him goodbye on the day he had driven with Max all the way to university lingered in Jeremy's head. "You've gone through a lot of things that were painful, Son," she had told him while cupping his face in her hands. "The doubts you have are not unwarranted, and I apologize for all the ways your father and I were unable to shield you from everything that chipped away at your faith, but we named you Jeremy for a reason. It means *elevated by God.* Someday, my son, you will see God's touch woven into the fabric of your life. You will hear His voice and have faith again. When that time comes, He will raise you up, and mark my words, Jeremy. Once the Lord comes for you, so He can lift you up, no matter how dark and heavy the situation, you will be light."

Those four words had stuck with Jeremy, because he had so longed for it to be true. For Mama's sake. Unfortunately, Jeremy had been spiraling toward the darkness long before college. He and Max had been good at hiding it — all their compromises and flirtations with what their religion considered to be of the dark.

Why Max was tattooing himself with innocence and purity baffled Jeremy as much as it baffled him that he would choose these four words to mark himself with when he felt like he was about to plunge headfirst into darkness. Maybe because part of him still believed in all that church had taught him since childhood. Was that it?

Jeremy didn't want to overthink it all. He just wanted to have fun. So, throughout his freshman year, that's what he did. He plunged himself fully into a hedonistic lifestyle — running after his own pleasures, not thinking of the consequences, and trying everything at least once, so he could say he had experienced it before making a decision. At first, Max was with him all the way, but after their first semester, the party lifestyle was clearly taking its toll on Max, who still managed to show up for all his classes and make good grades.

Then, Amie came along. This French-speaking girl from Madagascar. Amie had been the one who steered Max's path away from Jeremy's and back to God. Jeremy realized this upon waking up one morning to find Max bent over his study table, reading the Bible.

Jeremy blinked his eyes, unable to believe what he was seeing. They'd had conversations about Christianity — Max and him — but he never imagined Max would actually return to the faith.

Jeremy cleared his throat.

Max looked up. The tears in his eyes took Jeremy aback.

Jeremy had read the Bible multiple times growing up, and it never moved him enough to drive him to tears.

"Good morning." Max smiled.

"Do you like what you're reading?"

"It's powerful stuff." Max tapped the book with his fingers. "Remember when you first introduced me to the stories within its pages?"

Jeremy groaned inside. It was one thing for Max to return to Christianity, but would he try to bring Jeremy with him? "Mm-hmm," he replied. He rose from his bed and headed for his closet. "I still know the verses." He smirked as he gathered his belongings so he could head to the bathroom. "Like the one that says when I become a man, I put away childish things."

"Is that what we are now?" Max asked, amusement lacing his voice. "Men?"

"Heh. Good point." He clucked his tongue as he hung his towel over his shoulder. "I'm taking a shower."

When he returned from the bathroom, he walked back into their room and found Max on his knees, bowed down, deep in prayer.

That's when Jeremy felt like he lost his best friend to Jesus Christ.

A small voice within him coaxed him to follow Max, because Max had always been the smarter, more reasonable one between the two of them, but Jeremy backed away. The world still offered so much he wanted to learn about and experience. Max might be done with his venture into the world, but Jeremy's journey was far from over.

In the months that followed, Jeremy moved one way and Max moved the other. When Jeremy was out drunk and partying, Max was in a campus Bible study. When Jeremy was skipping class because of a hangover, Max was in class, drinking in as much knowledge as he possibly could. While Jeremy couldn't stand the idea of committing himself to a woman, Max was in a steady relationship with Amie, who kept challenging him to follow hard after God.

Jeremy began flunking his classes, and he barely cared. Life was too short and too fun to waste on being so serious and religious. Why follow all these ancient rules for living, when life had so much more to offer? Jeremy went through most of his first year in college, literally and figuratively high on all the experiences he had free rein to explore.

No one could talk him out of the life he had plunged himself into.

"She cries over you, Jeremy," Serene told him during one of their weekly phone calls. "She found out about what you've been up to out there, and she's heart-broken."

"It's not that deep, Serene. Stop reading too much into what I'm doing with my life. Tell her I'm okay. I just don't think I'm cut out for college, and I'm just having the most fun I can, because I doubt I'll continue after this year."

"Okay? What do you plan to do then?"

"I haven't figured that out yet."

"Jeremy, come on. Don't make the same mistakes I did. Why would you waste an opportunity to get a degree, especially when you don't have to go into debt for it? Believe me. I don't regret one bit that I returned to college to finish my degree. Even Nolan wishes he could have finished, if only to honor the sacrifices Nova made in helping him go through school. God has provided for us to—"

"Serene," Jeremy interrupted, "I love you. I respect your journey and that it took you back to Nolan and back to Christianity. I'm happy for both of you, I am, but let me walk my own path and make my own life decisions. It's me who will have to live with my choices, not you."

"Exactly. That's why you should make the right decisions. Why wouldn't you want to learn from those who have gone before you?"

"Because I want to live my own life, Serene. Remember what it was like when you weren't living yours? That time when you just followed the path Nolan set for you? Even if you were living a life a lot of people could only dream about, you turned away from that path, because you knew it wasn't your path to take."

Silence was the response. It took several breaths before Serene finally spoke up. "Jeremy, please reconsider. It'll break Mama's heart if she finds out this is what you plan to do. She is already under a lot of stress with people at church who are questioning their leadership because of the kind of lifestyles we both have embraced."

Jeremy rolled his eyes. "What are they going on about? You and Nolan are model Christian citizens now."

"Barely. There are people in church who still don't like that Nolan has decided to keep doing secular music instead of fully shifting into the Christian music industry."

"Serene, you realize telling me how people at church are rejecting your husband for the stupidest things doesn't help me want to go back to all this religious nonsense, right?"

"Sure, but you grew up in church and know enough about God and the Bible to understand that we're all works in progress. People in church, included."

"Right." Jeremy dropped himself on his bed and let out a sigh. "Grace and all that. Okay, fine. To get you off my back, I'll try my best to make it through this year without being a complete failure, but don't expect too much. And prepare Mama as much as you can, so she wouldn't take it too hard should I fail."

"We're praying for you."

That sentence irked Jeremy like nothing. They should pray for themselves. They were the ones who were all miserable and judgmental. "Thanks, Serene. I love you."

"We love you. Nolan says hi."

"Hi to him, too. Okay. I have to go. Let's chat again next week. Bye, gingerbrain."

"Bye!"

Jeremy hung up and checked his messages to find out if Max was going to the party with him. Max had sent a message saying he was with Amie and couldn't make it. Jeremy shrugged it off and headed to the frat party, where he could lose himself in a night of freedom and fun. After he won a game of beer pong and was high on his victory, his phone buzzed in his pocket.

It was past midnight. Why was Serene calling?

Before Jeremy even said hello, Serene's sobs pierced through the line and cut right through his heart. The foreboding built up within him, making him choke up before his sister could even say a word to explain her tears. He walked out of the frat house and to the lawn. "Serene, what happened? Why are you crying?"

It took a while for her to calm down. Once she did, she shattered Jeremy with her words. "We're at the hospital. Mama Aida suffered an aneurysm in her sleep..." Serene's words turned into static as she continued to speak. Jeremy didn't want to hear anything she was saying, so he tried to block her voice out, but whether he could hear or not, it was clear what Serene was trying to say.

Mama Aida was dead.

- JEREMY, 19 -

They lowered his mother's casket to the ground, and with its descent went what was left of Jeremy's faith. As steadily as it came down, it was neither grief nor the gnawing sense of loss that kept Jeremy company. What was growing within him, filling all his senses, was this boiling rage burning away every other emotion attempting to worm in and provide some form of reason for the tragedy he was facing. Anger was the one emotion that made sense to him, and at that moment, he was directing all the ire toward all these hypocrites surrounding him. He gritted his teeth at the cloying sound of Mrs. P's sobs right across the hole in the ground from where he stood. He made an effort to prevent himself from going to her side of the grave and pushing her right in there with his mother, because to him, she deserved to be there more than Mama Aida did. Everyone there talking about how Mama Aida had impacted their lives and made them believe in God's goodness and kindness made Jeremy want to vomit.

After all they had put his mother through? All the criticism they had thrown her way? Now when she could no longer hear them, when the life had gone out of her, now was when they wanted to talk about all the kindness they had experienced from her? His mother had loved every single one of them. She had poured countless hours serving them and praying for them. What had she gotten in return?

Jeremy's fists clenched, his nails digging so deeply into his palm, he was sure skin would break. When the casket hit the bottom with a thud, the finality of it hit Jeremy, and washed over his rage with this overwhelming sense of loss he didn't know how to handle. The tears came unbidden. His knees weakened, making him kneel on the ground, his fists digging into the grass beneath him. He stared at the wooden box containing his mother's remains even as memories of her smile, her touch, her words captured his mind. The sobs came, and his whole body shook as he let out the grief, the anger, the mixture of emotions that had taken hold of him and stolen his sense of control.

Dad laid a hand on his shoulder, firm but comforting. His father's touch irked Jeremy, because it made him feel like his father wanted him to stop grieving over the loss. How was he so solid at this moment anyway? Why wasn't he shedding a tear? Did he not care that he had just lost his wife? Intuitively, Jeremy was aware of how irrational his line of thinking was, but he allowed himself to sink into that mentality anyway. With this kind of pain twisting his heart, he was allowed to do whatever, think whatever.

"You will be light."

Jeremy's shoulders squared, and his spine snapped straight. Those four words said in his mother's voice were so vivid, he could almost feel her breath in his ears. This was his fault. How dare he blame anything on anyone, when all of this was his fault! Serene had tried to warn him. His spiral into darkness had been putting Mama under so much stress, but he had gone on living a life of vices, selfishness, and sin. She was where she was right now, because he cared about no one but himself. The guilt and shame accompanied the grief, and the pain in his chest increased to a point where he could barely gasp for breath between the sobs racking his body.

Ashamed to be around all these people claiming to be righteous, he slapped his father's hand away and ran off with no clue as to where he was going. He just had to get away, be on his own, lose himself in this all-consuming agony, twisting him inside. He ran fast and hard until any step farther would have stolen all the breath from his lungs. His legs slowed down to a halt, his knees shaking from exhaustion, his balance precarious. He laid a hand on the nearby acacia to give himself support before leaning his back on the tree's sturdy trunk. He sank down slowly, tears streaming down his face, crumpling into a mess of conflicting emotions — every single one crushing his soul and breaking his heart.

"You will be light."

What a lie. He had turned his mother's words — spoken with so much love and hope — into a lie, and what was grieving him the most was his refusal to amend his ways. All he wanted at that moment was to numb himself enough to believe that everything would be okay. He longed for all the pain, the guilt, the shame to go away.

The crunch of leaves on the grass indicated the arrival of company. Jeremy wanted to send whomever it was away, but he could barely breathe between his uncontrollable sobs, so he kept crying, kept letting it all out. His companion sat next to him and sighed. Jeremy didn't need to look to find out who it was. No one else would dare approach him in this state, other than Max. Perhaps his sister would, but she didn't have as imposing a presence as Max had.

Max didn't say anything. He just sat there and accompanied Jeremy in his grief.

Jeremy's tears subsided, and a long silence followed until the first thing that came out of Jeremy's lips was, "I hate God."

Max didn't immediately respond. He let the words drift into the air before saying, "You don't mean that. Can you imagine how Mama Aida would react if you said that to her?"

"It doesn't matter, because we're here and she's not. She's gone. God took her away from us. What kind of supernatural, all-powerful being lets something like this happen? God is more malevolent than He is benevolent."

His own words made Jeremy's skin crawl. His mother might be gone, never again able to hear his words, but was God hearing what he was saying? Would God let his mother know? The anger grew within him. God had taken his mother. She had loved Him so deeply, with all that she was, and in exchange, He stole her away from all who loved her.

Max stayed still. He didn't bother to defend God nor try to prove Jeremy wrong. Like the true friend he was, he just kept Jeremy company. There was no pity in his eyes. Just understanding and respect when it came to how Jeremy was processing what he was going through.

Time whiled away, meaningless to Jeremy. They could have been there for hours or minutes. He couldn't tell the difference. Eventually, Max suggested they go back to the Sinclairs' home.

"Everyone must have left already," he said. "It should only be Pastor Sam, Nolan, and Serene there."

Jeremy didn't budge at first. Did he have it in him to face his family? Did they blame him like he blamed himself? Out of mercy for his best friend, who had stuck with him for who knows how long, he relented, but when Max pulled over at their driveway, it was clear they wouldn't be alone with just Jeremy's family. People from church, friends of Nolan and Serene, and whoever else were still there.

"I can't be here." Jeremy squirmed in the passenger seat.

"Why not?" Max asked. "This is your home."

He shook his head. "Not when she's no longer here."

"Everyone else is still here, though. Your dad, your sister, your church. Me. We're your family too. You're home with us," Max said the words as gently as he possibly could, but the words stung, mainly because it was so simple.

Jeremy recognized all of it to be true, but how could Max not see it was different now that Mama Aida was gone? This place could never be home again. Not without her. Everyone at Connect Church was aware of that — none more than Jeremy. "Can you give me a moment to myself?" he asked. "Please."

"You'll be okay?" Max asked.

Jeremy forced a nod before saying something he wasn't entirely sure was the truth. "I'll follow you inside. I just need to pull myself together. Thanks for hanging around me through all of this, man."

"You know I've got you. Always."

The sentimentality irritated Jeremy. Max was his truest and most loyal friend, but there was no way he could always be there for Jeremy. He hadn't been these past months, because he was always with Amie and his Christian friends. Jeremy tried to smirk. "Don't go all sentimental on me now."

Max returned the smirk, probably relieved that Jeremy was still capable of smirking. "Dude, you've been sentimental all day."

Did he not have the right to be as sentimental as he needed to be? Jeremy's smirk turned into a frown. "Go."

Thankfully, Max got the hint and got out of Jeremy's car. Seconds later, he disappeared inside the house, leaving Jeremy with his anger and his sorrow. Jeremy shut his eyes and tried to search for any semblance of peace. When was the last time he had experienced that? It was hard to think, much less pray, given the chaos going on inside him. The car suddenly induced his claustrophobia, so he opened the door and took a step outside. He paced the front yard slowly, breathing in the fresh air. It helped enough for Jeremy to entertain the idea of praying, but that all went away when a gentle hand held his arm.

Rachel. She was a teenager now. How old was she? Fourteen? Fifteen? He had never doubted she would one day grow up to be a beauty, but she exceeded his expectations, as high as they already were. Today, however, given the situation, her beauty was no consolation to his grief, and her relation to Mrs. P made her the enemy.

"I'm sorry, Jeremy," she said.

He scoffed. "Are you, though?"

A short gasp threw Rachel's head and shoulders back. The hurt wasn't enough to mar her beauty as she narrowed her eyes at him. "Of course I am, Jeremy. I love Mama Aida."

"You were young back then, Rachel, but you were already old enough to understand all the things your mother has spoken against mine. I'm aware of how your family views mine. Don't assume Mama Aida wasn't aware either, so please. Spare me the false grief, Rachel. Stop being a hypocrite."

A tear ran down her pretty face, her blue eyes glistening with hurt, but she didn't withdraw her hand from his elbow. She just smiled at him — this soft, broken smile that made him feel so much worse than he already did. "You're hurting," she said. "I understand."

"What is going on here?" Mrs. P marched from the front door to them. She didn't sound mad, just curious, but Jeremy didn't care. His nemesis had just arrived.

"You!" He cussed out loud at the older woman, whose face contorted in shock. "Why are you here anyway? You've always hated my family. You've hated Mama Aida for years."

"That is not true!" Mrs. P clutched her chest. "Aida and I have been friends since we were teenagers. We came to know the Lord around the same time; along with your father, we started this church together. I love your mother."

Jeremy raised his brow. "You sure had a horrible way of showing that love. I grew up hearing all the nasty things you've said about my mother and my family, Rhoda. Stop pretending you care she's gone."

Rachel let go of Jeremy and hurried to her mother's side. Both had these hurt expressions in their eyes, making him feel, once again, like he was the villain. To his relief, no one else was around to see what was going on. Not that it mattered, because he was sure Mrs. P would tell everyone first chance she got.

Jeremy left them standing there as he returned to his car. Giving no space for hesitation, he backed the car out of the garage and drove away — aimlessly for a while, until desperation for relief brought him somewhere that would've further broken his mother's heart. He shoved the voice of reason back as he procured a small packet of something that would help him forget.

In a motel room an hour later, lost in a high, his grief fogged by psychedelic lights, he heard his mother's voice yet again, saying, *"You will be light."*

ten

THE ONE WHO LOST HERSELF IN COLLEGE

The stack of suitcases — pink, white, and lavender — was piling high in the Petersen's front yard. Rachel sauntered toward it and added one of the most precious things she owned — a bedazzled shoebox of cherished memories, containing letters, photos, and little nothings that would remind her of home. As she placed the box on top of a suitcase, Rachel bristled at the strangeness of the term. Home. The paradox she had been wrestling with for the past month caught up with her once more. On one hand, she couldn't imagine life without the community she had built around herself, right here, in this town she had lived in all her life. On the other hand, she couldn't wait to leave and experience what the rest of the world offered. The taste of freedom on her lips was almost intoxicating as she envisioned herself plunging into all the possibilities. Still, the juxtaposition of familiar and unknown left her with a yearning to go and a longing to stay.

Her friend, Sean, hauled the last of her bags from inside their house to the front yard. "If I didn't see your bedroom myself, I would think you packed every single item you own." Sean leaned on one suitcase as he caught his breath. "This is a lot, Rach. Have you seen the dorm rooms at our university? It's not even half the size of your bedroom, and you have to share it with another person."

Rachel laughed. "I'm aware." She rolled her eyes and tapped the edge of her memory box. "It's a lot, but it's all necessary, and trust me. All of it will find their proper place in time."

Sean chuckled and shrugged. "If you say so."

"You barely have any stuff, so worst-case scenario, I can use your dorm room as extra storage area."

Sean narrowed his eyes at her. "What do you take me for? I'm as much of a diva as you are, Petersen. Why would you assume I wouldn't have enough stuff to fill a house? Besides, that's a worst-case scenario for me, not you."

"True." Rachel swerved her hip to the side and winked at her friend. "But that's only because I find a way to make the best out of every situation." A soft smile appeared on her face. "All that to say, I'm blessed to be going to the same university as you. I wouldn't know what to do without my theater partner."

He grinned. "It's a relief for me, too. If I'm to direct a play once we're there, I will need you around to keep everything in order. There's no surviving, otherwise."

"Flattered to hear it, but you'll do fine without me."

"Where are your parents, anyway? And what will move all this stuff to the dorm? You might need a truck."

"Haha." She smirked. "My mom and dad picked up the RV they rented for the trip. It's overkill, sure, but they're excited about it, so I will not be the one to rain on their parade."

"Three-day road trip with the parents, huh?" He grinned. "You sure you don't want to fly with me?"

She pointed at her stack of suitcases. "The extra baggage fees will cost me half a semester in college."

He laughed. "That's true. Well, I guess I'll see you in three days then."

A loud honk jolted them both to attention.

She turned around to find her parents pulling up in the luxury RV they had splurged on for this trip. Rachel smiled and waved at her father and mother, whose faces were giddy with excitement as they waved back at her from the front seat.

A convertible and a pickup pulled up behind the RV, and a bunch of their high school friends arrived to bid Rachel goodbye.

"Rachel!" One of her friends from childhood, Erika, hopped out of the convertible to hug her. "I'm going to miss you so much!"

The next ten minutes ended in a flurry of hugs and well-wishes, as if all her friends hadn't already said goodbye to her during her numerous farewell parties and final outings at their favorite hang-outs. Their presence was a welcome embrace to Rachel, reminding her of how loved she was.

With the presence of more people to help, loading her suitcases into the RV was done in no time. Pictures were taken, hugs exchanged, keeping in touch promised.

Right as she waved her high school friends goodbye and the last of Mom's "food for the road" was brought to their rented ride, another van arrived. Out of it emerged Hannah, Knox, their three children, and Max. At the sight of their new youth-pastor-in-training, Rachel's heart smiled. Max's presence at church over the summer had brought about a wave of renewal and refreshment to all involved in ministry. Here was a man she could imagine a future with.

"We couldn't let you leave without saying goodbye!" Hannah exclaimed.

Rachel hugged one of her mentors. Hannah was the closest thing she had to an older sister, and having her there brought tears to Rachel's eyes. "I'll miss you, Hannah."

"I'm one call away."

After a long, tearful embrace with Hannah, Knox followed to give Rachel a bear hug. "Take care out there. If you need anything, let Hannah know, and we're there for you, you hear?"

Rachel nodded, wiping tears away.

Max stepped up and smiled at her. She blushed. It was no secret to the girls at church what a huge crush she had on Max. Whether he was aware of that or not, Rachel could only guess. He gave her a short hug, causing a surge of giddiness inside.

"Any advice for me?" she asked him.

He smirked. "Don't do anything you'll regret, Rachel, though I doubt you will. All of us are confident you'll do just fine."

Rachel wished she had the same confidence, but apprehension about the unknown loomed over her departure. What was she going to do without her church community?

By the time she climbed into the RV, her eyes were blurry with grateful tears. The farewell her friends had given her — both from school and church — made her feel hollow inside when the RV rolled on to get her to her dorm.

As they traveled through open roads to get to her university, Rachel's prayers helped her cope with one of the biggest changes in her life. God would surely replace whatever she might lose by leaving home. This was a new adventure, and she was going to face it with courage and a smile. Besides, though she would never say it out loud to anyone, she looked forward to being away from her parents. As much as she loved them, she was ready to have a little taste of independence.

Three days later, in the middle of the day, they pulled over at the dormitory parking lot. First, she had lunch with her parents before they helped take her things from the RV to her dorm room. It took another couple of hours before they finished cleaning, organizing, and decorating Rachel's side of the dorm room.

With nothing left to do, it was time for her parents to say goodbye.

Mom sighed. "I wonder who your roommate will be. I wish we could meet her before we go, so we can at least get to know who you'll be living with." She turned to Dad. "What do you think, Robert?

Should we stay another few hours to wait for Rachel's roommate? We can have coffee together while waiting."

Rachel's heart sank. She wanted some solitude before her roommate arrived, because she was sure it would be hard to have some alone time once the semester kicked in.

As if reading her mind, Dad stroked her mother's back. "It's time to let go, Rhoda. For all we know, her roommate might arrive tomorrow or the day after. Let's give Rachel her freedom. We have a long road ahead of us before we reach our first stop on our return home"

Mom's lips twitched as she stood on her spot, lingering long enough to give Rachel pause. Would Mom insist on her way? Her mother sighed and nodded. "Okay." The word had barely been able to get out of her mouth before a sob escaped her. For the first time in a long time, Rachel saw her mother cry. Rhoda Petersen. The iron lady of Connect Church. Her mother pulled her in for a long, suffocating embrace and cried.

Rachel did too, even if the larger part of her was ready to let go. She cried because she knew how difficult this was for her parents, and she could only pray for God's grace over them.

It took another half hour of farewells and Mom leaving her a list of reminders of things she needed to take care of. By the time she got the room all to herself, Rachel was drained from all the goodbyes. Still, she took one long breath and welcomed this new phase of her life. This was a precious chance for her to start a new life, to reinvent herself, and to make an impact on this world. It was just her and Jesus. The possibilities unfolded in her mind, and every single one made her smile, until finally, someone pushed the dorm room open and a blast from the past stepped in.

Rachel's mouth dropped open upon recognizing the familiar face. God had quite the sense of humor, because it turned out that Rachel's new roommate was none other than Crazy Jenna.

- ONE YEAR LATER; RACHEL, 19 -

Rachel clasped both sides of her head with her hands before dropping her entire weight on her bed. The soft spring mattress bounced beneath her. Her eyes rolled up to view the clear blue sky from the window above her head. Sunshine streamed through the sheer curtains, warming her face. Summer had arrived, her flight back home was tonight, and all she could think about was Jenna.

Where was she? She had promised they would spend the entire day together, but it was almost noon, and she was nowhere to be found.

Rachel curled up to her side, retracting her knees to hug them against her chest. "God, what is going on with me? Why am I like this? Why can't I get Jenna off my mind?" She bit her lip. Just saying it out loud felt like she was sinning. Most people around her wouldn't have considered any of this strange. Should she find the guts to mention it to anyone, they would even celebrate her. She was "coming out", so to speak. This was a good thing in today's society; it was an accepted ideology, sometimes even revered, but her upbringing and faith said otherwise. Her love for the Lord and His Word said otherwise. Yet, here she lay. Consumed. By an attraction for someone of the same sex. She further lifted her knees up, molding her torso against it to curl up into a ball. What would her church say if they ever found out what was going on within her? What would her family think? More than all of that, what was God thinking about her?

It wasn't like she had chosen to feel this way. Somewhere through the semester, whenever Jenna was around, Rachel's heart would skip a beat, and she would become hyper-conscious of her every movement, as well as Jenna's. Whenever

108

Jenna wasn't around, Rachel pined for her friend's company. She couldn't get Jenna out of her mind.

She had prayed and prayed, time and time again, to be delivered from this, but nothing happened. Her feelings for Jenna remained, and now, even with the guilt and the shame consuming her, her brain lingered still on how much she wished Jenna was here.

"God, why is this happening to me?"

The silence mocked her. Along with it came a voice telling her it was okay, it was natural, it was accepted. So what if she was bisexual or a lesbian? God wouldn't condemn her, because she was His daughter, right? She had served Him well all these years, hadn't she?

A gentle tremor swept through Rachel as she shook her head. Rachel pressed her cheek against the soft cotton of her bed cover. She was a woman, created for a man. That's what the Bible said she was, and that's what she believed she was. Right?

Rachel closed her eyes so tight, her entire face scrunched up, as she tried to focus on Jesus and dwell on things that were good, noble, and of good report. She began quoting Scripture to counter all the foreign thoughts and emotions coursing through her. "I am fearfully and wonderfully made. He knows when I sit and when I rise. He hems me in behind and before. Even when I make my bed in the depths, He is there. Even the darkness will not be dark to me. The night will shine like the day, for the darkness is as light to Him. My hope is in Him. He is the anchor of my soul."

Peace came over her. The Lord's presence did not manifest itself to her through some powerful sensation that gave her goosebumps or made her senses tingle. Instead, His presence settled within her — calm and steady amid the storm of emotion in her soul and the battle of reasoning in her mind. She wasn't lost, and whatever she was going through right now, it didn't change the fact that she was His. Rachel was a child of God, and her feelings did not define her. She had decided long ago that only God would be allowed to define her. Satisfied by faith in His abiding presence, Rachel smiled, but when she opened her eyes, Jenna was standing at the center of the room with a smirk on her face and a quizzical stare directed at Rachel.

"What are you doing, Princess?" Jenna asked. "The way you're closing your eyes like that, it's like you're trying to summon something."

Rachel gulped. The relief and excitement she felt over Jenna's presence warred with the peace God's presence had just established within her. Not moving from her position in the bed, she frowned at her roommate. "Where have you been? You said we would spend the day together. My flight is tonight."

Jenna laughed and dropped her weight on the edge of Rachel's bed, so that she was leaning her back on Rachel's waist. "You're not upset, are you?" She bounced on the mattress as she giggled. "We have plenty of time. I just needed an hour or two at the gym for a dance session to blow off some steam. You were asleep, so I figured I'd spend the morning there, so you could rest. Time kind of got away from me. Don't be mad, Princess." She rubbed Rachel's arm with her palm.

"I assumed you bailed on me." Rachel was acting like a pathetic whiny baby, and her recognition of that heightened the awareness that she was only comfortable acting this way around Jenna. With everyone else — especially people at church back home — she had to be more guarded, more careful about showing her true emotions. There was always this pressure to put up a front and keep up her smile. Not with Jenna. With Jenna, she could be as she was, without fear of judgment. Guilt took hold of her at the awareness of this reality. What kind of testimony did she have? How was it that Jenna was exhibiting more of God's life and freedom than she was? "You should have left me a note or a text message to let me know where you were."

Jenna playfully leaned her elbows on Rachel's arm and thigh — like she was on a couch — and let out a huge sigh. "Right. Didn't think about that." She tapped a finger on her temple. "But I'm here now, aren't I? Let's enjoy what's left of the day. We can go out for lunch, even go to a circus or something, whatever you want."

Rachel pouted. "Where are we going to find a circus?"

"Isn't there always one around?" Jenna wrinkled her nose. "Meh. Maybe not. Oh! I know! We can go to the aquarium. I've never been there. We can watch the fish and study their movements. It's for research."

"Research for what?"

"I'm taking swimming lessons this summer, and I want to learn how to swim underwater like a mermaid."

Rachel giggled and suddenly flinched when she noticed the way her fingers had started absent-mindedly stroking Jenna's hair. She stopped. "That's weird. Why do you want to learn to swim like a mermaid?"

Jenna shrugged. "It's visually stunning, and if all else fails in my life, I can fall back on being a stunt double for mermaid movies or shows. Also, I want to learn how to dance underwater."

"You and dancing. Sometimes, I wonder if you care more about dancing than you care about me." Rachel cringed the moment the words left her mouth.

"Aren't you clingy today? Where is all this coming from?" Without waiting for an answer, Jenna hopped to her feet. "We're burning daylight. I'm starving, and my research is waiting. Stop acting all spoiled and victimized, and get up, Princess." Jenna grabbed hold of Rachel's hand and pulled her up to her feet.

Rachel tried to resist, but given all the dancing Jenna did, she was pretty strong for her size. Jenna literally dragged Rachel out of bed and made her stand up.

"It will be a fun day." Jenna patted her on the cheek. "I'll drop you off at the airport later to make up for my absence this morning."

"My flight is almost at midnight. You don't have to."

Jenna laid her arm on Rachel's shoulder. "I want to. I don't believe in God, but if I did, I would thank Him for bringing you here. You kept me from losing my mind this year, which turned out great, and a lot of it is because of you." Jenna placed her palm over her heart. "Trust me. No one is surprised about that more than I am. Who would've imagined we would get along so well?" She dropped her arm off of Rachel's shoulder and skipped toward her closet.

"Are we going now? I'm hungry," Rachel said.

"So am I." Jenna opened her closet and took out some clothes. "But I need to take a shower first, because I stink. Wait for me."

Rachel's face blanked. "Fine. Go."

Jenna danced her way out of their bedroom, and it was that very image of freedom that attracted Rachel to Jenna. There was this childlikeness about her that Rachel had somehow lost as she was growing up. Jenna had always been true to who she was, unafraid to be her authentic self — even if her authentic self had been met with so much ridicule, some of which had come directly from Rachel.

She sat back on her bed and lost herself in thought as she clasped her hands together and laid them on her knees. Deep inside, she knew she loved Jenna, but if she wasn't careful, she would begin to love Jenna as more than just a friend, and she was afraid of what that would mean, not only for their friendship, but for Rachel herself. This would mean rebellion against so many beliefs she held close to heart. It would mean compromising what she believed to be her God-given identity. Full of conflicting and confusing emotions, Rachel knew in her core what had to be done. This wasn't something she could battle alone. She needed to tell someone this summer about what she was experiencing. Upon getting back home, she should confess this attraction to someone who could counsel her and pray for her, and if need be, she needed to prepare herself for the possibility of distancing herself from Jenna.

The idea hurt, because there was so much about Jenna that Rachel adored and appreciated, and not having Jenna in her life made her heart ache more than Rachel expected, but it was what she had to do. She had to be firm on this and stand on what was right, what was true. She squared her shoulders and made herself confident in her resolve.

When Jenna returned from the bathroom, all of that resolve melted away.

After all, Rachel wasn't home yet, and she still had half a day to relish every moment living vicariously through the wild abandon and *joie de vivre* of Crazy Jenna.

eleven

THE ONE
WHO WOULD
BE LIGHT

On a cool Friday night, in the middle of her summer back home, Rachel reluctantly dragged her feet from the parking lot to their church building. This was the last place she wanted to go to, mainly because she knew what typical youth nights were like. They would expect her to participate in whatever activities they had prepared, and she was in no mood for any of it. All she wanted was to stay in her room, curl up in her bed, and distract herself with something — that something would most likely be messaging Jenna or giving her a call. But that had been the way Rachel had spent half of her summer at home — "distracting" herself — and her parents were beginning to notice, so here she was. At church. About to listen to Max preach for the first time.

She was about to reach the door leading to the church lobby when a wolf whistle stopped her in her tracks. Who was that? She wasn't about to get cat-called in church, was she? A hooded figure emerged from the shadows, and she was about to hurry inside an empty church lobby to avoid the possibility of assault when the approaching stranger pulled his hood down to reveal his identity: Jeremy Sinclair.

"Jeremy?" Rachel winced. The first thing that came to mind upon seeing his appearance rushed out of her lips. "You look horrible."

His face was gaunt and pallid, his eyes bloodshot and sullen. Bags were under his eyes. He must have lost a ton of weight, because upon closer inspection, his once lean figure — supple and wiry — was now thin and sickly, his bones jutting out of his skin. He stopped right before he was about to step into the light coming from the lobby.

Rachel couldn't blame him for not wanting to stand in the light. She would hide in the shadows too, if she looked like that.

"It's nice to see you, Princess." He beckoned for her to come closer by curling his fingers toward himself.

If she was the princess, why was he the one summoning her? Wasn't he but a lowly knight? Also, why did he look like a hobo? Long beard, disheveled hair, hoodie several sizes too big for him.

Rachel hadn't seen him since Mama Aida's funeral, and he hadn't exactly left a good impression that day. There was no one in the lobby, so she wasn't sure if anyone would hear her scream in case Jeremy tried something unexpected. Should she approach him? She wasn't sure if she should. She didn't move an inch. "What do you want, Jeremy?"

He smirked. "You."

Rachel huffed and rolled her eyes. "Whatever." She pushed open the glass door to the lobby.

"No, Rachel, wait! I'm kidding. Come on." He took several steps into the light.

A clearer view of him made Rachel's face fall. It seemed he had aged thirty years in three. "Jeremy, what happened to you?"

He stroked his dark beard and shuffled on his feet. "I need a hit so badly."

"I think I can hit you, but I'm afraid that might be painful for my knuckles. Will you settle for a slap?"

"Very funny, Rachel."

"That's the only kind of hit you'll get from me, Jeremy." While a side of her feared his desperation and ability to overpower her, a larger part of her wanted nothing more than to hug him. How had he gotten to this level of self-destruction? She pointed inside the lobby with her thumb. "Do you want to come in with me? Max is sharing the Word tonight."

Jeremy shook his head. "Nah. I can't go in there. Can you let him know I'm here, though? I can't give him a call, because I lost my phone."

"What did you do? Sell it for a hit?"

"Heh." He forced out a scoff, but the way he averted his gaze told Rachel that was exactly what he had done.

"Come in, Jeremy. Please?"

His face fell. He didn't seem to know what to do, but there was a wild desperation in his eyes that told Rachel he didn't have anywhere else to go and didn't know what else to do. That's why he was there, and somehow, for the first time since she had arrived, someone other than Jenna was at the forefront of her mind.

Jeremy's head shook. "No, Rach. You know what our church is like. People will look down on me. If someone sees me and tells Dad or Serene about the state I'm in right now, it will break their hearts, and—" his eyes went wild "—you won't tell anyone you saw me, will you?"

"I won't if you don't want me to." She meant that. Despite her hesitation, she reached for his hand and squeezed. "No one here will look down on you, because no one here is above you. You've heard all of this before, Jeremy, but no one here is better than you. We're all sinners, and if you would only come, like I'm asking you to, then you can draw near to Jesus tonight." At the reminder of what she had been struggling with all summer — her growing obsession with Jenna — she bowed her head. "God knows I, too, need to draw to Him tonight, and I'd rather not be alone in doing it, considering how vulnerable I am right now, so what do you say? Aren't you my knight? If it makes you feel any better, we can find you a change of clothes to help clean you up a bit before we go in."

His gaunt face contorted in what looked like a real battle within.

Rachel squeezed his hand. *God, I hope he makes the right decision.*

Jeremy gulped. "Can you please call Max? I would feel better if he knows I'm here and if he thinks I should go inside."

That wasn't a no, so Rachel's hope remained. She brought out her phone and called Max. She pressed her phone against her ear in time to hear Max's voice on the other side. "Hello? Rachel?"

Before she could respond, Jeremy knocked her arm to the side and grabbed hold of her phone. He twisted on his heel and made a run for it.

"Jeremy!" Rachel yelled out, her heart sinking as she watched him speed away. "Don't do this!" Tears rushed down her cheeks, not because she had lost her phone, but because of the disappointment she felt on his behalf over the wrong choice he had made, but how could she blame him for that, when she herself had been making one wrong choice after another? "Lord, have mercy on Jeremy. Have mercy on me. Don't let the enemy win tonight."

Right as she finished whispering her prayer, just as Jeremy was about to exit the parking lot, he stopped running. For one brief moment, his shoulders sagged, and he bowed his head. He just stood there for several minutes, until, to Rachel's amazement, he turned — one hundred and eighty degrees — and walked back to where she was standing. His eyes unable to meet hers, he flinched before lifting his arm in front of him, her phone in his hand.

"I'm sorry," he said. "I shouldn't have done that."

Rachel took the phone. The screen revealed that there was still an active call with Max. Again, she pressed the phone against her ear. "Max?"

"Rachel? Is that you? Where's Jeremy? Is he there with you? Make sure he doesn't leave. I'm heading for the lobby right now."

"Okay." Rachel glanced at Jeremy, who was now sitting on the pavement, his arms wrapped around his knees as he rocked back and forth. "I don't think he's going anywhere."

Within seconds after she hung up, Max appeared from the hallway leading from the main sanctuary to the lobby. He ran toward them and knelt in front of his best friend. He pulled Jeremy into a hug. Assured of Max's presence, Jeremy fell into a heaping, crying mess against his best friend's embrace.

"I need help, Maximus. I need help," Jeremy kept repeating.

"We'll get you help, man," Max responded. "We'll get you all the help you need."

Rachel didn't know what it was about this precious scene between these two childhood friends that hit her so hard. She had witnessed firsthand the brotherly bond they had developed while growing up. There was something true, pure, and eternal about the love these men had for each other. It never needed to be romantic. Something within Rachel snapped, as she recognized the lie she had been believing.

Just like Jeremy, she needed to step into the light, so the moment she got home after their gathering, Rachel sat down with her mother and confessed everything she had been going through with Jenna.

Just like Jeremy, that evening, Rachel got the help she needed.

- JEREMY, 23 -

His craving for relief, for another high, drowned out Rachel's pleas for him to return. He would've stolen from Max instead, but Rachel was right there in front of him, showing off the solution — temporary as it was — to his need. This was what Max had never been able to wrap his head around. Jeremy didn't just want to get high; he needed to. Otherwise, life was a nightmare. Getting high — no matter the substance — was his only means of escape.

Jeremy promised himself he would make it up to Rachel someday, but even his desperation-clouded mind couldn't allow him to fool himself into believing that to be true. There was no way he would come back from this. Rachel must think the worst of him now, but he had already gone past the point of no return. So, he took flight, hankering for another shot of whatever drug he could get hold of that night. He was about to reach the exit of the church parking lot when a voice on the phone crackled in the air.

"Rachel? Hello? Are you there?" The voice was definitely Max's. Jeremy slowed down, partly because of his curiosity about what Max was about to say and partly because he had run out of breath. He couldn't keep running anymore. "I hope you come tonight, Rachel," Max said on the phone. "We would all love to see you. I can only guess what you're going through right now, but I hope you know you will always have a family who loves you right here at Connect Church."

Why was Max saying these things to Rachel? Jeremy hung his head. The slightest hint of emotion moved his heart, already numbed by life. If even Princess Rachel was struggling through something, maybe Jeremy wasn't as alone as he had assumed. Still, that hit. Her phone would get him high for at least another week. His mind was too clouded to reason him out of the temptation of an entire week of losing himself in drug-induced bliss. The drugs would quiet down the tug of conscience weaseling its way into his consciousness. Jeremy didn't want to help Rachel. He just wanted to get high, so he took another step forward, ready to run when...

"Rachel? You there? Remember what Mama Aida used to say about you? How she believed you are the type of woman who would not only be able to overcome but can also help others overcome? I believe that to be true, but I hope you know it's okay to ask for help, too."

"Is it?" Jeremy asked out of pure impulse, barely aware that he had said the words out loud.

"Huh?" Max paused. "Who is this? Jeremy, is that you?"

He hung his shoulders. Even if getting to his next high consumed his mind, his feet suddenly felt too heavy and unable to move. He turned around and saw Rachel still standing there, her golden hair illuminated by the light coming from their church. She was like some beacon of light forcing out the clouds in his hazy mind. With every step he took forward — back to Rachel and the church — clarity came.

"Jeremy? Are you still there?"

"Yes, Max. I'm here. I stole Rachel's phone," he confessed.

He continued moving forward, even if every step seemed heavier than the last, like his body was actively fighting against his deliverance, but the sliver of reason still left in him gave him the will to keep going. By the time he got to his destination, his mind was clear as a summer blue sky, and he had no question whatsoever about what he needed. Help. He needed help. This realization broke him, and by doing so, it saved him.

One week later, in the throes of pure anguish, where his entire body was raging war on him, punishing him for his substance abuse, Jeremy opened his eyes to see pure light shining right at him. It burned his eyes, so he shut it back again. He writhed and twisted on his bed, his own sweat soaking him. Where had his mattress gone? Why was his bed made of nothing but wood? He clutched his stomach and groaned. "Enough. Please. Enough of this. Just one hit. All I need is one, and everything will be okay."

"Shh..." A cool, soft hand pressed against his burning forehead. "You will be all right, Jeremy."

"Mama?" he whimpered. "Is that you?" That was it. He had gone to heaven. He could go see Mama now. And Jesus.

"You will be all right."

No. That wasn't right. What Mama said was he will be light. This must be an impostor. He had gone to hell, and an impostor had come to torment him. Darkness was about to swallow him.

Jeremy's eyes shot open as a controlled yelp escaped him. Sure enough, it wasn't Mama. It was someone else. Someone clothed in light. The light burned his eyes so badly, but he couldn't afford to close his eyes, because he needed to see who had come for him. Was he going to hell or to heaven? He scrambled away from the feminine touch until his back hit something hard. Was it the bed's headboard or the wall? Or was he somewhere else entirely? Where had they taken him?

A soft touch squeezed his arm. "Oh, Lord, help Jeremy."

His vision cleared, and relief washed over him when he saw an angelic face hovering over him. It wasn't a demon, after all. No impostor. It was this beautiful woman. Not an enemy. It was Rachel.

He agreed with her prayer, because should the darkness come for him, even her light wouldn't be able to ward it off. Only God could help him now. Jeremy calmed down, his tension washing away. He curled up in a ball on the hard surface he was lying on. Whether it was the bed or the floor, he didn't care. He wasn't in pain anymore. For now.

"Jeremy, Max and I will come back for you, okay?"

"You're not alone in this, Bro. We're all praying for you."

Jeremy whimpered as he forced himself to look at the person whose hand still held his arm. "Rachel?"

"Yes?"

"Go out on a date with me?"

She laughed. What a sweet sound. "How about you get well first before you start asking random people out, huh?"

"Okay."

They left him alone, and fear tried to creep its way in, but he remembered her prayer. *"Oh, Lord, help Jeremy."* In their absence, he sensed another presence — One holier, more faithful, ever gracious. *I will never leave you, nor forsake you.* It was a presence that had always been there, even when Jeremy had been too stubborn to recognize Him. The cycle of pain started again, but Jeremy wasn't alone anymore. He had Someone to cling to, Someone Who was Helper and Comforter. His Word was steady and enduring. *Like a mother comforts a child, so will I comfort you.* Jeremy wrapped his arms around himself and embraced this cross, and in the throes of withdrawal, he somehow managed to give his life to God again.

Two weeks after Max and Rachel's first visit, Jeremy woke up with tears rushing down his eyes. Dread filled him over the day ahead. The past twenty-one days of withdrawals had been pure hell. Not one minute passed by when he didn't regret his drug dependence, but neither did a minute pass by that he didn't cling to the Man on the cross, his Tree of Life.

Lying flat on his back, a cold sweat broke on his brow, and Jeremy shuddered as he braced himself for another day of struggle, but it didn't come. Instead, there was just light. For the first time since he had checked into *Hope's Well*, the presence of light no longer burned Jeremy's eyes. He got up from the bed without pangs of anguish shooting through his body. He looked out the window at the beautiful day outside.

The lightness within him surprised him. It had been a long time since he had ever felt this way. Free from any burden, unencumbered by fear and anxiety. He traced his fingers on the words tattooed on his arm. *I will be light.*

It was the first time he had looked at that tattoo and believed it to be the truth of today, and not just the hope of tomorrow. He held on to the back of a chair set in front of an empty wooden desk. From his view through the window of his second-floor room, he could see two familiar figures walk from the parking lot to the rehab facility.

Max and Rachel.

Instead of dread and shame, Jeremy's heart leapt with excitement upon seeing his friends. He couldn't remember feeling this way over anything other than drugs for the longest time.

As if sensing his stare, Rachel looked up and locked gazes with him. She smiled and waved. He waved back.

Thirty minutes later, they were at the rehab center's visiting area, sharing a breakfast of orange juice and sandwiches, while laughing at his memory of Rachel hopping around like a rabbit when she was a toddler.

Once the laughter died down, Max took on a more serious tone. "Pastor Sam says he and your sister — possibly Nolan and Lily Red, as well — want to come visit you. They want to make sure you're willing and ready to face them."

Jeremy clenched his jaw. The resistance inside was undeniable, but he couldn't keep putting this off, so he nodded. "Whether or not I'm ready, it's time to face them. Please let them know I will look forward to seeing them."

"That's great to know." Max grinned. "I'm sure they'll be happy to hear that."

Rachel tilted her head to the side and traced her finger over his tattoo.

"It was Mama Aida who said that to me. When she did, I could tell she believed the words with all her heart."

"Because it's true, Jeremy," Max said. "You will be light."

"I already am." He shifted in his seat. "Look. I've already surrendered my life to the Lord while going through withdrawal. He held my hand through it all, but I want to make it official today. How about you lead me in the prayer of salvation, Max?"

His eyes moistened. This man, this brother of Jeremy's, had been fighting for him and praying for him for years, and now, he got to return the favor Jeremy had given him all those years ago in their school playground. That afternoon, Max led Jeremy to the Lord, and finally, Jeremy became — once again — a child of light.

part one

PRESENT DAY

CIRCA
LATE 2010'S

twelve

THE ONE
WHO DANCED
ANYWAY

- JEREMY, 27 -

Jeremy snapped one photo after another. It was all beautiful. The people in his life were beautiful, and he thanked God for the ability to recognize that. How had he missed out on all of this for almost half his life? He had been so selfish, so caught up in his own victimhood, that he hadn't recognized just how blessed he had been all along, how God had given him much more than he ever needed.

"It's time for the toast," Rachel told him. "Should you go first? Or should I?"

"You should go before me, so I can copy what you say." Jeremy grinned.

She rolled her eyes. "Like anything I say would be anywhere near your style."

"Heh. Point. Go make your toast then. Take your time."

Rachel motioned to go.

"Wait." Jeremy took a couple of steps forward. "Look at this shot first." He showed her the latest photo he had taken of Max and Jenna. It was a shot of both of them laughing over something — Jeremy could only guess what. The couple seemed to have way too many secrets and private jokes already. Kind of like Cody and Lena at the airport this morning.

Jeremy had to grin at the idea of what the bride and groom would be like as an elderly couple.

"They're so lovely!" Rachel pressed her palm against her heart as she stared at the photo. Her smile was still there, but Jeremy caught how her eyes twitched when he showed him another photo of the newlywed couple. Was he just seeing things, or was Rachel still into Max?

She sighed, her smile growing as she relaxed her shoulders and squeezed his arm. "You take the most amazing shots."

"Thanks." His brows met. "Go do your speech, so I can take another amazing shot of you."

Rachel curtsied. "Happy to oblige." With that, she headed to the front of the tent and took the microphone and tapped on it. Within seconds, everybody's attention was on her.

As she talked about how she and Jenna met, Jeremy continued taking pictures. He had been so focused on that, he hadn't quite noticed the woman standing next to him.

"You haven't said hello to me yet, young man."

Jeremy tried not to visibly cringe at the voice. He turned to find Rhoda Petersen giving him a smile. "Mrs. P! I meant to, but—" he lifted his camera with one hand "—I got caught up in all the wonders of this wedding."

Mrs. P shot a cold stare at Jeremy. "She is a wonder, isn't she?" She then glanced at her daughter to make her point.

Jeremy threw his head back in surprise. For a breath, he debated with himself if he should get away from her if he could, but this was Rhoda Petersen. He had grown up with this woman. He could handle a few minutes with her. "She's stunning, Mrs. P, but you are aware we're just friends, right? If I had any intention of pursuing your daughter beyond friendship, trust that I would seek your blessing. Based on Max's experience, I'm aware of what you and Mr. P prefer."

"Is that what you're doing right now, Mr. Sinclair?" Mrs. P tilted her head back, her chin upturned. "Are you asking for my blessing to pursue my daughter?"

"No, ma'am. I'm just here to attend my best friend's wedding and to take photos to encapsulate these memories. I also happen to enjoy taking pictures of Rachel, because she photographs beautifully, which I'm certain you're aware of."

Mrs. P's shoulders relaxed, similar to how Rachel's had earlier. "Yes, yes. She's exquisite in photos, isn't she?" She eyed his camera. "Do you mind showing me a few photos of her?"

"Not at all." He rolled through the photos he had taken and stopped to show Mrs. P his favorite one. The one where Rachel wasn't smiling, as she watched Max and Jenna dance.

At the sight of it, Mrs. P's countenance darkened, like she was in pain. She closed her eyes and pressed her palm against Jeremy's arm, leaning her weight against him. "God, preserve our children," she whispered loud enough for Jeremy to hear. "Don't let them be led astray in any way."

"Amen," Jeremy said, though he wasn't sure what had caused the sudden prayer.

Mrs. P opened her eyes and tapped his arm. "You are a talented photographer, Jeremy. Truly."

"Thanks, Mrs. P. Always a great feeling receiving a compliment from you."

"Yeah. Well, don't let it get to your head, okay?"

"Of course."

As if she had suddenly gone weak, Mrs. P walked away and returned to her table without another word his way. Jeremy looked at the picture on his camera. Something was definitely going on between Rachel and her mother, but he couldn't quite dwell on that, because Rachel was tearing up in front and that could mean he would be up next soon. Jeremy pressed the back button of his camera several times to get to a photo he had snapped of Cody and Lena de Leon, the couple he had met earlier. He rushed to the tech guy handling the projector and asked him to show the photo on screen once it was Jeremy's turn to give a speech. They both figured everything out in time for Rachel to gesture for Jeremy to come up front.

Jeremy jogged toward her and gently laid the palm of his hand on the small of her back. He whispered in her ear, "I think your mother is having a moment. You should go check on her." Her face fell as she handed him the microphone. Whether Jeremy liked it or not, after a few conversations with the right people, he would most likely find out at some point what was going on between mother and daughter. For now, he had a speech to make. He pointed the microphone toward his mouth and grinned at his best friend.

"I was almost late for this wedding," Jeremy said. "If it weren't for our lovely maid-of-honor and her quick thinking, I wouldn't have made it here on time. To be fair to me, however, I had several good reasons to be late. One of them was an old couple I met on the plane. Cody and Lena de Leon. I plan to release a video of them on my channel, which I will not shamelessly plug here today, because this isn't about me. No. Today is about my best friend, Max and his beloved Jenna. Today is about love. Which brings me back to Cody and Lena, who traveled all the way to their home state to visit the places they used to hang out in when they were younger. It was a way for them to remember the many ways God has been good to them while they still could. As they shared their story for my video, I kept thinking of my man, Maximus, and his now wife, Jenna. What would they be like once they grow to be like the picture you see on the screen behind me?"

He pointed at the screen, and as he did, he caught a glimpse of Mrs. P and Rachel at a table, arguing. Had he just directed Rachel to walk right into a trap?

Jeremy cleared his throat and tried to focus on the speech. "I believe they will get there, Max and Jenna, because I know Max and how loyal he is. They both are blessed to have found each other. Also, to be honest, Max has always been smarter than me." He grinned. The crowd laughed. That seemed to get Mrs. P's and Rachel's attention, distracting them from their argument. "No objections, eh? Yeah, well, it's true. As smart as Maximus is, though, I saw this—" he pointed at Max and Jenna "—way before he did. I wear that as a badge of honor, because it's the first time I was ever ahead of him in anything, and that shouldn't have been the case, because Max has overcome a lot more than I have. When I first met Max, he was this traumatized kid who liked staring at his feet. Never understood why until I realized how large his feet were." Again, chuckles filled the room. "It was much later in life that I found out what he had gone through as a boy. Max is a survivor. More than that, he is an overcomer. I'm glad I got to stand witness to how he went from that traumatized boy to this dashing man about to start a family with his lovely bride."

Jeremy bowed his head at Jenna. "I have to confess that as a kid, I thought you were a little cuckoo, and if anyone then would've told me we'd be here now, I wouldn't have believed them. But, today, I can honestly say how grateful I am to you, Jenna, because I've never seen him as happy as he is now. The way he looks at you and the way you look at him, I have no doubt you have found something special in each other. I'd like to believe it is Christ. Cody and Lena, the couple you see in the photo on screen, just in case you forgot—" he pointed at the screen again "—told me that was the secret to their enduring marriage. It is their love for Jesus. That's who I see in both Max and Jenna. That's why I believe they will make it. As a final word, Maximus—" Jeremy looked his best friend straight in the eye "—you saved my life, and I can never thank you enough. I'm so happy for you both. With all my heart, thank you. I wish you both all the joy heaven can give."

As the audience applauded, Max stood up and approached him. They hugged.

"You haven't changed at all," Max said. "You still always manage to steal the show no matter where you go — even if no one could quite figure out it was you who stole it."

"I don't know what that means, but it sounds like a compliment, so I'll take it."

"It's a compliment." Max clapped his shoulder before returning to his bride.

Jeremy passed the mic on to the host, who announced that Jenna was about to dance with her father, Paolo. After Jeremy retrieved his camera from the tech guy, he caught sight of several latecomers familiar to him, sneaking inside the tent all the way to the back of the reception area. Serene and his niece, Lily Red, had just arrived. When his older sister caught sight of him, she waved. Jeremy rushed toward them.

"If it isn't my beautiful sister!" He wrapped her in a huge hug. "Thank you for coming! This way, I get to say I'm not the last person to show up."

"I can't believe you're here! Did you arrive on time for the ceremony? What time did you land this morning?"

"You don't even want to know how crazy this morning was." Jeremy gave her a once-over, his hands still on her arms. "Let's just say I'm jet-lagged, but the adrenaline is doing its work, so it's all good." He lifted his niece in the air and carried her in his arms. "Who is this pretty little lady who looks so much like her uncle?"

"Uncle Jeremy!" Lily Red exclaimed. "I was supposed to be the flower girl, but Dad's tour bus took forever to get here."

"We hit so many roadblocks." Serene shook her head as Jeremy led them to their father's table. "We tried to get here on time, but yeah."

"It's a wonder Rachel isn't upset with our entire family. Mrs. P seems to be, though."

"When is she not?" Serene rolled her eyes.

"Where's Nolan?" Jeremy asked.

"He just dropped us off. He still has a lot of miles to cover if he wants to get to his concert tonight."

"Still living the rock star lifestyle, huh?" His gaze lingered on Serene. "How are you coping with all that?"

A dry chuckle escaped her lips. "It has its challenges, but it's the life I have, and there's a lot to be thankful for."

"Good." Jeremy nodded. "I'm glad to hear that."

"Is that my granddaughter?" The way Dad's face lit up at the sight of Lily Red made Jeremy smile. There was so much about his niece that reminded them all of Mama Aida. Speaking of mothers, Jeremy scanned the tent to check on Rachel. He winced at the intensity of their expressions as Rachel and her mother stood in a corner of the tent by the buffet table.

"Catch up with Dad," Jeremy told Serene. "I'll let Rachel know you're here."

Serene nodded him away.

Jeremy weaved through the tables, waving at acquaintances, and stopping by to have a little chat with friends, before reaching Rachel and Mrs. P, who had her back turned on him. He slowed down when he started hearing what the mother and daughter were arguing about.

Mrs. P stomped her foot. "Why are we even having this conversation? Are you developing feelings for Jeremy?"

"Mom, how is that even possible?" Rachel blurted out. "He just arrived this morning. How can I develop feelings for him while the wedding is happening? What do you take me for? I can't—" Rachel gasped upon catching sight of Jeremy about to twist on his heel and turn back.

Mrs. P turned around. Upon seeing Jeremy, she threw her hands in the air. "Of course. You are an adult now, Mr. Sinclair. All this time, I think you should've already learned not to listen in on other people's conversations."

At that, Jeremy could only chuckle in response. She was upset? All this time, had she not learned not to talk negatively about other people? Especially when she had no clue what she was talking about? "I'm just here to let Rachel know Serene and Lily Red have arrived. They can explain themselves why they weren't able to arrive in time, but right now—" Jeremy smirked at the older woman and extended his hand toward Rachel.

She stared at his hand like it was about to bite her. "What?" she asked.

Jeremy was probably being petty, knowing how much it would irk Mrs. P if Rachel said yes, but he was Jeremy Sinclair. Everyone knew he liked to stir the pot a little whenever anyone gave him opportunity to. "We haven't danced yet, Rachel. I believe the best man and the maid-of-honor usually get one dance?"

Rachel's focus switched from his hand to her mother, then to his face. Her eyes narrowed at him. To his surprise, she shrugged, flashed her mother a smile, took his hand, and said, "Yes."

She shouldn't have done that. Immediate guilt slammed against Rachel's chest the moment they walked away from her mother. Rebellion wasn't her thing, and for good reason. Rebellion was an assault against the kingdom of God. It wasn't God's way. It wasn't Rachel's way, either.

Proving yet again how well he knew her, Jeremy agreed with that realization. "I wasn't expecting you to say yes."

"Why did you ask then?" They reached the middle of the dance floor. She faced Jeremy, who held her waist as she laid her palms over his shoulders.

He shut one eye to give her a lopsided facial wince. "I wanted to see the expression on your mother's face."

"Do you enjoy provoking her or something? There's something about you that riles her up, and I've never fully understood it."

"Same here. Your mother has never liked me, and I've kind of gotten used to it by now." Jeremy shrugged. "Growing up, I didn't give her many reasons to be a fan of me, so it's all good. And no. I don't enjoy provoking her. Most of the time. As a teenager, maybe, but now, it's my intent to always extend the right hand of fellowship to her no matter what she throws my way."

That confounded Rachel's mind, mainly because not many people in church would have intentions like that toward her mother. Only a select few — the ones who had Rhoda Petersen's approval — got along with her mother.

Jeremy was one of Mom's regular targets, yet even then, Rachel had to admit Jeremy had taken all the criticism and passive-aggressive remarks in stride. Why? And how much of what they had been talking about had he overheard? How was he okay with any of that? In his shoes, Rachel would have been mortified.

"I'm sorry, Jeremy," she said. "I'm not sure how much of our conversation you heard, but it wasn't right, and to be clear, I didn't develop feelings for you in the span of one morning."

He laughed. "Ouch. How will I ever recover?" He pressed his palm over his chest before an easy grin appeared on his face, his eyes twinkling, like all of her drama gave him amusement. "Don't worry about it. It's not like I had any delusions about that. Not sure why Mrs. P thinks you have feelings for me."

"This dance certainly isn't helping."

"Do you want to stop?

Rachel was about to say yes, but there was something relaxing about being on the dance floor with only Jeremy able to see her face clearly. She didn't feel the need to smile, especially since her mother might mistake her smile as some sort of interest in him. "No, we're already here. Let's finish the song. I can use the peace and quiet."

"So I'm right, huh? You and Mrs. P are having some issues. Like way before I even showed up?"

Rachel nodded slowly.

"I'm not sure what's going on, and I'm not going to ask, but I do understand why your mother would caution you to be careful around me. If you were my daughter, I wouldn't trust me with you either."

"Don't say that. You are amazing, Jeremy. A lot of people in church may not recognize it yet, but I do. You've changed a lot from what you were before you returned to Christ."

The smile Jeremy gave her in response convinced Rachel of her own words. She would never have seen him smile like this before he started following God again. Not since Mama Aida's passing.

"I mean it. You're like Knox 2.0. Only he used to be a criminal and an ex-convict, and you never were."

"Only because I never got caught." Jeremy smiled. "I was a drug addict, Rachel. I've been at rock bottom more times than I care to remember, but that's beside the point. God has been faithful to redeem both Knox and me, but I still have a long way to go before I can say I'm completely on the straight and narrow. I live by God's grace every day. My point is your mother may be rough around the edges and more than a little tactless and critical at times — no offense —"

"None taken."

"—but if there's anything I'm sure of when it comes to Mrs. P, she loves God, she loves Mr. P, she loves the church, and she loves you. I'm sure she's just looking out for you and praying for what's best for you. I would even dare say the only reason she's so sharp and vigilant in rebuking and reprimanding people is because she desires the best for our church and for them."

Rachel wasn't expecting Jeremy, of all people, to say that. He was siding with her mother? What would that mean for her plans to flee the country with him? Also, had no one told him of what had been going on at church lately? Not Pastor Sam or Serene? Not even Max? How could Jeremy not know that Rachel's parents currently had plans to split the church he was saying she loved? "You have no idea what has been going on lately. I'm sure you won't think so highly of my mother once your family updates you on current events."

His brows met. "What do you mean? What's been going on?"

"Oh no." A wry chuckle came out of Rachel's lips. "You won't hear anything from me. It's best for you to have this conversation with your father." She braced herself to resist in case Jeremy tried to push and crack her resolve, but he just shrugged and changed the topic.

"So, when will you inform me how I'm supposed to make it up to you for having abandoned you these past three months? Do you have a list of demands I can sort through? Knowing you, the list is probably already in order of priority."

"No list." Rachel gulped. "Just one giant favor I beg you not to say no to."

The casual, easygoing expression on his face turned serious. He squinted an eye at her, as if to assess her. "You're making it sound so ominous. Do I need to sit down for this? What is it?"

"Wherever you're going a week from now, whether in China or the Philippines, please take me with you."

His face crumpled in an expression of confusion. He let go of her waist and stepped back to give her a long, solid look. He shook his head and then laughed. "Very funny, Rachel. No. No way."

All of Rachel's plans crashed all around her, but it took a few breaths before she recovered from the surprise. She flashed Jeremy her most alluring smile, while in her mind, she set her face like a flint. She was Rachel Petersen, and she took after her mother. When she set her mind to something, she wasn't willing to take no for an answer.

This was her one shot at a secure escape from all the chaos about to ensue, and Jeremy Sinclair wasn't about to leave her hanging dry. So, she linked her arm with his and walked in stride with him toward his father and sister's table. She then said in as sweet a tone as possible, "Remember how much you owe me, Jeremy?"

thirteen

THE **O**NE
WHO **T**OOK
SHOTS

To call Rachel relentless was a huge understatement. The woman was downright ruthless, but even she couldn't make Jeremy back down from a challenge. If he could stay unoffendable with the mother, surely he could stand unwavering in his decision to not let the daughter rebel against anything — whether it was her parents or whatever else it was she needed to escape by running away with him.

He had learned the hard way what the consequences of rebellion were, and he wanted no part in Rachel's rebellion. He would be the immovable object to Rachel's unstoppable force. Or something like that. However, to characterize Rachel as a force would be to do her a disservice. She was more like a gentle wave, tantalizing one to float with it wherever it chose to go.

"Lily Red!' Rachel carried Nolan and Serene's daughter and twirled her in the air.

"Rachel!" Lily Red squealed. "I missed you!"

"I missed you too! Where did you run off to?" Rachel hauled the six-year-old in her arms and rocked her from side-to-side. "I was so excited to see you as a flower girl, but I guess your dad had to whisk you away to wherever."

Lily Red nodded excitedly. "We went everywhere!"

"You did?!" Rachel pouted. "I want to go everywhere too, because I'm always stuck around here."

"You should travel too, Rachel." Lily Red pressed her palms on Rachel's cheeks. "We flew all the way to Ancoria, and I got to see the prince and princess!"

"You did?! That's amazing!"

Lily Red tilted her head to the side, her dark curls swaying in the air. "You're as pretty as the princess was, Rachel."

"Oh yeah? What was her name?"

"Princess Talia!" Lily Red said.

"That's a pretty name."

Serene nudged Jeremy. "When she first saw the royal family, Lily Red kept mentioning how much Princess Talia reminded her of Rachel. She says that out of all the people in church, she loves Rachel and Jenna the most."

Jeremy raised a brow. "Well, Rachel has lived up to her name. She's always been Princess Rachel to us, so it's appropriate."

"Have you ever been to Ancoria, Jeremy?" Rachel asked.

"I joined a team led by Knox and Hannah once."

"Isn't that cool?" Rachel wrinkled her nose. "I've never even ridden an airplane."

"Why not?" Lily Red mimicked her expression. "It's super fun."

"I've never been outside the country," Rachel said, "but I might travel overseas soon, if I convince one of my friends—" she winked at Jeremy "—to take me on a trip to Asia."

He smirked before taking a sip from his glass of water.

"I've never been to Asia." Lily Red turned to her mother. "Have we been to Asia, Mommy?"

"Yes, poppy, we have. We went to Japan once, remember? Actually, we've been to several countries in Asia. It's a huge continent."

Rachel put Lily Red down and hugged Serene. "I'm glad you guys were able to make it here."

"We're so sorry we couldn't make it to the ceremony. We tried our best to get here on time."

"From the beginning, you made it clear it's a long shot, so believe me. Max and Jenna understand."

Rachel glanced at the newlyweds. Max pointed at the cake. Rachel nodded. "I think it's time to cut the cake." She signaled the host to make the announcement and lifted a finger in the air as a signal for Serene to wait. "Have they served you any food?"

Serene shook her head.

"There's a buffet table you can get your food from—" Rachel huffed upon seeing that the caterers were already packing up "—I'll find someone who can take care of you, help you get you anything you need."

"Rachel, you don't have to. We're fine. We can grab something to eat after the wedding."

She smiled at Serene in acknowledgment, but as she sauntered away, her stride confident and sure, something told Jeremy she would still try to find someone. He was surprised she didn't just decide it should be him.

"She's quite something, isn't she?"

Jeremy pried his eyes away from Rachel and directed it toward his father. "She is. If one didn't know any better, one could easily assume she is living a life as perfect as the appearance she projects."

Dad's brows flicked up. "Why do you say that? Do you think she's going through something?"

"Is she? I've only been here a few hours, and I've already been hearing some whispers."

Dad and Serene exchanged looks, confirming Jeremy's suspicions that something was astir at Connect Church. However, regret gripped him. Why hadn't he kept his mouth shut? He wasn't willing to dive into drama just yet. In his week-long stay there, he would doubtless hear plenty about what was going on.

To his relief, Serene chimed in and directed the conversation elsewhere. "Rachel is a strong one, that I can say for sure."

Dad nodded. "She was one of your mother's favorites, for a reason. Aida used to have nothing but good things to say about Rachel."

"Heh." Jeremy grinned through the bittersweet taste in his tongue at the mention of his mother.

"Mama Aida used to have nothing but good things to say about everyone. Growing up, I never heard her put anyone in a bad light."

Dad's face softened, convincing Jeremy of how much his father still loved his mother. It had been years since his mother had passed away, but her memory and legacy still lingered fresh in their hearts and minds.

Not long after the bride and groom cut their cake, Rachel returned to their table and sat next to Jeremy. "The caterers have been informed," she told Serene. "They should arrive with your food any time now."

Serene smiled. "Thank you, Rachel."

Lily Red, on the other hand, left her chair and climbed onto Rachel's lap. "Your dress is so pretty, Rachel. You look so perfect. I think you should be a princess, for real."

"I should go to Ancoria then. Do you know someone there who can turn me into a princess?"

"You're already Princess Rachel, remember?" Jeremy grinned. "You don't need to go overseas for that."

Rachel laughed. "I wouldn't call myself a princess. My gap year will be over soon, and executive assistant to my dad's boss isn't exactly princess-like."

Executive assistant. It sounded like the perfect job for Rachel, considering how organized and good with people she was. Why then did the idea of Rachel working an eight-to-five put Jeremy off?

"Robert did mention something about that the last time we talked," Dad said. "Something about the current executive assistant waiting for you to get on board before retiring? It's rare for a company to be willing to wait a year for someone to take a job. It's unheard of. They must really want you, which says a lot about your capabilities and your father's good standing with the company. What favor the Lord has granted you!"

Rachel squirmed in her seat. "Right, Pastor Sam. The Lord has been good to us."

"You don't seem as excited as most would expect you to be," Serene said.

"I don't know. Something about it feels off. My dad's boss has always been kind to us, to me, and I'm sure it's a job that will expand my capabilities and challenge me, but—" Rachel shrugged "—I'm not sure it's what I want to do."

Jeremy rolled his eyes. "Millennials."

"Is Rachel a millennial?" Serene asked. "Doesn't she count toward the next generation already?"

He shrugged.

"Oh no," Rachel answered for herself. "I'm not Gen Z. I'm among the last of the millennials."

"Have you spoken to your parents about your reservations?" Dad asked, veering the conversation away from which generation Rachel belonged to.

She nodded slowly. "They know."

She didn't need to explain any further. They also all knew her parents well enough to guess what their reactions could be.

She widened her smile before nudging Jeremy's rib with her elbow. "I was hoping Jeremy would take me to the Philippines with him before I commit to a lifetime of corporate drudgery. It would do me well to get involved in missions and see life from another perspective. That's good, right?"

"I think that's great." Dad's eyes twinkled as he spoke. Any talk of helping spread the Gospel anywhere made him come alive. "It would benefit you to spend the rest of the summer on the field before you get tied to a job that will make it more challenging next time. Besides, Jeremy usually works with teams, so it won't put you both in a compromising situation." Dad turned to Jeremy. "What do you think, Son?"

Jeremy gave Rachel a sharp side-eye.

She grinned at him, her perfect teeth mocking him. "Yeah, Jeremy. What do you think?"

"I already told you what I think," he said.

"And that is what?" Serene asked.

"I think you should bring Rachel on a plane with you, Uncle Jeremy," Lily Red said, swaying her legs as she leaned against Rachel's torso. "She's never been on one before."

How had Rachel somehow rallied his family against him in this? All in the span of several minutes. Oh, wow. She was good at this. He should never underestimate her. "Let's just say I have reservations about it for a reason. Rachel knows what those reservations are, but she and I can discuss it within the next few days, because this wedding is about to end. Right now—" he stood up and retrieved his camera from the table "—I need to take photos of the waterfall before this event wraps up."

"Wait." Rachel straightened in her seat so suddenly, she almost knocked Lily Red off her lap. She wrapped her hand around Lily Red's waist to hold her the child steady. "You're the best man. You can't leave. What if Max needs you?"

Jeremy pointed at Max, who had his eyes set on his wife, whispering something in her ear, both barely aware of anyone else around. "He can do without me at this point, Rachel. I doubt they even remember any of us exist. Things are winding down, the toasts have been made, the cake has been cut. There'll probably be a little more dancing. That means I'm running out of time, and I want photos of that waterfall."

"At least let him know where you're going."

"Fine. If it gives the princess peace, why not?" He swept a nod at his father, sister, and niece. "I'll see you guys later. Dinner? At Serene's or Dad's?"

"Serene's," Dad said.

"Copy that."

"Aren't you going home with us?" Serene asked.

Jeremy shook his head. "Knox lent me his motorcycle for the rest of the week, so there's no way I'm riding anything other than that beauty while I'm here."

"Can I ride with Uncle Jeremy?" Lily Red asked.

All the adults around her said, "No," in unison.

"Phooey." Lily Red scowled.

Jeremy headed for Max. He hadn't gone far from his family's table when Rachel, for some reason, caught up with him. "Is this how my week is going to be, Rachel? Are you going to stalk me until I agree?"

"Come on." She sped up to match his strides. "Don't you trust that I wouldn't do something this drastic unless I had good reason to?"

"I don't think traveling to the other side of the world to avoid your parents is a good reason, Rachel. Besides, your mother is already freaking out about how something might be going on between us, and we've barely spent time with each other. Mrs. P will think we've eloped or something."

"So what if she thinks that, Jeremy? It's not the truth."

"You would do that to your own mother?"

"Please." She grabbed his elbow, forcing them to stop walking. "I need this. You don't understand how much." Her blue eyes glistened from the tears threatening to fall down her cheeks.

Why did Jeremy feel like such a villain at that moment? "Give me time to pray about it, Rachel. A day or two. Something about this doesn't sit well with me."

Rachel nodded, gulped, and backed off. "I can do that. Just know that I'll prepare everything anyway. I'll pack my bags. I'll do everything."

He raised a brow. "Don't take this as me saying yes, Rachel, but if I agree to this — and odds are low that I will — bring only whatever you can carry yourself. This isn't a luxury vacation we're going to."

Her face lit up, her tentative smile quivering into a confident one. "Noted."

Jeremy huffed. Had he just given her hope? So much for being an unwavering and immovable object to her unstoppable force. He proceeded toward Max's direction, with Rachel still striding next to him. Why she was still following him was anyone's guess, but if she wanted to trail behind him everywhere, he wouldn't stop her. Her company was pleasant enough to have around, and he could probably even convince her to let him take a few shots of her at the waterfall.

Finally, he reached his best friend. "Hey, Maximus. I'm heading to the waterfall to take a few shots before everything wraps up and you whisk your bride away for your honeymoon. Is there anything else you need?"

Max stood from his seat. "No, man." He tapped Jeremy's back. "Thank you for coming. We both appreciate it a lot."

"We're saying goodbye already?" Jeremy asked.

"Just in case you don't get back in time before Jenna and I have to leave. I think the limo's waiting outside already."

"Got it. Have an amazing time."

"I'm going with Jeremy to see the waterfall," Rachel told Jenna. "I'll try to get back in time to say bye."

"Don't worry about it." Jenna jumped to her feet and gave Rachel a hug. "Thanks for everything. You are so amazing."

Having received the groom and bride's permission to leave, Jeremy focused on the matter at hand: the waterfall.

Once they reached the stunning scene of that body of water dropping from a woodsy cliff onto an otherwise peaceful lake, none of the tension Rachel had earlier was present. Of course. This was Princess Rachel, the little girl from his childhood years, who basked in all the attention people showered upon her. He didn't need to ask to take shots of her. The moment they arrived, Rachel slipped her shoes off and waded into the water, the waterfall as her backdrop.

"Take a photo of me! Quick!"

Jeremy already had the camera aligned for a perfect shot. Rachel Petersen was a natural at this. Pose after pose, shot after shot, she delivered a stunning photo. With the gown she had on, the glow of natural sunlight on her skin, the foggy backdrop of the waterfall, and her innate beauty, Rachel looked nothing short of ethereal, like someone out of a fantasy novel. He only directed her once in a while, but she had creative ideas of her own regarding where to go and what to do to get unique, breath-taking shots. At one point, she stood on a rock right in front of the waterfall, not caring if her gown got wet, not at all scared that she might slip. She stretched her arms on both sides, perpendicular to her body, and looked up.

Jeremy gulped as he took shots from several angles. With the sun's rays radiating on her and the raging waterfall as her background, the shot made her appear almost angelic. Or maybe it was something else. Something a lot more heavenly. After taking a final shot, Jeremy took a moment to just enjoy the scene. That's when he realized what was causing her radiance. Rachel was a daughter of the Most High, one who was her Father's delight.

His heart swelled, almost as if God allowed him to share a fraction of the affection and delight God contained in His heart for Rachel.

Rachel dropped her arms and turned her head to look at him. "Are we done?"

His breath was stuck in his throat, so Jeremy nodded in response, before scrolling through his camera to check the photos he had taken. Each shot was a piece of art.

"Can I see?" Rachel spoke from behind him, before leaning against his shoulder to get a peek at the photos. "Did we take good shots?"

"Gorgeous," he said. "Come on." He pulled his shoes and socks off and threw them on the nearby grass, close to where she had thrown hers. He sat on a nearby ledge, where his feet could hang over and touch the water. When Rachel sat next to him, he showed her the photos.

Her smile was brilliant and genuine as she scrolled through his shots. "These are amazing, Jeremy," she said. "You have to send some to me, so I can post them."

"Sure. Let me know which ones you want."

"All of them, I think." She chuckled as she continued going through every photo.

As she continued to browse, Jeremy took time to admire the scenery. It took several minutes before she handed the camera back to him. He took the device and laid it over his lap. A moment of comfortable silence followed, a moment to appreciate the wondrous world they lived in.

Jeremy swayed his legs, shoveling water with his feet, before speaking his mind. "What are you running from, Rachel? Is it just your parents? Or is there more?"

"It's not just them." Rachel fixed her focus on the tip of her right toe, which she was swirling around in the water. "It's a lot of things, for sure, but I'd like to think I'm running toward something, not running from whatever."

"And that something is? What are you searching for?"

"God? Myself? It's hard to explain. I understand if I'm not making much sense to you, but this is something I need to do. Even for just one summer."

"Try to help me understand."

"I don't know how."

"Try."

She let out a long breath. "All my life, there has always been a script to follow. As a kid, I believed with all my heart that if I followed the script, everything would turn out fine, and it did for a while, but these past years, the more I try to follow the script, the more I wonder if I'm missing out on something greater. A corporate job is the next scene in a script my parents have written for me. It makes sense, but it's not what I want to do."

Rachel's hooded gaze and the way she looked in profile made Jeremy want to snap another shot, but he recognized a preciousness to the moment that made him pause. It was a moment that didn't need to be photographed to be remembered, because he doubted he would ever forget the way she looked at that moment.

"Take your time to decide," she said. "I respect you enough to believe you are trying your best to walk the straight and narrow, but please don't dismiss this as me rebelling against my parents. That's not my heart. God knows how challenging this whole wedding has been for me, and it's not just because you've been M.I.A.. I joke about that a lot, but it's a variety of things that have been breaking my heart."

So, it was true. She really had fallen so deeply in love with Max, hadn't she? "The right guy is out there for you, Rachel. He will show up unexpectedly, and when he does, you might be surprised who it is. For all we know, he might be someone who has been right beside you all along."

Rachel gave him a funny look — stoic but questioning, like she didn't have the slightest idea what he was going on about.

"Of course, that's assuming Mrs. P doesn't get ahead of you and arrange a marriage to fit that script you're talking about."

She laughed. "I wouldn't put it past her to pull something like that. My mother is relentless."

"Kind of like you."

"What? How so?"

He gave her a pointed look. "You've barely left my side since I said no to the favor you asked."

She giggled. "What can I say? I'm desperate. I can go on my own, sure, but it's much safer if I go with someone I trust, and I trust you, so—"

Jeremy couldn't deny how good it felt to hear her say that, even if he wasn't sure he deserved it. "I'll pray about it, Rachel," he assured her. "I'll get back to you in a few days."

She opened her mouth to say something, but before the words came out, someone spoke up behind them.

"Mind if we join you?"

Jeremy grinned at the immediate recognition of the voice. Sure enough, Max and Jenna were walking toward them, holding hands.

"What are you doing here?" Rachel asked. "You should be in the limo by now."

"We asked the driver to wait." Jenna bunched her fingers on the sides of her skirt and lifted it up before performing a pirouette. "This place is beautiful, and we didn't want to miss the opportunity to enjoy it with our best friends." She tapped both Jeremy's and Rachel's shoulders to signal for them to scoot over to give her space. Both moved to the edge of the rock to make enough space for all four of them to sit. Jenna sat right next to Rachel and leaned her head on her maid-of-honor's shoulder. Rachel leaned her head on top of Jenna's. Meanwhile, Max took his seat between his wife and best friend. He brought out his phone and stretched his long arms to take a selfie of all four of them.

Right before he pocketed his phone, Max and Jenna exchanged looks — the kind Jeremy had seen his father and mother give to each other multiple times. The scene tugged at a longing Jeremy had shoved to the side many times over. Was he ready for marriage? Was it time to be more intentional in praying to God for a partner? The desire stirred inside him, and it only kept growing as they spent the next half hour laughing over numerous inside jokes, taking photos, and reminiscing over their childhoods and how far God had taken them since then.

That afternoon, Jeremy's heart opened to a possibility he had often felt inadequate to entertain — the possibility of being a husband, a father, the leader of his own family.

Later, leaning against a borrowed motorcycle, he scrolled through his photos and stopped to stare at one of his favorites: the one with Rachel basking in sunlight, with the waterfall gushing behind her, lost in a gesture of surrender. The image struck him with realization: the daughter whom God delighted in had looked Jeremy in the eye and had told him she trusted him.

From Rachel, who was as straight an arrow as one could get, the trust was a boost of confidence Jeremy hadn't even been aware he needed. The temptation to say yes to her, go on a trip halfway across the world with her, would be so easy to give in to. But no. Not without the Father's approval. He couldn't mess up where Princess Rachel was concerned, so Jeremy shut down his camera, placed it securely in the motorcycle's container box, and rode as fast as he could away from the living temptation that was Rachel Petersen.

fourteen

THE ONE
WHO NEEDED
TO GO TO THEIR
HONEYMOON

Rachel buried her face in her pillow to block out the sun. What time was it? Why was the sun up so early? Rachel blindly grasped for her phone on her bedside table before forcing her eyes open to check the time. A few minutes past ten o'clock. What?! How had that happened? She had set her alarm to wake her up at six o'clock. Had it not gone off?

She checked her alarm settings and discovered that it had gone off as expected. A vague recollection of her hitting the snooze button several times drifted through her mind. "Ugh." She rolled onto her back, making her bed bounce beneath her. "How on earth am I going to work a nine-to-five when I can't even wake up before ten?"

How had she been so disciplined in waking up early and doing her morning devotions when she was a child, only to be this lazy and undisciplined as an adult? She felt more like a child now than when she had been an actual child.

Rachel forced herself up and dragged her feet on the floor to fix her bed. At least she was still consistent in doing that. Every move she made carried a weariness she couldn't quite place, the building pressure within her chest threatening to make her burst at any given moment. Still in her nightwear, she put up her hair in a messy bun just to get its strands off her face. She didn't bother to look in the mirror because she didn't have to worry about the way she looked or how people perceived her.

She brewed herself a cup of coffee and enjoyed the warmth of the mug on her palms for a few seconds before heading to her living room. The night before, she had left her journal and Bible on top of the coffee table. She lifted her bare legs up the soft couch, positioning herself comfortably before taking a long sip of her coffee as she listed in her mind all the things she needed to do that day.

Jenna and Max were calling from their honeymoon at eleven o'clock. Rachel wasn't exactly sure if she was looking forward to that, but they had sounded excited about getting in touch. Curiosity was enough to push Rachel to want to talk to them. Besides, she already missed her best friend. She gulped. God, have mercy on her.

Next on her schedule was lunch at twelve-thirty at Serene's house. After that, Rachel planned to hit the gym if there was still time. It would all depend on how much time she would end up spending with Serene, because she needed to go to dinner with her parents in the evening. That last appointment, she dreaded the most.

Overall, though, it wasn't too busy a day.

She had cleared up most of her freelance work to have time to rest after Jenna's wedding. Her clients would have to do without her for a while should her trip to the Philippines with Jeremy push through. "Lord, I hope he has already changed his mind about letting me go with him." He was leaving a week away from the wedding. That was four days from today. Rachel winced. He was cutting it close. It had been so hard to get in touch with him over the weekend. Was Jeremy deliberately avoiding her? Did he not care that she still needed to book her flight?

Rachel cringed.

This trip would wipe out her savings. Hopefully, she could make up her losses quickly after returning from the trip — assuming she would go, assuming she would return. What was she saying?! Of course she would return! This trip was just a temporary reprieve, a chance to sort herself out.

Rachel sighed and laid her mug of coffee over the floral coasters on top of her hardwood coffee table. She then picked up her Bible and opened to where she had left off the day before. Romans 8 was one of her favorite chapters, but the whole passage flew over her head, because her mind kept traveling to other places, like how she shouldn't be lounging around. She hadn't even prepared an outfit for the day yet. Was she really going to face Serene — former rock star, renowned artist, and creative entrepreneur — looking like a person who wakes up at ten in the morning? No way. She should look sharp and presentable. She replaced her bookmark in her Bible, marking the passage as unread. A quick prayer and a few scribbles in her journal to explain why she wasn't able to spend more time with God — and how she would make up for it — completed her morning devotions, before she rushed to the shower to prepare herself for the day.

By the time she opened her laptop and laid it on top of her island counter to chat with the newlyweds, anyone could assume Rachel had woken up to the most productive of mornings, based on how sharp she looked in the pantsuit ensemble she was wearing.

"Rachel!" Jenna squealed the moment she caught sight of Rachel's face on the monitor.

"Hey, Mrs. Owens! How's the honeymoon going?"

The couple exchanged lovey-dovey looks that made Rachel all giddy, but the giddiness dissipated when a stray thought repeated itself in her head. This was Max and Jenna — the only two people in the world she had ever been infatuated with. The reality of those words made Rachel sick to her stomach. *God, forgive me. How do I even have thoughts like this in my head?* Rachel's smile faltered.

"You okay?" Max coughed.

The screen showed the couple's heads squished together, both their eyes narrowed at her.

Rachel blinked away the melancholy. "Hmm? Yes! I'm fine. Sorry."

"Good." Jenna pouted. "We were saying that we're having a great time, and it's amazing here, but you left us behind and traveled to space on your own. For a moment there, it looked like you were about to throw up."

Rachel forced out a chuckle. "I'm fine. I just have a lot on my mind. Stuff I need to do today." She tightened her lips and tilted her head to the side to indicate her reluctance over everything she needed to do. "How can I help two of my favorite people in the world?"

Jenna giggled. She couldn't stay still in her seat, like she had been possessed by unbridled whimsy, making her husband laugh. "You should come here tomorrow, Rachel!" she was finally able to say. "It will be fun!"

Despite all her practice putting on a happy face, Rachel was unable to hide her horror. "What? Why? It's your honeymoon. No one in their right mind would want to be the third wheel in someone's honeymoon."

Max chuckled. "Jenna's getting ahead of herself. Let me explain. Nolan is having a concert here tomorrow. It's perfect timing, because his label is planning an after party to celebrate his latest single going platinum — whatever that means. The label offered to fly Serene and Lily Red over to surprise Nolan, but instead of doing that, they decided to take a road trip with Jeremy tomorrow. We figured you might want to travel here with them. You can stay the night, so all four of us can hang out before Jeremy flies back to wherever. What do you think?"

Why did the idea sound so alluring and dreadful at the same time? Also, she hadn't realized until then that neither Max nor Jenna knew of her plans to fly off with Jeremy. "I'm having lunch with Serene and Lily Red in half an hour, so I'll discuss with them if it's okay for me to go. It's a long drive too, so I wouldn't want to impose on them if they'd rather spend time together just as family."

"Oh, come on." Jenna waved dismissively at the screen like Rachel had just said something utterly ridiculous. "You're family to everyone at Connect, Rachel."

Was she? Did Max and Jenna have any idea what her parents were planning to do? How could they? Even Rachel couldn't fully wrap her mind around why her parents would seriously consider splitting the church she had grown up in. It was equivalent to splitting their family apart. How had it even come to this?

"Rachel?" Max and Jenna said her name in unison.

"I'll let you know if I can go. Hopefully, it'll all work out, because it will be so fun if we pull this off!" Rachel tried to sound excited, but her tone sounded fake, even to her.

"Well, we thought we would run it by you, just in case you're interested," Jenna said in a tone a little more sober. "It will be great to have you here, Rach."

"I know! I want to go, but I don't want to get too excited, in case it doesn't work out." That was somewhat true. Part of her wanted to go — mostly the part that loved hanging out with her friends. "Serene and I will talk it over and see what happens."

Jenna clapped her hands. "Perfect!" She had never looked happier than she did then.

Rachel exhaled after ending the call and shutting down her laptop. Was this wise? Wouldn't this trip only fan the flames of her mother's growing ire toward her? Was it rebellious of her to keep choosing her friends, even if it triggered her family's spite? What if her mother would once again get notions in her head that Rachel might still be attracted to Jenna? She winced. Was that why Mom was so resistant to her helping out with Jenna's wedding?

Or what if Mom would once again imagine this non-existent attraction between Rachel and Jeremy? Should Rachel go on a road trip with him instead of spending more time with her parents before flying to the other side of the world with him?

She caught herself.

Jeremy hadn't even agreed yet. This trip might be a great opportunity to get him on board with Rachel's plans.

But was she running from her parents again? How had her family and home become such a source of discomfort that she was making up any excuse not to have to be with them?

As she rushed toward her car to get to her next appointment, Rachel shed a tear, which she dabbed away carefully, so it wouldn't mess up her makeup. During the short drive to Serene's home, she decided she wasn't going. After lunch with Serene and Lily Red, Rachel decided she wanted to go. After dinner with her parents, Rachel was sure of it. She needed to go.

So much was happening, and if things fell apart, which seemed inevitable, it might be a lot more difficult and complicated for Rachel to spend time with Jeremy, Max, and Jenna in the future.

The Ducati's smooth roar faded as Jeremy pulled over at Serene's front yard. He caressed the polished exterior of the vehicle before letting out a sigh. "I'll miss you so much, but I'll see you in a couple of days—" he harrumphed "—right before I leave again."

The paradox of Jeremy's life hit him right then — the paradox that no matter where he went, he was always home and never home at all times. The past three days since he had arrived, he enjoyed the familiarity of everything around him. Communication wasn't a struggle. There was no confusion or fear of offending in the process of understanding and assimilating to local culture. His family and friends were around — just a call or drive away. Yet, a huge part of him was only home when out in the unknown, where God had called him to be. Out in places that weren't his comfort zone, but represented places that could be home if he could only advance God's kingdom there.

Something about the atmosphere within his family, and even in Max's and Jenna's wedding, heightened Jeremy's awareness of this paradox. No one was telling him anything, but something was amiss, and he fully intended to use this road trip with his sister to find out what was going on.

He climbed the steps of the mansion his rock star brother-in-law and artist savant sister owned. The luxury made him bristle. Their home was a far cry from what he had grown accustomed to over the years. Of course, he couldn't hold this against his family, because Nolan and Serene were also generous in their giving to charity, the church, missions, and God's call upon Jeremy's life.

Everyone had their calling. Theirs was to give and to send. Jeremy's was to go.

He opened the front door without knocking and found a drowsy Lily Red sitting at the bottom of the staircase, hugging her stuffed elephant. Her eyes were drooping close while the grandfather clock above her head ticked five-thirty, almost as if it was taunting her. Her head fell on top of her elephant, turning it into a pillow before Jeremy could greet her good morning.

To give her a few minutes of rest before they had to leave, he tiptoed to the kitchen, where Serene was already stuffing a large bag full of food for their road trip.

"Good morning, gingerbrain," Jeremy greeted.

"Oh my. You haven't called me that in years!" Serene didn't even bother to look up from what she was doing. "Come, be helpful and help me pack those sandwiches." She pointed at the dining table where there were at least a dozen grilled ham and cheese sandwiches on a large plate. Squares of parchment paper lay beside it.

"Why are we packing so much? It's a six-hour drive. I eat a lot, but I don't need to eat that much, and you and Lily Red will most likely barely finish one sandwich." He washed his hands at the sink. "Also, if we leave on time, we can even make a few stops to grab as many donuts as I want and still have plenty of time to prepare for Nolan's concert."

"I know. It's just for emergencies, in case something goes wrong. We've been on the road with Nolan enough to know that plans can go awry on these road trips. Also, with Rachel going with us, we'll have an extra stomach to feed. Don't let Rachel's size fool you. She can eat quite a lot. That woman's metabolism is worthy of envy."

Jeremy threw his head back as he returned to the table to start wrapping. "Rachel's coming? Why?"

"We had lunch yesterday. She said she chatted with Max and Jenna, and they floated the idea of her going on the road trip with us, so you four can spend time before you leave on Saturday. Rachel was hesitant, saying she's preparing for a trip and has a lot on her plate, but I suggested it might be better if she takes advantage of going while things are still at an impasse between her mother and the church." Serene winced. "And that's more than you need to know."

Jeremy was already wrapping his third sandwich. "I disagree. You should tell me more. Trouble ahead?"

"It's all rumors, at this point. Dad and Mrs. P have been at each other's throats a lot lately. You know what she's been like since Mama passed away. It's like she's trying to take over the role Mama had and has been frustrated that people at church aren't embracing her the same way they did Mama."

"Heh." Jeremy rolled his eyes. "It's impossible. Mama was something else."

"Mrs. P finds statements like that upsetting. She says we've all immortalized Mama into this saintly figure, and she insists Mama was human like everyone else. She keeps bringing up stuff from their past when they started the church way before we were born. Dad has tried to be patient over the years, but she's wearing him down. He hasn't been able to hold his tongue against her as much as before."

Jeremy scoffed. "Can you blame him? After years of bearing her criticism, anyone would cave. Still, what does all of this have to do with Rachel spending more time with Max and Jenna?"

Someone pulled over in their driveway. It could only be Rachel. Jeremy quirked a brow at Serene. "Well? Is anyone going to tell me what's going on?"

His sister sighed. "It's not for me to tell. I've already said too much. It's better you hear it from Dad." She placed the fruits she was slicing into a container, which she then added to her growing bag of goodies. "He asked us to drop by before we head off."

"Doesn't he want to go with us?"

Serene shook her head. "He said he didn't want to take such a long trip. He has been different lately. More irritable, gets more tired easily."

"It's probably age." Jeremy finished packing the last of the sandwiches and brought the plate to his sister, who added it to her bag of food.

"He isn't getting any younger, for sure," Serene said.

The doorbell rang, but Rachel walked in without anyone opening the door for her. She and Serene exchanged a nod before Rachel directed her full attention to waking Lily Red up. While Jeremy thought the interaction odd, he focused on more urgent priorities. The next fifteen minutes were a mad scramble to make sure they had everything they needed and that Rachel's car and Knox's motorcycle were parked safe inside the garage, because they were taking the Stones' family van on the road trip.

Half an hour after they left, Jeremy parked in the driveway of his childhood home. His presence there always brought back so many memories — both good and bad — and for some reason, Jeremy always choked up at the sight of the path leading from the street to their front porch, where Dad was already waiting.

Perhaps it was his conversation with Serene earlier, but Jeremy was suddenly so fully aware of the gray in his father's hair and the wrinkles on his face. Lily Red was quick to get out of her car seat with Rachel's help. She scrambled to the pavement and rushed past the front lawn to her grandfather.

"Grandpa!" she exclaimed before leaping into their dad's arms.

Serene trailed behind her while Jeremy and Rachel hung back, waiting to be acknowledged.

"We can't take too long, Dad," Serene said as she hugged their father. "We'll need to get on the road, if we're to make it in time for Nolan's concert."

"I'm aware. No need to keep reminding me, Serene." Dad nodded as he rocked Lily Red in his arms. "My granddaughter is so lovely, isn't she?" His eyes sparkled as he sought out the faces of Jeremy and Rachel. His gaze lingered on Rachel, and for a moment, the delight turned into hurt.

She flinched beside Jeremy. What was going on?

"It's good to see you, Rachel. What an exquisite young woman you are. No wonder my Aida adored you. She always spoke highly of you." Dad reached out to her and hugged her.

When Rachel stepped back, Jeremy caught sight of the tears she quickly wiped away.

"How about you guys come in for a minute?" Dad placed Lily Red back on the ground. "I have juice in the fridge and a popsicle stick for Lily Red. I'd just like to speak with Serene before sending you guys off."

"Dad." Jeremy stepped forward. "Can I be there to hear what you have to say to Serene?"

Dad and Serene exchanged glances. She nodded.

"Sure." Dad sounded nonchalant, but there it was again, the sadness in his expression, but it turned into delight when Lily Red grabbed his hand and pulled him toward the house. Serene followed after.

Jeremy walked on, but Rachel stayed rooted to her spot.

"Aren't you coming in?" he asked.

"I should probably hang back." She sounded choked.

"Okay. This is ridiculous." Jeremy shook his head. "Something is obviously going on, and no one cares to tell me what is happening."

"Your father will let you know now." Rachel's somberness unsettled him. "Whatever he tells you, I hope you'll see things from my perspective and let me leave with you. I still need to book a ticket, Jeremy, so don't take too long to decide."

"Right," he said. Whatever was going on, it was clear from the absence of Rachel's smile that this was bothering her greatly. "I'll let you know by the end of the day. Right now, I just need to figure out what's going on. Aren't you coming in?"

She didn't budge from where she stood.

This was more than strange behavior from the walking model of confidence that was Rachel Petersen. "Come on, Princess Rachel." Jeremy extended his hand for her to hold. "If anything goes wrong, I'm your knight, remember?"

Rachel's lips quivered at his gesture. Jeremy questioned whether he would be able to handle Rachel's tears. This was so unlike her. To his relief, she nodded and took his hand before he led her inside the house.

While Rachel looked after Lily Red, Serene and Jeremy entered their father's study, where the reason behind Rachel's tears unfolded for Jeremy.

"Since you're going to see Max and Jenna—" their father leaned back in his favorite recliner facing the couch where brother and sister sat next to each other "—I wondered if it would be wise to discuss what's going on with them, before the rumors get to them first. I'm sure at this point, they already have questions. As much as I don't want to put a damper on their honeymoon, I do feel like Max, especially, has the right to know."

"Wait." Jeremy huffed. "What is going on?"

Dad nodded at Serene, who repositioned herself on the couch, so she was at a sideways angle, able to look Jeremy in the eye. "Dad made an announcement among the core leadership of the church that he plans to retire from his position as pastor, and after spending time in prayer, he believes the Lord is leading him to train Max to take his place."

The news hit Jeremy like a lightning bolt. While it made complete sense to him that his father would choose Max, it also clarified the trouble he had been sensing among church people. "I'm guessing Mr. and Mrs. P aren't okay with this?"

"Along with several other elders of the church, at first." Dad sighed. "We've had several discussions about this, but none of them could agree on a replacement either, so I told them finally that I can only go by how I believe the Lord is leading me. I requested they all pray about it, as the last thing I want is to cause division in the church. This was a month ago. I expected everyone to pray about the situation and seek God's will, so we can all gather together to talk. Instead, rumors went flying that Robert and Rhoda have been meeting with church members and telling everyone that if Max becomes pastor, they will leave and start their own church."

"After all that," Jeremy said, "you're still planning to endorse Max as the head pastor?"

"How can I not? Those who were opposed at first — like the Grants, for example — have been praying about it, and after they sought the Lord, they changed their minds. Marcus and Naomi even came over a few weeks ago to break bread and apologize for the negative things they've said about me. It's only been Robert and Rhoda who have remained firm in their stance to resist this. Meanwhile, every time I pray, it's still Max whom the Lord is placing in my heart to train up for leadership."

"Does Max know about this?"

Serene nodded. "He was reluctant, at first, but before he asked Jenna to marry him, he made sure this was the path God was leading him to tread. He didn't want to pull Jenna into a marriage without preparing her for what could happen."

"And Rachel?"

"She's caught in between." Dad leaned forward, his one elbow on his knee. "She has been trying her best to stay neutral, but it's come to the point where lines are being drawn, and it looks like no matter what we do to compromise, the church is about to experience its first split."

"Just like that?" Jeremy clenched his fists, unsure of what to do with the swirl of emotions going on inside him. "It's not just rumors? It's going to happen?"

"The Petersens made it official last night," Serene said. "Rachel had dinner with them and called me right after. She was asking if we still wanted her to go with us. She's heart-broken about it."

Dad's hands balled into fists, mirroring Jeremy's. "This never would have happened if your mother was still here."

"Dad—" Serene's voice broke.

A tense silence followed before, for the first time in a long time, Samuel Sinclair broke down in front of his children. Jeremy sat frozen in his seat as Serene rushed forward to embrace their father. How had it come to this? If only he had been obedient, if only he had been more cooperative, if he had submitted to authority and supported his parents' ministry, if he hadn't gone astray, would his mother have not died? Would all of this have been avoided?

There was no way to know now. What was clear was that the church he had grown up in was breaking apart, and it felt to him like his father's and mother's legacy was breaking right along with it.

fifteen

THE ONE
WHO WANTS
HIM BACK

By the time they left Pastor Sam's house to commence their road trip, Jeremy's sullenness had convinced Rachel that their family home contained some sort of trigger, bringing out Jeremy's irritation toward her. The last time she had been to that house was after Mama Aida's funeral, and the confrontation between him and her mother still lingered fresh in her mind.

Jeremy was in many ways different now than he had been during that time of his life. But given what he had been through, could anyone blame him for his erratic behavior back then? He had lost his mother so abruptly, and despite Rachel's defensiveness for her own mother at that time, she couldn't deny how she too had grown up hearing Mom say all sorts of negative things about the Sinclairs. Now that news was spreading about her parents trying to instigate a split at their church, Rachel understood why, after leaving his father's study, Jeremy could barely look her in the eye.

Lily Red yawned as she drummed her fingers on her legs, bopping her head from side to side. Serene hummed a tune in the passenger's seat while Jeremy brooded silently as he drove. There was still a lot of highway ahead of them before they would reach their destination.

"Rachel, are you still okay back there?" Serene asked. "We can still switch if you want to."

"No," Jeremy blurted out. "Stay there, Serene. She's fine."

Serene attempted to twist her torso to face Rachel, her seatbelt not giving her much wiggle room. "We packed plenty of food. It's all in there." She pointed at the large, colorful bag next to Lily Red's car seat. "In case you're hungry."

"I'm fine." Rachel's stomach grumbled. She hadn't actually eaten breakfast before rushing to meet with them. "For now."

Serene's stare lingered on her, and she looked almost sorry about something. What that something was, Rachel could only guess. Lily Red drifted off to sleep, making Rachel want to doze off as well, if only to escape this awkward car ride with a family who had every right to hold umbrage against hers. She leaned her head against the leather-padded car interior, her gaze set on the scenery they were passing.

To her relief, Serene put on some music to help get rid of the uneasy silence. Rachel yawned and within a few minutes of the soothing acoustic music, she was fast asleep.

Lily Red's giggles awakened her. Rachel blinked her eyes open as her brain clamored to orient herself regarding her whereabouts. She was in the Stones' family car. Where were they now? How long had she been asleep?

"Rachel's awake!" Lily Red exclaimed.

"What time is it?" Rachel asked.

"It's about two o'clock. We've already eaten lunch," Serene explained. "You were so out of it, so we decided not to wake you up."

Lily Red laid her palm over her chest. "I wanted to wake you up, Rachel, but Uncle Jeremy didn't want me to."

Rachel cast a glance at Jeremy, who fixed his eyes on the road. He didn't bother to explain why he had asked them not to wake her. "I wish you would have woken me up," Rachel said. "It would have been nice to have lunch with you guys. I can't believe I slept that long."

"You must have needed the rest," Serene said. "If you're hungry, there's food in the bag. Donuts, too. We still have two hours before we get there, so it will do you well to eat something."

"Thanks, Serene." Rachel rummaged through the bag for something to eat and found a sandwich. She unwrapped it and took a bite before daring another glance at Jeremy, whom she caught looking at her from the rear-view mirror. She smiled at him. He shifted his gaze. She squirmed in her seat. He had most likely just found out what her parents had been doing, what they were planning to do. Was he mad at her because of it? She bit her sandwich angrily before chomping on the cold ham and cheese. Why would he punish her for what her parents were doing?

Jeremy switched on the radio. The first song that blared out of it was one familiar to all of them. *Rocking Serene*. It was the song that had launched Nolan and Serene to musical fame as *Red & Ice* when they were still barely out of their teens.

"Do you want me to change the station?" Jeremy asked his sister.

"Yes please." Serene nodded emphatically.

"No!" Lily Red objected. "That's Daddy's song! I like it."

"Your mom is already so tired of hearing it. I kind of am, as well," Jeremy said.

Lily Red pouted. "I'm not. Can we keep playing the song, Uncle Jeremy? Please, Mom? I haven't heard it in forever! Are you sick of this song, Rachel?"

She shook her head. "Not at all. I love that song. My mom's not a big fan of it, though." She bit her lip. Why did she have to say that? She wished she could take it back.

"Why's that?" Jeremy asked, the edge in his tone unmistakable.

Rachel shrugged in an attempt to play it off as nothing. "She says it's rebellious."

"It's a love song Nolan wrote for Serene. How can it be rebellious?"

"As I said, I love it." Why did it sound like Jeremy wanted to instigate a fight, or at least an argument, out of this? The looming confrontation made Rachel squirm in her seat. "I think it's romantic how a song Nolan wrote to express his love for Serene launched them to fame."

"To be fair to Mrs. P," Serene chimed in, "the song is kind of rebellious, considering where Nolan and I were at in our relationship when he wrote it. He meant it as a song of defiance toward religious mindsets and whatever else was keeping us apart. I think it's part of the reason I have trouble listening to it after all these years. It reminds me of a Nolan who didn't love God the way he does now. We were so in love back then, so idealistic, but in so many ways, we were missing the point of life. It's not just about rocking the norm or causing a stir, though kingdom culture could be quite disruptive, sometimes. Life is something more than all that. It's about something deeper and much more enduring. I find it sad that the song has now become some sort of anarchist anthem, when it was never meant to be that."

"Pfft." Jeremy scoffed. "How people interpret the song is entirely up to them. Nolan didn't originally intend for it to be perceived that way, and the original intent of the artist should matter. The song is a testimony of how far God has brought you and Nolan. I mean, come on. It paved the way for Nolan to rock the norm and cause a stir in a way that eventually glorified God. The fact that all Mrs. P or people like her can get from the song is that it's rebellious is to discount what God has done through it. He can make all things beautiful in its time, remember? He's done it for me. Why can't your mother see that, Rachel?"

Her breath hitched. If only she could turn back time and take back her words. Clearly, her mother was not a topic to be broached without expecting shots fired by Jeremy Sinclair — at least during this road trip. Rachel suddenly missed the cool and carefree version of Jeremy at Max and Jenna's wedding.

"Obviously, this isn't about the song anymore." Serene lightly slapped her brother's arm. "What has gotten into you? Rachel stated that she doesn't agree with her mother."

"I just find it infuriating how we let Mrs. P get away with all the shade and criticism she throws at us. She and Mama were supposedly best friends, yet she always says something snide about our family. We've made our mistakes, but hasn't she? She has been a walking mistake for decades, while she goes around like a hypocrite, correcting everyone's faults and acting all high and mighty. She—"

"Jeremy!" Serene's cheeks flushed red. "That's enough."

Silence followed. This wasn't the same Jeremy who had many times shown kindness to Rachel, and this outburst certainly had nothing to do with Nolan's song. This was coming from somewhere much deeper. Rachel shut her eyes. *God, he is right. We have been critical of him and his family. Forgive us, Lord. We are no better than anyone. Especially considering why I'm on this trip to begin with.*

Lily Red grabbed her stuffed elephant from the side of her car seat and hugged it against her chest, her face crumpling with genuine confusion. She leaned forward slightly to check on her uncle. "You can change the song, Uncle Jeremy. I'm sorry it upset you so much. Just don't be mad at Rachel now, okay? I'm sure she's sorry too, aren't you, Rachel?"

"I am," she croaked out. "Sorry I said what I said. It was inappropriate for me to bring up my mother's opinion on Nolan's song, especially considering how precious that song is to Nolan and Serene's story. Please forgive me."

"You don't have to apologize, Rachel," Serene said before glaring at her brother. "Right, Jeremy?"

He didn't respond. Another uncomfortable silence followed. How much time did Serene say they had left before reaching their destination? Two hours? Rachel sighed. Might as well be an eternity.

When Jeremy pulled over in front of their hotel, a collective sigh of relief filled the SUV. The tension had been unbearable inside, and Jeremy could only blame himself for that. Serene and Lily Red had tried to diffuse the tension as best they could, but Jeremy was unwilling to acknowledge Rachel's apology or apologize for his own outburst, so the rest of the drive had been uncomfortable for all of them.

As Jeremy was about to get out of the driver's seat to help Serene unload the bags, Serene gripped his arm. Rachel slammed the door shut in the backseat, after already having helped Lily Red get out.

"What?" Jeremy asked, even if it should be clear what Serene was about to speak to him about.

"Stop acting like a jerk, Jeremy," Serene said. "I vouched for Dad to tell you everything, because I thought you would be able to handle this like a mature individual. What Dad told us earlier is a lot to take in, but you don't get to vent out your frustration on Rachel. She has nothing to do with what's happening. It's already tough enough being caught in the middle of all this mess, and it wasn't like she was aware of everything her parents had been up to, because she was pouring all her energy and time on putting together your best friend's wedding. Remember how she covered for you all that time. Stop punishing her for the many ways her mother has offended you. She doesn't deserve that."

Jeremy opened his mouth to respond, but Serene lifted her finger and pointed it at him to shush him.

"Lily Red and I are going to check in for all of us. You and Rachel go ahead and meet Max and Jenna, but before you do, apologize to Rachel, and be nice to her. She is not her mother. Remember that. Now, broaden your shoulders and man up."

His shoulders squared as an automatic response to the challenge. Jeremy rolled his eyes. It had been a long time since Serene talked to him this way. "You done?"

"Don't give me attitude, Jeremy. You know I'm right. Stop being rude to Rachel. Even my six-year-old noticed, and that is unacceptable. There will be a lot of explaining to do to her about this, so you better apologize to her as well."

Jeremy sighed. "You're right. I was out of line. I'll say sorry to Lily Red once we get back."

"And Rachel?"

"I'll apologize to her too." It didn't feel good saying that out loud, but there was no arguing with this side of Serene. "And I'll be nice."

"Good. Now, stay there." Serene got out of the car. Outside, hotel bellboys were already all over Rachel, each of them more than willing to do whatever she told them to do, like the princess that she was.

Jeremy had to give it to Rachel. No matter what she was going through, she had a way of getting things done while still looking like she had done it all without effort. Once the hotel staff had gotten all their bags out of the vehicle, Serene said something to Rachel, who nodded and hugged his sister. While Serene and Lily Red headed inside the hotel, Rachel headed back to the car, taking her place in the passenger seat in front.

Like nothing had happened earlier, she smiled at him and said, "Let's go?"

Jeremy started the car and remained silent, allowing himself to brew in his own thoughts, while his ego tried its best to prevent him from blurting out a much-deserved apology to Rachel.

"Max already sent the location. Can you check my phone for it? The map app should already have it."

"On it." Rachel took his phone from its holder and launched the app. Minutes later, they were driving toward the coffee shop where the newlyweds were already waiting for them.

Spending the next few hours with this tension brewing between them was far more uncomfortable than holding on to his pride, so after taking a few minutes to gather his courage, Jeremy sighed and said, "I'm sorry, Rachel. I shouldn't have said all those things. There's a lot happening, as I'm sure you're aware, and I'm struggling to process it in a Godly way."

She didn't respond immediately. Instead, she sat there like she hadn't heard anything, with her gaze flitting between the road ahead and the phone in her hand. When she finally spoke up, Jeremy exhaled with relief.

"It's fine," she said. "Apology accepted. Completely forgiven. How about my apology?"

"Unnecessary," Jeremy said, "but sure. Forgiven."

"I have to say, as unexpected as it was to hear you say all those things — you're usually cooler than that — you had several fair points. Especially after the things you heard my mother say at Max and Jenna's wedding. I was wondering how you were able to smile through all of it. You kind of just took it to the chin and carried on."

"Part of it is because I've already accepted Mrs. P as she is. She's always been this way, and Dad and Mama — especially her — loved her anyway. It's just that this morning, after the news Dad gave us—" Jeremy clenched his jaw. "Let's just say it triggered a lot of junk I thought I already dealt with. It's no excuse. I was wrong, but you deserve an explanation."

"So, Pastor Sam told you, huh?"

"About your parents wanting to leave Connect, because my dad plans to endorse Max as the next lead pastor?"

"Yes. That." Rachel's posture collapsed, like she had just given up on something. "It's a large part of why I wanted to leave with you, Jeremy. It's going to get messy around here, and I don't think my heart can handle the fallout."

"I've never pegged you as the kind of person who runs away from trouble, Rachel. That's more my M.O.. You're the one who faces challenges head on with a smile on your face and a tiara on your perfectly coifed hair."

"Coifed? Really?"

"Tell me I'm wrong."

"First, it's been a long time since I've worn a tiara."

"Oh yeah? When was that?"

"Prom queen." She waved a hand the way pageant girls do. "That's not the point, though."

"Yeah? What is?"

"As much as I appreciate your vote of confidence, I'm just—" she inhaled and exhaled "—exhausted. I can't explain how much I want to get away from all of it."

"Can't you convince your parents not to push through with this? It's not Biblical, and Max may be young, but bias aside, don't you think he would make a great pastor?"

"The sleeve of tattoos on his arm alone makes my parents think of him as unqualified." A wry chuckle came out of her mouth. "You think you know how stubborn my mother is, Jeremy, but you don't have the slightest idea what she's like when she fixates on something. For some reason, she has taken it as a personal affront that your dad would choose Max as lead pastor over my dad."

"Wait. What? Your father wants to become head pastor?"

Rachel shrugged. "My dad is as low-key as my mother is high-strung, but apparently, he's been expecting Pastor Sam to choose him, because he has been studying for the position, even if he had never quite functioned as one at church."

"Rachel, no offense—" Jeremy cringed "—he's your father and all, but I have trouble seeing him as lead pastor of Connect. It would be more like your mother will be the one running the church."

"Whether or not that's true isn't for me to decide. I've tried to talk them out of it. I spent all night last night doing that, and now, it just feels like I've somehow betrayed them, because they interpret my actions as me not taking their side. What they don't get is I'm not taking any sides. I don't want a part in any of this. It's too much pressure to handle. On top of that, my gap year will soon be over. Max and Jenna's wedding gave me an excuse to not commit to a job at my dad's company, but it's over now, so my parents have expectations. I told them I don't want to take the job, and—" Rachel bowed her head. "Let's just say they're not happy with me right now."

"Wow. That's a lot. I'm sorry you're going through all that." Jeremy slowed the car down to follow the GPS directions to take a turn toward an area with a group of restaurants clustered close to each other. Within the cluster was the coffee shop where Max and Jenna were waiting.

"So, now that you are aware of my situation, does that mean you will let me go with you? Will you rescue me from all this trouble?"

Jeremy grinned. That was smooth. He chuckled. "While I would love to be your knight-in-shining-armor and come to your rescue, Princess Rachel, one of my many concerns is that I am a man, and you are a woman." He parked the car as he spoke. "Don't you think taking you with me will only fuel rumors and leave us in a compromising situation? I get now why you want to go so badly, sure, but given the already heated atmosphere here, won't your escape just fan the flames? To be honest, I couldn't care less about rumors going around about me, but you're Little Miss Perfect. Your reputation at our church is squeaky clean. Do you want your pristine image tarnished?" He stepped on the brakes. "Here we are."

"Can we just talk a bit more and settle this before heading off to meet Max and Jenna? They're newlyweds. They're probably so absorbed with each other, they won't even notice we're late." Rachel cast him a pleading look. "Please. I need to know if there's a chance you'll agree to take me with you."

"If I say no?"

"I think I'll find an escape some other way — get Knox to sign me up to join a missionary ship or something — but I'd rather go with you."

"Okay, but I told you my concern, and I think it's a valid one. Aren't you worried about the optics of all this?"

"We're not doing anything wrong. It's not like we'll be living together on our own once we get there, and it's not like you've ever seen me that way."

Jeremy bristled. Something in his expression or reaction must've given him away, because Rachel furrowed her brows at him.

"Right, Jeremy?"

"Come on. I'm not blind. I see you, and I'm not immune to how attractive you are. Not only that, there's so many things about you and your personality that I admire. This shouldn't even be news to you. I've already asked you out once, and you said no."

"Jeremy, you were delirious the one time you asked me out."

"Doesn't matter. It's out there now. I'm attracted to you, Rachel, so I think you should take that into consideration. Ask yourself if it's wise to go halfway across the world with me."

"If that's true, and it's something I need to worry about, why haven't you tried to pursue me?"

"Should be obvious." Jeremy shrugged. "You're your mother's daughter, Rachel. I know how Mrs. P sees me, how you see me. I didn't think I would ever stand a chance, especially since you already said no once."

"Because you were in rehab and going through withdrawals! No woman in their right mind would have taken you seriously."

"So, if I ask you out now, would you say yes?"

Based on the way her lips tightened and her shoulders tensed, it was clear the question had thrown her off, but her quick recovery was admirable. "Are you? Asking me out?"

Jeremy scrunched his nose to give it some thought. "No."

"Then what's the problem? You are attracted to me, fine. Whatever. So was Max, remember?"

"And so many other guys at church," Jeremy added.

"Not all of them acted on the attraction. Max did, but it didn't take long for the attraction to wear off when he realized how incompatible we were. I am more than whatever it is about me you are attracted to, Jeremy. You probably realize that, which is why you never acted on the attraction. People at church underestimate you because of all your missteps, but I recognize God's wisdom in you. All those years of Sunday School, all the services you sat through... His Word never returns void. Now that you're living a life for God, I have no doubt I can trust you to be a gentleman throughout this trip. I can trust you, right?"

"Sure." Jeremy nodded. A lump had formed in his throat as he listened to her words. He never imagined he would ever hear her say those things about him.

The corners of Rachel's lips tugged upward, her hair cascading to the side, as she tilted her head to give him her plea. "So? You're taking me with you?"

His brain tried to come up with more reasons not to, but the truth was he had been praying about this since the wedding, and if it hadn't been for what his father told him that morning, he would have already said yes. What was he doing? Why was he prolonging Rachel's agony? He drummed on the steering wheel. "Fine. I'll send you my flight details tonight."

The brilliant smile on Rachel's face made him feel like a hero. "Thanks, Jeremy. You don't know how much this means to me. I'd hug you, but it's kind of difficult to do that here. I'm just glad this is settled." She unbuckled her seatbelt. "Let's go see our best friends?"

Jeremy grinned. "Right. Let's go." He got out of the car, shut the door, and rushed to open the door for Rachel. The moment her feet hit the ground, she threw her arms around his neck and breathed out a thank you yet again.

"I'm glad to have you back," she added as they walked away from the car.

"What do you mean? We've been together all day."

She lowered her gaze, smiled, and waved her hand in the air. "Never mind."

On the short stroll from the parking lot to the coffee shop, Jeremy's heart opened toward a possibility he had never seriously considered before. By the time he opened the cafe's door for Rachel, he already had a seed of hope within him and a silent prayer he wasn't even aware he had kept in his heart until that moment. *God, is there a possibility that Rachel might be the woman for me? If so, open my eyes to all the ways we are right for each other.* The prayer felt right, so much so that Jeremy wondered what had kept him from pursuing her for so long. Was it just because of Mrs. P or had something else been holding him back until now?

Upon reuniting with their best friends, Jeremy remembered why. At the first sight of Max and Jenna together, Rachel winced. That was why Jeremy had hesitated for so long. From his perspective, it was pretty clear: Rachel still had feelings for his best friend.

sixteen

THE ONE WHO BROUGHT HER PEACE

Jeremy leaned back in his seat and took a sip from his mug of plain brewed coffee. Across the coffee table from him, Max and Jenna exchanged affectionate gazes, hands clasped tight, like they had glued their palms together, never to let go. Beside him, Rachel shifted in her seat and straightened the hem of her blouse over her thighs for the fourth time. Jeremy had been counting. She then took the bright yellow pillow with swirly white patterns and placed it over her lap before picking up her chilled mochaccino, touching her lips with the straw, not sipping anything, then replacing the drink back on the coffee table. All of this discomfort, she masked with that brilliant smile of hers — the one she had practiced and polished like a pro-smiler — hiding the way she gulped every time she said anything.

Did she feel like throwing up or something?

At the sight of Max's and Jenna's intertwined fingers, Rachel's lower lip twitched ever-so-slightly, it was barely noticeable. In fact, her discomfort since they had gotten together with their best friends had been quite subtle. The only reason Jeremy could spot the hints was because he had always been alert around Rachel, mostly because growing up, he had been careful not to misbehave around her, lest she report his misdeeds to her mother. This afternoon, he was even more alert than usual, and there was no denying it. Rachel wasn't herself.

"So, how's your first few days as Mr. and Mrs. Owens?" she asked.

Wrong move. Jeremy smirked. Why would she ask about that if she would only be bothered by their answer?

Max let go of his wife's hand — not glued, after all — and laid his arm over her shoulder, his thumb brushing against her shoulder blade. "She keeps me on my toes, that's for sure."

"Literally!" Jenna exclaimed. "I'm trying to teach him how to execute a perfect pirouette."

At that, Jeremy had to laugh. "That, I have to see. How about a demo?"

"No!" Max scowled at him. "Don't give her any ideas about me trying to do what she does in public. She might run with it."

"He's actually getting better at it," Jenna said.

"Not true." Max shook his head. "I have big feet, and I don't dance. Still, she insists."

"Only because it brightens your mood—" Jenna giggled "—every time."

"True. It's a good distraction."

That made Jeremy's ears tingle. What would they need a distraction from? He, for one, needed a distraction from Rachel, whose straight posture, crossed legs, hooded gaze, and reserved laughter hadn't escaped his scrutiny. The coffee shop's modern millennial couches and seating were designed for relaxation and comfort, and the rest of them had felt right at home from the get-go, but not Rachel. Her absent stare made it clear she wasn't as invested in this conversation about Max learning to pirouette, even if she was the one who had led the topic there.

Was he the only one noticing Rachel's unease around Max and Jenna? Wasn't Jenna her best friend? Sure, Jenna was in love and all googly-eyed for Max, but how was she not seeing this?

Max cleared his throat. "Enough about Jenna and me. How are you guys?" His eyes lit up with interest as he leaned in to listen to their response.

This was one of the many reasons Jeremy believed his best friend could become a great pastor. Max genuinely cared about people. Time and time again, he had invested his hours, emotions, and prayers into the lives of people God had placed in his life. "I'm sure a lot has been going on with you both. Jenna and I have been so busy with the wedding and now, our honeymoon—" Max looked at Jeremy "—we've barely had the time to catch up."

Rachel didn't respond to Max's question, so Jeremy did. "Cut yourself some slack. You just got married. No one expects you to focus on anything or anyone other than Jenna here."

"Still, we're here," Jenna said, "so we would love to hear from you guys."

"Nothing much to say," Jeremy said. The elephant in the room was that Rachel's parents were splitting their church up, but was that what he wanted to start with? "I'm leaving for the Philippines in a few days. Joshua and Vienna are leading a team there, and Rachel here—" he pointed at Rachel with his thumb "—has decided to go with me."

"Rachel!" Jenna's jaw dropped. "What?! Why didn't you tell us? That's great news! Is this your first time going overseas? I'm so jealous. I've never been outside the country." She grabbed her husband's arm. "Have you?"

"No, but I'd love to go someday. Amie still has an open invitation for us to visit Madagascar."

"Who's Amie?" Rachel asked.

"Max's ex," Jeremy and Jenna answered in unison.

"I would actually love to meet her," Jenna said. "She sounds amazing."

"She and Max dated for a bit in college," Jeremy explained. "Amie plays a part in Max returning to God."

Rachel's lips formed an O, her eyes wide, like she had been backed into a corner. Her lips twitched before that smile of hers snapped right out, covering up whatever was going on in that head of hers. She tucked her blonde waves behind her ear. "That's awesome. I didn't know that."

Jeremy stared at her. Hadn't Max mentioned that to her when they were dating?

"But enough about that," Jenna said. "You're going to the Philippines with Jeremy? How did this happen? Your mother's okay with this?"

Rachel cast Jeremy a cold glare. Only then did he realize she might have wanted to keep that life tidbit a secret. Oops. "My parents don't know yet. Jeremy just agreed to take me right before we came here to meet you guys, so I haven't had the chance to tell them. I wanted to go, because I figured I should grab the opportunity before committing to a full-time job, which seems to be where my life is headed next."

Max set his jaw firm as his eyes lingered on Rachel, as if to assess her. He exchanged glances with Jenna before adjusting his position — elbows on his knees, palms pressed together, fingers pointed at Rachel — to show she had his full attention.

Jeremy's breath hitched at the sudden shift of tone, like they had gone from pirouettes and exes to something more serious and relevant.

Rachel blushed at the intensity of Max's stare. "What?"

"Is that the only reason you want to fly halfway across the world?" Max asked.

Rachel lowered her eyes. "What other reason would there be?"

Max hesitated, his gaze drifting from Rachel to Jeremy to his wife, then back.

Jeremy leaned back, curious about what would happen next. Where was this conversation going?

Finally, Max came out with the topic they had all been circling for the past half hour. "I assume you've already heard of everything going on at Connect. Is that one reason you're leaving?"

Jenna's hand sought her husband's arm, as if to give him support.

Jeremy had just assumed they were having the time of their lives, because they had just been married! That was what Jeremy would have been doing if he was on his honeymoon, but Max wasn't that type of guy. He wasn't the type to drown grief or sorrow or responsibility by diving into whatever would distract, numb, or please. No, that guy was Jeremy, not Max.

Rachel once again straightened her blouse beside Jeremy. She sure was taking her sweet time to respond. He could only assume she was choosing her words carefully. She slowly nodded before finally answering the question. "Among other things, yes. I want to get away from the pressure of feeling like I have to take sides."

The newlyweds exchanged looks. Jenna opened her mouth to say something, but sealed her lips soon after, choosing not to say it. Heaviness replaced the levity that usually marked moments their group of four spent together.

The tension was more than Jeremy could bear, so he let out a laugh, more out of nervousness than anything else. All eyes went toward him. He shrugged. "Did you think this was what you were signing up for when you became a Christian?"

All stares remained blank until a glint of amusement appeared on Max's face. "Not at all. This is tough, to be honest."

Jenna nodded. "Heart-breaking."

"Painful," Rachel added.

"Necessary," Jeremy finished.

Max's brows furrowed. "Why do you say that?"

Jeremy smirked.

Three pairs of eyes widened at him like he had gone mad.

"We all grew up in church. That means we've seen it in its highs and lows, and we're familiar with its ins and outs. We've experienced firsthand how broken the Body of Christ is, and we know God's people aren't perfect, and that's okay, because it's not up to us to perfect God's people. We can't even perfect ourselves, so why are we sulking around like this is something that's unthinkable?"

"Because this is our church, Jeremy," Rachel said. "This is our family, and it's breaking apart. Don't you think that's something to grieve over?"

"All I know is that our family hasn't broken apart yet, so instead of grieving like we've lost it already, we need to find a way to fight for it. I mean, Scripture warned us about this. As the return of the Lord draws near, we will encounter more and more of these situations, but we take heart, right? He has overcome the world. Come on, guys. Are you really surprised this is happening? I mean, yeah." Jeremy rolled his eyes. "It is surprising, because this is the church we all grew up in, and no one ever expected something like this to happen to Connect — most especially Rachel here, who was far more faithful to the church than all three of us combined."

Jenna giggled. "True. Rachel was a good girl." She tilted her head to the side as she reached across the coffee table and squeezed Rachel's hand.

"Little Miss Perfect?" Max grinned.

"Princess Rachel," Jeremy added. "We were her knights."

"I was her dragon." Jenna nodded.

Max's eyes narrowed. "Weren't you a dinosaur?"

"Meh." Jenna's nose scrunched up. "To-may-to, to-mah-to."

Rachel laughed, but it didn't take Jeremy's brilliant observational skills to figure out it wasn't a real laugh. She hung her head and pulled her hand away from Jenna before clasping her fingers together over her lap. Her lips quivered, and a tear ran down her cheek. She wiped it away quickly before raising her eyes to look at Max and Jenna. "I'm sorry, you two," she said. "I never imagined it would get to this. For all it's worth, I think you'll make a wonderful pastor, Max. I've tried to talk my parents out of this, but—" She shrugged. "I wish none of this was happening."

"Rachel," Jenna spoke up, "Max and I have been praying for you, because you are precious to us both. You have inspired us in our relationship with the Lord in so many ways, and it breaks our hearts to find you caught up in this mess. We know how much you love your parents and how much you love us, so please know that if you choose a side or if you don't at all, it doesn't change the way we see you. I'm sure there are a lot of factors involved in you feeling this pressure to pick a side, but I hope Max and I aren't among those factors. We respect you and believe in your discernment and ability to listen to how God is leading you."

Rachel trembled as Jenna spoke. She tightened her lips, as if she was making an effort to hold back tears.

Jeremy stroked her back with his palm. He exchanged glances with Max and Jenna as Rachel let out a sniffle.

"Should we pray?" Jenna asked.

Both men nodded. They all held hands. Max bowed and spoke out a prayer that started with, "Lord, have mercy on us."

The moment those words came out of his lips, Rachel started sobbing. Jeremy's heart went out to her, but at the same time, a peace came over him — the kind that transcended all understanding. It brought about a trust in God to be her Comforter through this challenging season of her life.

By the time they finished praying, it was time for them to head off to Nolan Stone's concert, the venue of which was within walking distance from the coffee shop. With the women walking ahead of them, arms linked together, and Jenna's head leaning on Rachel's shoulder, Jeremy took the opportunity to check on his best friend.

"How are you dealing with all of this, Maximus?" he asked. "Must be tough to have to go through this, when you should enjoying your honeymoon."

Max shrugged. "It's a lot, but it's not like Jenna and I didn't see this coming. I'm just relieved that I discussed this with her before we got married. All of this would have been a lot more challenging for both of us if I married her and dragged her into all this drama without her knowing beforehand. We've both prayed over this, and we trust God's hand in it all. I'm more worried about Rachel. She's in a tough spot. I wouldn't know how to handle being in her position."

"Right." Jeremy nodded slowly. "Especially considering her connection to both Jenna and you. I didn't give it much thought before the wedding, but it is kind of weird that her ex married her best friend."

"Yeah?" Max chuckled. "It hasn't been an issue for me and Jenna, mainly because Rachel had a hand in bringing us together. Just like you, she saw me and Jenna being a couple before either of us started seeing each other that way. It never felt like an issue, because Rachel never acted like it should be an issue."

Jeremy rubbed the back of his neck and stroked the stubble on his chin. "So, you believe completely that Rachel no longer has feelings for you? I mean, you were her first boyfriend."

Max's brows met as he gave Jeremy an odd look. "What are you trying to get at?"

"The possibility hasn't crossed your mind?"

"Not at all. Rachel and I never would have worked out as a couple, and we've made it clear to each other that we believe it was the right decision to break up and go our separate ways — at least as far as a romantic relationship is concerned."

"Hmm." Jeremy decided to let it go. "Good to know that's settled, then."

Max nudged him. "How about you?"

"What do you mean?"

"Do you think you and Rachel could work as a couple?"

"That question came out of nowhere." Jeremy chuckled.

Max smirked. "Still, the question stands."

Jeremy didn't quite know how to respond, so he pointed at the five-thousand-seater theater ahead of them. "There's the venue. Ready to rock out to Nolan Stone's music?"

Max gave him a knowing look before nodding his head. "Yeah, yeah. Sure." To Jeremy's relief, Max let it go, because the only honest answer Jeremy could have given Max was "yes". By the end of the night, one thing was clear to Jeremy: he had a lot of praying to do, because if Rachel was no longer in love with Max, what was stopping Jeremy from taking his shot at a future with Princess Rachel?

Rachel never imagined a day would come when she wouldn't be able to stand listening to Nolan Stone's music. He was in top form on that stage. A born performer and a musical prodigy, he was clearly in his element, and because they were friends with the rock star himself, they got to have the best seats in the house, but at some point in the show, the strobe lights, the beating drum, and the hyped-up crowd exaggerated the impending implosion of pent-up emotions within her.

With Serene hidden away back stage with Lily Red, the only person Rachel could think of to inform that she wanted to take a breath of fresh air was Jeremy. The man, however, was fully into the music, fist-pumping to the rhythm, and singing right along with Nolan, who had complete command of the crowd, except for one. Rachel.

She squeezed Jeremy's arm to get his attention.

He turned to find out who it was, and his eyes lit up at the sight of her. A soft smile appeared on his lips as he quirked his brow up at her. With Nolan on stage hitting skyscraper notes to a frenetic song, it was almost impossible to communicate. Rachel leaned over so her lips were right in front of Jeremy's ear.

"I'm going outside!" she yelled. She was about to give him an explanation why, but before she could, Jeremy tapped Max's shoulder and made some exaggerated gestures meant to inform Max they were going outside. Max glanced at Rachel, then at Jeremy before nodding.

Jeremy placed his hand on Rachel's back and motioned for her to follow him. Rachel furrowed her brows. She didn't want him to go with her. She needed this time alone. How could she object, though? Jeremy was already using his full body like a snowplow, pushing past Nolan's fans to create a path for her to pass through, and if she trailed too far back from Jeremy, the path would close in a matter of seconds. A sigh of relief escaped Rachel once they were able to get past the crowd and were able to walk normally without getting glares from the people they were passing by.

Without a word, Jeremy walked alongside her toward the exit, like some sort of bodyguard tasked to protect her. Despite how flustered she was by the surprisingly monumental task of getting out of a theater full of die-hard Nolan Stone fans, a small smile snuck in at how Jeremy was stepping into the role of being her knight.

Once they were out of the theater, by an empty sidewalk next to a quiet parking lot, Rachel let out a long breath, as if she had been holding it in the entire time.

"You all right?" Jeremy asked.

"I am. It just felt like I might implode in there. Love Nolan's music, but there's just too much going on in my heart and in my head to fully be there."

"Heh." Jeremy stood straight and crossed his arms over his chest. "There's a missionary called Jim Elliot. One of his most famous quotes goes, *wherever you are, be all there*. I've tried to live by that ever since I stepped into the mission field. Whatever is going on back home or within me, I try to set it aside, so I can be all there, wherever I am. You'll need to learn how to do that on this trip."

"I don't know how you do it." She shook her head. "With everything that's happening, I'm always second-guessing if I'm doing the right thing. When I take time to just breathe and pray and grab hold of moments like this, I do find God's peace, but it seems to disappear the moment I'm back in the rush of things. I'm not sure how to 'be all there' when I feel like I'm constantly being torn apart and swept away in a million different directions."

He chuckled and bumped his arm against hers. "Come on, Rach, haven't you learned to *let go and let God* yet?"

Despite herself, Rachel echoed his chuckle. "We're going to dive into Christianese clichés? Is that what we're doing?"

"Hey. If the clichés still help, can we really overuse them?"

"I guess." She shrugged. "All I know right now is that I can't wait to get out of here."

"Piece of advice, Rachel, not that you're asking for it."

"I'm listening."

"Once we're out there, try to get the most out of the experience." He ran his hands up and down his arms and sighed. "Be all there."

Rachel was about to tell him she intended to, because the whole point was to take herself away from all the issues here, so why would she dwell on those issues once she was out there? Before she could speak up, however, she realized that was exactly what she was doing that evening. She couldn't quite focus on the moment, because her troubled mind was worrying over her parents' reaction to her leaving.

"I'll try." Rachel said it more to herself than to Jeremy. "I'll try to be all there." She then bumped his shoulder like he did to her earlier. "When did you get all wise and knowing, like some sort of owl?"

"You learn a thing or two when you've been to hell and back, but that's one journey I would never recommend you to take."

"No, I guess not..." Her words trailed away when she caught sight of what was written in ink on his right arm. "I will be light. Interesting. You've had that tattoo forever, I'm sure, but it's only now that I actually paid attention to what was written on it. It's actually quite beautiful."

"Also, one of the many reasons your mother isn't a fan of me."

"She'll come around." Rachel shrugged. "Max has a lot more than you have, and she got over it, eventually. Though it might be one of the reasons she thinks he can never be a pastor."

"Possible." Jeremy's jaw tightened. Max being the lead pastor and her parents' objection to it were still sore subjects for everyone. He quickly recovered and traced a finger against the blue sun on his wrist. "This was done on a whim. The last thing Mama Aida said to me before I headed off to college was that I will be light, so I had myself permanently marked with those words. That's how impulsive and reckless I was back then, and I've many regrets because of it, but this one. This, I don't regret."

"I never asked you what happened to you all those years you bailed from college. What were you doing the entire time? I find it hard to believe you were just in some dark alley, getting high, all those years."

"Embarrassing to say—" Jeremy scoffed "—but that might be accurate. Only it was in dark alleys all over the world. Globe-trotting on a budget. Running all the time, wandering and restless, trying to numb the pain by chasing highs." He snorted at himself before narrowing his eyes at her. "Is this really how you want to spend the night? You would rather miss out on a Nolan Stone concert and listen to my tragic life story?"

"I've been to Nolan Stone concerts before." Rachel sat on the edge of the sidewalk and tapped on the space next to hers. "I've never just hung out with you and listened to your story. I'd rather be with you here than be with a crowd of strangers in there."

"Okay." Jeremy sat next to her on the pavement. "So, where do I start?"

He spoke to her of his lowest points, but he also told her of the unique characters and experiences he had encountered as he explored the world. Her fascination grew as she listened, more so because of how faithful God had been to redeem Jeremy from the darkest, most hopeless moments of his life. She had expected Jeremy's stories to awaken in her an appetite for adventure, a thirst to experience the world like he had, but that wasn't what happened.

Instead, sitting on concrete pavement next to a quiet parking lot with Jeremy, she listened to his stories about God and His faithfulness to him. Without her being fully aware of it, Rachel forgot about the trouble in her mind and the weariness in her heart. In Jeremy's company, peace allured Rachel and spoke gently to her, bringing about a necessary calm to her restless soul.

seventeen

THE ONE WHO WASN'T ALL THERE

The extravagant homes in Nolan and Serene's luxury neighborhood never failed to take Rachel's breath away. As the SUV rolled past the gated estates and over-the-top architecture, a part of her fluttered with dreams of a future living in neighborhoods like this. Somehow, it didn't seem too far out of reach for her, but something about it also made her feel out-of-place, like she knew deep in her core that Nolan and Serene's world wasn't hers. She was a princess without a palace, and she was okay with that. Then again, she seemed to know instinctively what she didn't want, but never what she actually wanted.

Jeremy parked the car in the driveway, and they spent the next fifteen minutes helping Serene and Lily Red bring all their stuff inside the house. Once the mother and daughter were settled, Jeremy and Rachel headed for the garage to get in their vehicles.

"So, are you going through with this?" Jeremy asked as the garage door rolled up.

Rachel nodded. "I booked the flight last night. Right after you sent me the flight details."

"No way to convince you to change your mind?"

"Is that what you want?" Her brow quirked up, but a smirk was on her face. "For me to change my mind?"

"Honestly?" Jeremy stroked the growing stubble on his jaw. His green eyes swept over her, the right corner of his lip tugging upward, making for a lopsided and imperfect smirk that brought out his charm. "I look forward to seeing you out there in the wild. It'll be interesting to see how you cope."

"Wild? You make it sound like we're going to a jungle."

"Odds of that are low, but it's better to be prepared for anything if I were you."

"Prepared for anything—" she lifted both hands, palms up, as if to weigh something "—but bring only what you can carry."

"It's a life skill that can be quite useful if you decide to travel more." Jeremy's gaze lingered on her, as if assessing her. For what, she could only guess. Suddenly, he tapped the top of her car. "Well, I'll see you at the airport on Saturday, then. Message or call me if you need anything, okay?"

Rachel nodded as she clicked the button on her car key to unlock the vehicle. He rounded the hood to open the door for her. He certainly was no longer the Jeremy from her eighth birthday, who couldn't be bothered to open the door for anyone. As he waved her goodbye, reality hit Rachel. She was going through with this. Everything was in place. Her passport, her ticket, her luggage — well, some of it — were all ready and waiting for her to just fly off to her first trip abroad.

Once again, she came face-to-face with that paradox between familiar and unknown, even more so when she got back to her apartment where, within minutes of her arrival, her parents came knocking at her door. Upon seeing her parents standing there, all her resolve to leave evaporated. Did she have it in her to hurt them this way?

"Where have you been?" Mom brushed past Rachel and dropped her bag on top of Rachel's kitchen counter, so she could face-off with her daughter with no encumbrances. "Did you go on a road trip with Sam's children? What has gotten into you, Rachel? Why didn't you tell us you were doing this? You had dinner with us the night before you left! You could have told us beforehand."

"Hello, Rachel." Dad laid a hand on the small of her back and kissed her temple.

"Hi, Dad." Rachel gave him a smile before closing the door, bracing herself for the inevitable confrontation awaiting her.

"Don't do that, Robert." Mom stomped her foot on the floor. "Don't undermine my authority by acting like the nice guy while painting me as the bad guy. You were as upset as I was about what Rachel did. Don't act like you weren't."

"I'm not acting anything, Rhoda. I can disagree with my daughter's actions and still be happy to see her." Dad plopped himself on the living room couch. "A glass of water, please, Rachel. Ice cold, if possible."

"Do you want anything too, Mom?" Rachel asked.

Mom sat next to Dad and waved her hand in the air to shoo Rachel away. "Just hurry. We have a lot to talk about."

Rachel disappeared inside her small, but cozy and functional, kitchen. She hadn't prepared herself for this. She had been ignoring all calls from her parents throughout the road trip. This would not be an easy confrontation. Rachel pressed her palms against the fridge for support. *I'm not alone in this. Lord, You are with me. Give me wisdom on how to handle my parents. Give me courage, if it's Your will for me to tell them what I'm planning to do.* She stayed still for a moment and tried to listen, but there wasn't a response. Still, Rachel had enough faith to believe God had answered her prayer. He would give His answer in due time. She pulled the fridge open and retrieved a pitcher of cold water. She poured out a glass, added some ice, and placed the glass and pitcher on a tray, along with two empty glasses for herself and for her mother. They all might need a drink after this. After breathing in a deep sigh, as if to inhale courage, Rachel returned to the living room and set the tray on the coffee table.

"Thank you, Rachel," Dad said, after taking the glass from Rachel. He took several gulps of water, finishing half of it before placing it on a coaster on top of her coffee table.

Rachel sat in a chair facing her parents. "Mom?"

"Explain to me, Rachel. Why are you acting the way you are? Ever since you became friends with those people, you have changed so much!"

"Those people?"

"You know who I'm talking about. Max, Jenna, and Jeremy. You may not see it, but they have been such negative influences in your life. You used to be so obedient to your father and me, but now we barely know who you are."

Rachel found in herself an urge to defend her friends more than she had the urge to defend herself. "This is why I didn't tell you about the trip, Mom. I didn't want you to think that I was choosing them over you. It was just a spontaneous trip to celebrate Nolan's success and to have a few hours with Max and Jenna before Jeremy and— before Jeremy leaves." Her breath hitched. *Jeremy and I.* She had almost slipped and told her parents about her plans to go with Jeremy. Was it wise to just let them know? It would hurt less on their part, and it was better to walk in the light than to hide in the shadows.

"We didn't raise you this way, Rachel," Mom said. "I am so disappointed in you."

Rachel flinched. All her life, Mom had never said those words to her.

"Rhoda. Come on. That's uncalled for."

"She needs to hear the truth. This is a challenging season in our lives, and I would appreciate having my own daughter's support, but no. What does she do instead? She goes on a road trip with the very people who have caused us all this hurt!"

"Mom—"

"Listen to me, Rachel." Mom pointed a finger at her. "I raised you to be honest. I taught you to honor your father and me, because that's where God's blessing is. You may not understand our choices right now, but you will respect us. Do you understand?"

The war within Rachel escalated as she kept her head bowed, her eyes downcast. Was she being rebellious by trying to run from all this chaos? Was she making a huge mistake by doing this? How was she supposed to respond? "I understand, Mom. I'm sorry. This is a tough time for you and Dad, I know, and I'm certainly not trying to hurt you. The last thing I want is to disrespect you, but—"

"But what, Rachel? But you think we're wrong?"

"I didn't say that."

"Then what are you trying to say?"

Rachel balled her hands into fists over her lap as she shut her eyes. *Jesus, what do I say? How do I assure my mother?* Right then, one image drifted through her mind. It was of Jeremy's tattoo. The blue sun and the words that said, *I will be light.* The message was clear. She had to walk in the light, so she looked her mother straight in the eye. "Mom—" she looked at her father "—Dad."

"Rachel," her father responded.

"I love you both, and Mom is right. I don't understand why you are making this decision, but I know you both well enough to believe you wouldn't do something like this unless you genuinely believed it was God leading you to do it." Rachel clutched her knees, her fingernails digging into her leg. "But Mom is also right. I need to be honest with you both. I will not be taking sides. Not yours. Not Pastor Sam's or Max's. I don't even think there should be sides, and it breaks my heart that we have come to this. To avoid all the pressure of having to pick a side, I have decided to remove myself from the situation."

"What do you mean?" Mom frowned.

"Joshua Grant is leading a team on a mission trip to the Philippines. Jeremy is flying there on Saturday, and I booked a flight to go with him. It's a three-week trip with an open possibility for us to go to China after to see the work Josh and Jeremy are doing there."

"No. This is unacceptable." Mom shook her head. "No. You will not do this, Rachel. Your father and I need you here." She shifted on the couch to face Dad. "Robert, say something."

"Who will you be traveling with, Rachel?"

Mom's face drained of blood at her father's question.

Recognizing a window of hope, Rachel was quick to answer before her mother could object. "Only Jeremy and I will be on the flight from here to the Philippines, but once we're there, we will join a team of five women and three men, not including Josh. He will lead the team."

Dad sighed. "Despite everything going on, Joshua Grant is a solid man who has done a lot to serve the Lord and advance God's kingdom."

"You can't be seriously considering this, Robert. This is not the time to—"

"Rhoda, I'm trying to gather facts, so I can make an informed decision. Rachel rarely makes impulsive decisions like this — that, we need to give her credit for. I want to understand why our daughter believes this to be a proper course of action for her."

"This is madness. It's as simple as us not allowing our daughter to gallivant around the world with a former drug addict!"

"Mom, that's not fair." Rachel squirmed in her seat, an indignant defensiveness rising within her on Jeremy's behalf. "The man has cleaned up his act and has been serving the Lord overseas. Don't undermine God's work in his life, because you're upset about something Pastor Sam did."

"Do you see the way she talks to me after spending time with that man?"

"Rhoda." Dad sighed. "Enough."

Her father's demeanor gave Rachel hope that this could go her way. It was rare for her father to take on this tone with her mother, but every time he did, it silenced Mom, with no fail. This case wasn't any different. Mom huffed in protest, but she backed off immediately.

"What about the job we've been discussing, Rachel? What should I say to my boss?"

"Dad, I've been praying about that job offer the entire year. I don't have peace about taking it on. I don't think it's what God is leading me to do at this time. Sorry if I led you and Mom on, but there has been so much pressure from you both to take the job. I couldn't find the courage to tell you it's not what I want."

"Then what do you want, Rachel?" Dad asked. "How do you intend to make a living?"

"I don't know."

"Rachel—" Dad leaned in, his face a mask of seriousness "—that's not acceptable. You went through four years of college for a degree in finance and graduated with honors. Now, after we have allowed you the space to decide what you want for an entire year, you're telling us you still don't know what you want. Not only that, you drop on us that you're flying halfway across the world with Jeremy Sinclair. Don't get me wrong, Rachel. I believe he is sincere in his pursuit of God, but I hope you recognize why your mother and I have reservations about him. He has proven problematic in the past, not to mention what's going on between his father and us right now."

Rachel was at a loss for words. It stung to hear about her shortcomings from his perspective. Every word he had said rang with truth. Yet, something about him asserting himself in this situation made her proud of him. It was easy to ignore him sometimes, because he was a reserved and quiet person, often outshone by Mom's big personality, but though he wasn't like Max in terms of charisma and ability to draw people in, her father had wisdom Max didn't have. Years of faithful Christian living and persistent Bible study had helped him in that regard.

"Rachel," her father continued when she didn't speak up, "you're not a child anymore. Your savings will only go so far. With this trip, I imagine you've already spent most of it."

She flinched. She couldn't find an appropriate rebuttal. He was right. Simple as that. Should she call Jeremy to back out?

Her dad sat up straight and looked her straight in the eye. "Rachel, we need to come to some sort of compromise, so here's what I propose..."

Rachel gulped, bracing herself for the worst, but when she heard what her father had to say, all she could do was agree to his terms. There was an authority he had as the head of their household that Mom never had, no matter how much she tried to assert control over situations. By the time her father finished laying down his terms, all Rachel could do was agree. After they left, Rachel had never been more torn. Was Pastor Sam making a mistake in choosing Max as the lead pastor of Connect? He was so young, so inexperienced. Her father would also make a great pastor, a different kind than Pastor Sam was or Max could be, but a great one, still.

Rachel tossed and turned in her bed that night, unsure of what to do. Somehow, what had been easy for her as a child proved to be a lot more difficult as an adult, because for some reason, she could no longer figure out which way was the right way to go.

eighteen

THE ONE
WHO TOOK
FLIGHT

After all the fuss Rachel had put up about going on this trip with him, was she really going to stand him up, last-minute?

Jeremy brought out his phone and checked for a message from Rachel. Nothing. What was going on with that woman? Was she okay? His heart sped up and adrenaline rushed through him, making him take stock of where he was at when it came to Rachel Petersen. He had been looking forward to this trip with her. Spending time with her had opened his heart up to so many possibilities of a future he hadn't thought he was ready for. How would he handle it if she suddenly bailed on him? This was so unlike her.

Jeremy paced the floor, not far from the check-in counter that would get them to their flight. He hadn't even checked in yet. Last night, when he had given her a call, Rachel had begged him to wait for her before checking in. This, after all, was her first international flight, and she wanted someone to accompany her through the motions of checking in, security, finding their boarding gate. He tried calling her again. No answer. They had an hour left before the flight. There were barely any people left in line at the check-in counter. Thank God for the forethought to check in online the night before to secure their seats; otherwise, they would have the worst seats imaginable on a fourteen-hour flight.

He stared at the airport entrance, almost willing her to show up. Just when he was about to give up, there she was. Shock overpowered his relief, because Rachel wasn't alone. Right behind her was her father, pulling a huge light pink suitcase behind him.

Rachel arrived, disheveled and unkempt. Her usually perfect hair, not a stray strand in sight, was in messy pigtails hanging on either side of her shoulders. Her face didn't have a single trace of makeup, and it was clear from the tear stains on her cheeks, she had been crying.

Jeremy's shoulders squared and his fists clenched. Something about her appearance brought about a visceral — almost violent — response from him. What had happened to her?

"I'm sorry I'm late," she said, her voice hoarse.

"Not gonna lie. You cut it close, but you're here now. I'm relieved." Jeremy gave her father a curt nod. "Mr. P." They shook hands. "Is Mrs. P here?"

Mr. P shook his head. "No. She's a little under the weather right now." He tapped Rachel's back. "It's been a tough few days for our family."

Jeremy cast Rachel a concerned look, but her smile was back. "Do I have time to do my makeup?"

"No," he said, his tone firm and authoritative. "You can put on make up once we're on the plane, though you'll spend most of the flight asleep, so it won't matter what you look like."

"It's my first flight overseas. I will not sleep."

Jeremy grimaced. "Why? It's nighttime. There's nothing to see out the window. Once morning comes, it'll mostly be clouds and sky. That's gonna get old fast, believe me."

"What happened to enjoying the beauty all around us?" Rachel laughed. "Wasn't that what you were saying when you made me panic over how late you were to your best friend's wedding?"

He smirked at the role reversal. She had made him panic over her lateness, and he hadn't felt that way in a long time. He tried to play it cool, though, by shrugging a shoulder and rolling his eyes. "No matter how beautiful something is, Rachel, you can't stare at it for fourteen hours straight without the novelty wearing off."

The genuine laugh that came out of her lifted his heart. "Are you challenging me?"

Mr. P cleared his throat. Jeremy froze. He had forgotten he was even there. He could so lose himself — for fourteen hours straight, even — in the easy rapport that had somehow been established between him and Rachel.

"Thanks for coming all the way here, Dad." Rachel hugged her father.

"Message me as soon as you arrive in Manila."

"I will."

Mr. P turned to Jeremy. "I trust you to take care of my daughter, Mr. Sinclair. You're aware of how precious she is to her mother and me."

"Of course." Jeremy nodded. "You can count on me, Sir. If it helps to give you more peace, I can even send you updates, complete with photos of places we go to, people we've met."

"Rhoda and I would appreciate that a lot." Mr. P pointed at the large digital board displaying departure times. "You should check in now. You don't want to miss your flight."

"Right." The strangeness of talking to Robert Petersen like there wasn't this huge issue hanging over them wasn't lost on Jeremy, but part of him appreciated seeing how Mr. P loved his daughter enough to take her to the airport even if he might not agree with her decision to go. Was that the case, though? Or did Rachel find a way to get her parent's blessing when it came to this trip?

"Bye, Dad." Rachel embraced her father one more time, before they rushed through all the rigmarole of getting from the departure area to the boarding gate. By the time they reached their gate, their names were already being announced as the last two passengers left to board the plane. Finally, they were seated inside, with Rachel in a window seat and Jeremy in the middle seat beside her.

Only then could Jeremy ask, "What happened? For a while there, I was afraid you changed your mind."

"For a while, I did," was her honest response, "but after we prayed together as a family, I was so sure I had to go, so Dad let me. He said that with everything that's about to happen, it was better for me to take flight. So, here I am."

"And your mom?"

Rachel's smile faltered, her lips quivering, before her face fell. "Let's just say she's not thrilled with either Dad or me right now."

Jeremy could only imagine what she had gone through the past few days, but he could already tell it would be a challenge for Rachel to immerse herself in this trip. After all, given what was happening back home, it wouldn't be easy for anyone to "be all there".

Despite her proclamation that she wouldn't sleep throughout the flight, Rachel dozed off soon after dinner. By the time she woke up, the first light of dawn was already peeking through the clouds outside her window. Next to her, Jeremy was watching something on his phone, a big goofy smile on his face, and a hint of a tear in his eye.

"What are you watching?" Rachel asked as she drew her knees to her chest, her feet curling beneath her, as she shifted to her side, her head leaning against the backrest of the seat, so she could face Jeremy.

"It's the video I made of Cody and Lena." He wiped a tear away before it could fall to his cheek. "I finished it right before heading for the airport. I plan to upload it next time we get access to Wi-Fi. Do you want to see?"

"Sure. Give it."

He restarted the video and gave her one of his earphones so they could watch together.

"This was the couple you mentioned in your best man speech? The ones to blame for your lateness?"

"The exact ones." He pressed the play button and sentimental piano music started playing.

An elderly couple, probably somewhere in their late sixties, showed up on screen. The man was brushing his fingers against his wife's silver hair. She was straightening his shirt. He had a huge, satisfied grin on his face, and her eyes showed nothing but affection behind those big grandma glasses.

"Awww…" Rachel cooed. "They're cute."

"One afternoon," Cody explained to the camera, "Lena and I were browsing through some of our old photographs. Our families, our friends, our children's children."

"Oh!" Lena exclaimed as she reached for her purse. "I have pictures of our grandkids. We should show Jeremy. One of them was born just last month."

Cody held her hand. "We can show Jeremy later, honey."

"I'd love to see them, Lena," Jeremy said from behind the camera.

Rachel giggled. "That's why it took you time to finish?"

Jeremy nodded but couldn't keep his eyes off the screen, the smile still on his face. "So many pictures."

On screen, Cody and Lena locked gazes before Cody sighed. "As we looked at old photos of our parents, we both realized that my mother and her father both suffered from Alzheimer's later in their life."

"So," Lena said, tilting her head to the side and smiling, "we got to questioning, Cody and I. Is that sort of thing hereditary? We went to see our doc, and he said there was definitely a risk, though he said the risk is higher for Cody than it is for me. He said something about copies. Cody has more copies. I don't remember."

Information about Alzheimer's and the risk of inheriting it flashed on screen.

"The doc assured us though that it wasn't a certainty," Cody said, "but Lena and I have such beautiful memories and plenty of time, so we decided to go on this trip."

Lena's smile grew wider. "We want to go to the places of our youth, to where we first met, where we had our first date — can you believe that bowling alley is still there, Cody?"

"Maybe we should find out if we're still good at it. What do you think?"

"Don't be silly." Lena shook her head. "I can't carry those heavy bowling balls anymore."

"I meant dancing. Bet they still have that old jukebox over there."

Lena's face lit up. "I love dancing." She shimmied her shoulders and laughed before saying to the camera, "We're also going to the church we got married in before we moved to another state. Cody already talked to our pastor there. Oh! It will be so nice to see him again, after all these years!" She clapped with delight.

Cody faced the camera. "It's our trip down memory lane, Lena and I. We want to remember all the good things, because there's a risk we might forget."

"And we're hoping that if that should happen, if Cody and I forget, we will have people around who can remember for us."

As the music soared, the shot shifted to their children and their families waiting at the airport for them. Three generations, all in all. They traveled from different parts of the country and the world to meet Cody and Lena there, so they could all remember together.

Rachel sniffled as she watched Cody and Lena hugging their kids and grandkids. After, Jeremy showed photographs of their trip down memory lane sent to him by their youngest son. The last frame of the video was a picture of the entire family along with the words, *Remember Love.*

The video ended and Rachel grabbed a pack of tissue from her backpack and wiped her tears away. Her eyes cleared, she noticed Jeremy was crying, too. She giggled and handed him a tissue.

"That last part gets me every time," he said. "Aren't they just the most adorable old couple ever?"

"They are. That was lovely." She gave him a quizzical stare. "Never pegged you for a sentimental person, Sinclair."

"You should get to know me better then, Petersen."

She let her stare linger on him for a few seconds. "I'd like that," she said, and for the first time since their childhood, Rachel wondered what it would be like to spend a lifetime growing old and remembering love with Jeremy Sinclair.

nineteen

THE ONE
WHO WAS ALL
HERE

The Jim Elliot quote Jeremy had shared to her at Nolan's concert became somewhat of a mantra to Rachel during her first week in the Philippines.

Wherever you are, be all there.

She kept whispering it to herself whenever she found her heart and mind drifting back home, making it a struggle to stay present and immersed in what they were doing as a team. Their first three days, they helped a church organize and staff a citywide youth event. After that, they spent two days in an orphanage, a day visiting historical sites while praying for the city, and one day resting.

On the evening after their rest day, the team gathered in the spacious living room of the three-floor transient home they had hired for the duration of their three-week stay in Manila. Their team leader, Josh, and his wife, Vienna, sat smooshed together in a loveseat, while the rest of the team were in various positions — some on individual chairs, others on the sofa, others on the floor. Rachel sat in between Jeremy and her newfound friend, Malaya Cortez. Josh instructed everyone to share about their experiences so far, so one by one, people started mentioning things about the trip that had touched their hearts and moved them in one way or another.

Rachel's heartbeat sped up as her turn to speak came closer. How could she tell everyone that she was finding it hard to connect with anything they were doing? Nothing about the trip had hit her beyond a superficial interest over the places and people they had encountered. By the time Jeremy started gushing about things that had impacted him — and there were always plenty — Rachel's plastered smile was wavering. When he finally finished, all eyes fixed on Rachel, and for the first time since her birth, she didn't enjoy being the center of attention.

Her mind went blank, and it was as if their stares on her had morphed into symbols of all the expectation and pressure that Rachel had lived through for years. She fought to keep her smile, but her eyes watered and her lips quivered.

"Rachel?" Vienna shifted to the edge of the loveseat, her hand on her husband's knee. "You all right? Anything you would like to share?"

Jeremy's hand ran up and down her spine. She glanced at him, hoping to draw from his strength.

"You're safe here," he said, like he was reading her mind. "No need to put on a brave face."

A tear dropped down her cheek as she twisted her lips. "I don't know what to say," she admitted. "To be honest, I didn't come here with a mindset toward missions. I just kind of wanted to find myself." Another tear fell. Almost like a knee-jerk reaction to the sense of vulnerability sweeping over her, she grabbed Jeremy's wrist and clung to him for support. "Don't get me wrong. I want to serve here. It's been quite an experience, but I'm not all here. I'm still praying and asking God to show me what He wants to teach me through this trip. There has just been a lot of confusion, both around me and within me, and it has been overwhelming." At this point, the tears were running down her cheek, pooling on her chin, and dropping to her lap. Jeremy handed her a tissue, which she used to wipe her tears away.

An awkward silence followed, making her feel foolish, like she was some sort of nuisance who thought she could join a mission trip and make it all about her. She was about to apologize when Vienna rushed to her, knelt in front of her, and gave her a hug.

Rachel clung to Jeremy's wrist, but he gently pulled his hand away, squeezing her hand before letting go. Never having been in a situation like this, Rachel didn't know how to respond. She was used to being the strong one. Could she break down now without fear of repercussion? What choice did she have? All the ladies gathered around her to pray for her. She realized that was why Jeremy needed to let go of her, to give space for the women to minister to her. That's when Rachel let go. She eased herself into Vienna's embrace, and it was as if all the fear, trauma, and pressure caused by everything she had experienced at home and at church suddenly found release. As the team prayed over her, Rachel fell to her knees and asked God for forgiveness for thinking herself able to achieve perfection apart from Him, for her self-reliance, for her pride and vanity, for all the things she had hidden in darkness when she was supposed to be a child of light.

Rachel surrendered the title of Little Miss Perfect to God. She couldn't even remember how she had associated that term with herself, yet there it was. A lifetime of pressure cocooned in three words. Little Miss Perfect, no longer.

No. She was Princess Rachel, not because of anything she had done, but because she was a daughter of God, beloved of the King.

It felt like hours, the time she spent on her knees, loved on by Vienna and the other women on the team, but it wasn't even ten minutes. When it was over, Rachel was convinced she had just experienced a touch of eternity. Her heart was light, her soul was free, and the first person she could think of to share her joy with was none other than Jeremy.

A short ride on a passenger motor boat got them to the other side of a murky river intersecting the bustling city. The stench of the trash floating in the water and lining its banks assaulted Rachel's nostrils as the boat's motor roared to a halt beside a wooden ramp. One by one, their team filed out of the boat, careful to keep themselves balanced so as not to rock the wooden vessel. Rachel was the last to get out. At the pointy head of it, just as she was about to hop off the boat and onto the ramp, she wobbled enough to fear she might tip over and fall into the dirty water. Thankfully, Jeremy grabbed her wrist to hold her steady. She held on to his arm and hopped to the ramp that would lead her to solid ground.

"Thank you," she said once her feet landed on the pavement. She breathed out a sigh of relief. The rest of the team was already way ahead of them as they made the short walk toward one of multiple towns — *barangays* — clustered close to each other.

"How are you holding up so far?" Jeremy asked. "Last night must have been intense for you. I was wondering if you would ever run out of tears."

"It was intense, yes, but it was also necessary." Rachel pulled out a white satin handkerchief from her back jean pocket and wiped sweat from her brow. The humidity had a way of making the blazing heat worse. "The tears needed to come out. I felt a lot lighter after."

"Glad to hear that."

"How about you?" Rachel had a skip in her step. "Excited about the day ahead?"

"I'm not sure 'excited' is the word," Jeremy said. "Based on the last time we visited, it will be a lot to process." This was a surprise coming from carefree Jeremy.

"Is it that heavy?"

A reserved smile appeared on his face. "You'll see."

They waled side-by-side toward the direction the rest of the team had gone off to. The homes surrounding them were made of wood, others of concrete blocks. Each home was painted in loud colors of blue, green, or yellow. Almost every home was covered by tin roofs. The homes were quaint and so close to the other homes, sometimes, the only way Rachel could tell the houses apart were the different paint jobs and window designs.

"Do you know where we're going?" she asked.

Jeremy nodded. "Yeah. We'll get there. Did the girls tell you anything about where we're headed?"

"Malaya said something about spending some time with teenagers and children in a slum area in Manila. Is this it?"

"Not yet. This is the better part of the neighborhood, actually. The place we're going to is not too far from here. Be forewarned, though. It can be more than a little overwhelming — it's poverty unlike what we see back home."

Rachel squared her shoulders as a way to physically brace herself for what was ahead. She kept in step with Jeremy, as they both turned a corner and started down a path, stony, muddy, and unpaved. She wrinkled her nose. Why had she worn her white Vans today? They would be impossible to clean later. She giggled at herself. She was surrounded by all this poverty, and all she could think about was how to clean her shoes?

The houses got smaller and smaller as they walked farther down the road. At some point, they couldn't even be called houses anymore. Just boxes of wood, cardboard, and tin patched together to create some form of dwelling.

Jeremy nudged Rachel and pointed his thumb at a house with no door. Inside, a family of at least five were all huddled together on the wooden floor, watching a Filipino TV program on a large flat-screen TV on the wall. The juxtaposition of the expensive television set and the house of wood and tin threw Rachel's head in for a loop.

"I don't understand," she said to Jeremy in a hushed voice. "Is it rude to ask about the TV? Am I wrong to think it looks completely out of place?"

"Strange, right? That's a family with six children — the oldest is a fourteen-year-old, the youngest is at around two. The mother is jobless and is pregnant with a seventh child. The dad is a drunkard who does odd jobs here and there. I met the fourteen-year-old, Alex, last time we came here. We've kept in touch over the past year. He'll be here to meet us later."

"How are they surviving?" Rachel grimaced. "And what's with the TV?"

"To help make ends meet, Alex dropped out of school and is helping his uncle with seasonal construction jobs. As for the flat-screen, the dad won it from a raffle draw. Alex said they plan to pawn it off once they're desperate enough for money. For now, it's a source of entertainment, and to some extent, prestige around the neighborhood."

Rachel bit her lip as she tried to make sense of what Jeremy was saying. "They're not desperate for money now? Shouldn't they just sell the TV, so their kid could go to school?"

"The poverty spirit is a strange beast, Rachel. It's a mix of keeping up with the Joneses and a complete disregard for the principle of delayed gratification. Strange as it may seem, a lot of the kids here aren't dreaming of getting out of this community. They're okay with life here. It's their community. They belong. A lot of them drop out of school to take jobs that pay a pittance — just enough to get them through a month, a week, a day. They eventually get someone pregnant, get married, build up their own little shanty wherever, then the cycle continues for another generation."

Jeremy might as well have been speaking in another language, because Rachel's mind struggled to grasp what he was saying.

A little boy, who couldn't be any older than three years old, ran up to them and smiled. Dirt smudged his face, and a soiled white shirt draped loosely from his shoulders down to his knees. He had one rubber flip-flop on his foot, while the other was on his hand, and he was waving it at them like some flag meant to welcome their arrival.

Rachel waved back at him. Where were his parents? He had such an innocent and childlike joy about him that was making her heart ache.

Jeremy extended his hand for the kid to high-five. The boy leapt to his feet — one slippered, and one barefoot — to high-five him, before taking his hand and pulling him toward a wooden stall selling food. Rachel remained where she stood, in the middle of a muddy clearing, surrounded by dozens upon dozens of square wood, tin, and cardboard shanties. Everything she laid her eyes on shocked her — visual overload of something so foreign to her, she never could have imagined it. The imagery consumed her for a few minutes, but what surprised Rachel the most were the smiles on people's faces when they noticed the foreigners visiting their town.

"Barbie doll!" A little girl yelled at Rachel like she was accusing Rachel of being a toy. She then giggled, looked at the woman she was with, pointed at Rachel, and yelled, "Mama! *Amerikana o!*"

"There you are."

Rachel flinched when someone touched her arm. She turned to her side to find Malaya casting a concerned look at her.

"Are you okay?" Malaya asked.

"A little shocked, to be honest."

"Ah yeah. I get that. It's a lot to take in." Malaya nodded. "I was the same when I first joined the team last year. We're meeting with our contacts for orientation. Where's Jeremy?"

Rachel pointed at him. He was carrying the boy in his arms and was chatting with the store owner like they were long-lost friends. It struck her then how much he looked so out-of-place yet so in his element all at the same time.

"Jeremy, come on! You can chat later." Malaya waved at the store owner. "Hi, Dante! We'll drop by later to catch up!"

"Welcome back!" the store owner said, a brilliant smile on his face.

Jeremy passed the boy to the store owner and signaled for Malaya to give him two more minutes as he nodded at Dante to finish what he was saying.

"Are there many places like this in the Philippines?" Rachel asked Malaya.

"Unfortunately, yes. Especially here in Metro Manila. The poverty rate is high, and the capital is congested. To be honest, it's hard even for me to imagine this exists, because I grew up in another country, and our relatives here are considered upper middle class. Not all of the Philippines is like this, certainly not my hometown, but yeah. Places like this do exist, and there are more of them than I'm comfortable to think about."

Jeremy approached them and clapped his hands together. "Let's go?"

Rachel grimaced upon seeing a smudge of dirt on his cheek. She brought out her handkerchief. "You have something on your—" Without thinking, she just started wiping it off. "There. All good."

The stare Jeremy gave her made her bristle. "What?"

He smirked. "Nothing."

"Can we go now?" Malaya sounded irritated and amused all at the same time.

She walked ahead, and they trailed behind her. They passed through a narrow alleyway, the distant end of which went right back to the river they had crossed earlier. Malaya entered a small house. Rachel followed and was surprised to find the house air-conditioned inside. The cool air gave her relief. The heat had been punishing. They all squeezed into one small room with an alcove to the left that served as a kitchen and a staircase to the right that led to a second floor. On the staircase sat a couple. The woman had an infant in her arms. Meanwhile, the team sat on mattresses filling the available floor space — about fifty square feet all in all.

Vienna waved at Rachel and patted the space next to hers. Rachel sat next to Vienna and Malaya.

Josh stood by the stairs to give them instructions. "We have a long day ahead of us, so I'll make this quick. We've been working with our hosts, Phil and Claire Rodriguez—" Josh gestured at the couple on the stairs "—for a few years now. We used to perform skits, conduct prayer walks, and give away food and supplies, but this year, they asked us to do something else. Something more personal. So, we will group by teams of three. Because there are more women than men, Vienna and Malaya have divided us into groups of one man and two women. Our goal is to go to at least two homes, get to know the family, and pray for their needs. If there is an opportunity to share the Gospel, go ahead. We're in the Philippines. It's not a restricted country, people are generally open and welcoming, but still, be wise and discerning. Finally, Phil and Claire's local church will hold an evangelistic event here on Saturday, which we will all attend and help out with, so let us invite as many people as we can to the event. Any questions?"

No one brought up anything, so Josh clapped his hands and said, "Great! Malaya will group everyone up and announce who will be leading each team. After that, Jeremy and Malaya will lead us in one worship song; we all pray by teams, and off we go. We all come back to this spot exactly three hours from when we separate into groups. If you finish earlier, this is the place to go. Phil and Claire will be here to host you. Everything clear?"

"Clear!" several of them said in response.

Rachel expected to be teamed up with Jeremy and Malaya, so it came as a surprise when they teamed her up with Josh and Vienna instead. She couldn't complain, though. The couple had been doing trips like these for years now. She could learn a lot from them.

With groupings finalized, Jeremy took the space upfront. Phil handed him a guitar. She hadn't even known Jeremy could sing, much less play an instrument. Why did that come as a surprise? Jeremy was Serene's brother, and she had some pipes as well.

Jeremy strummed a familiar worship song from at least a decade ago. The song hit Rachel a different way this time. As she sang about how God was mighty to save, her heart expanded for the people around her. Somehow, for the first time since she had landed in the country, Rachel was completely there. She was in Manila with this team — heart, soul, and mind. Not a single part of her was still back home, worrying about what was happening there.

After worship, while an awkward shuffle of positions ensued around them, Vienna nudged Rachel. "I'm glad you're with us."

Josh squeezed himself into a cross-legged position in front of the women. "So? Is there anything you would like to share before we pray and head off to our assignment?"

Vienna nodded. "I've been reflecting on what Rachel shared last night, and it reminded me of the Jim Elliot quote. *Wherever you are, be all there.*"

Rachel had to smile at the mention of the quote. She glanced at Jeremy, who was already praying with his group, before returning her focus to Vienna.

"This trip has been a struggle for me, more so than usual. It's the first time Josh and I are traveling without the kids, and since we arrived, all I've wanted was to get back to our children. I'm sure they're safe with our church family in Ancoria, but it has been hard for me to be 'all here'."

"Next time, we should bring the kids," Josh said.

Vienna laughed. "Easier said than done, but I agree. Part of why I'm struggling is the thought that they would have loved to be a part of everything we've been doing here. Zoe would have loved the orphanage."

"Micah would have loved this town," Josh said.

"It's a shame we didn't bring them." Vienna sighed. "Still, as I said, I need to be here right now and open myself up to whatever God wants to accomplish while we're here. I had to ask forgiveness from the Lord for being so... detached." She squeezed Rachel's arm. "I have to thank Rachel for sharing what she did last night. It helped me realize I was going through something similar."

Vienna's words struck Rachel even as she smiled at a woman she had always looked up to. Was it possible Rachel's vulnerability was more relatable, more encouraging than her attempts at perfection?

"How about you, Rachel?" Josh asked. "How's your first glimpse into what Jeremy's life is like outside of home? At the very least, I hope hearing Vienna talk about missing our kids gives you a picture of what a kingdom family on the mission field can be like should you and Jeremy have one in the future."

Heat rushed up Rachel's cheeks. "What?"

"Honey, Rachel and Jeremy aren't a couple," Vienna said.

Confusion wrinkled Joshua's face. "Are you sure? All the while, I assumed—" He scratched his head. "Sorry, Rachel. I must have misinterpreted."

Vienna's face brightened, despite her husband's embarrassment. "Now that Joshua mentioned it, though..." She grinned at Rachel. "Do you see Jeremy that way? Is it something you would consider?"

That triggered a whirlwind in Rachel's mind. "I— Uhh..."

Jeremy's head popped up from his group. "I heard that, Vienna. It's a cramped space, you realize?"

Vienna laughed. "Sorry! We'll pray now." She winked at Rachel and whispered so only she could hear, "I totally see it. You and Jeremy."

Rachel gulped. Did they not know what was happening back home? At this point, she and Jeremy were pretty much the Romeo and Juliet of Connect Church. "We're just friends."

"Of course." Vienna patted Rachel's hand. "We should pray now. Hon, do you want to lead the prayer?"

Relief washed over her as they bowed their heads. Somewhere in the middle of it, though, Rachel snuck a peek at Jeremy, only to find him sneaking a peek at her too. As soon as their eyes locked, they both smirked and shut their eyes. Despite her amusement at the idea of dating

Jeremy, a question lingered in her mind. Was a future with him possible?

Unable to come up with a definitive answer to the question, Rachel focused on the task at hand. As they made their way through the neighborhood, an overpowering sense of helplessness gripped Rachel. This was a world, a setting, and a mindset completely foreign to her. She couldn't think of a way to help out other than to throw money at the situation and return to her home country, back to a setting that was so much easier to comprehend and deal with, because it was much more familiar. Despite all the troubles back home, at least it wasn't as confusing as this place and this different way of life God was now introducing her to.

As they walked on, Rachel kept a prayer in her heart for the places they were passing: *Lord, lead us to the right people, to the ones in whose lives we can make a difference. I feel ill-equipped to help, but You know the best way we can make the most of our time here. Help us make an eternal impact on the lives of the people we meet.*

Josh turned around to face them and pointed at a rickety house made up of patched wood, hollow blocks, and tin. "How about this one?" he asked.

They walked in, and the people they met proved to be the ones who made an eternal impact on Rachel's life. By the time they left the community, Rachel's pockets were empty, but her heart was full of hope. God's light truly had a way of shining even in the darkness. She couldn't wait to tell Jeremy all about it! Upon returning to their meeting spot, however, Jeremy's countenance told her he was in no mood to listen. He was leading a prayer with Phil and some of the other guys who had gotten there earlier. Fury was in his expression, and battle was in his posture. For some reason, though she couldn't tell for sure what they were praying about, Rachel found herself drawn to this image of him, mainly because she wouldn't mind fighting life's battles alongside someone like Jeremy.

THE ONE WHO MADE AN IMPACT

Bone-weary and overwhelmed by the experience of revisiting the slums and his friends back there, Jeremy withdrew to the room he was sharing with two other guys the moment they arrived at the transient home. He dropped himself on the bed and stared at the ceiling. Exhaustion took its toll on him, and he dozed off within minutes. By the time he woke up, the room was dark and his roommates were snoring. Hungry and unable to get back to sleep, he took a quick shower before grabbing his camera and making his way to the small living area on the second floor of the townhouse. He plopped himself on a couch and scrolled through the photos in his camera. What a shame that he wasn't able to bring it to the slums.

Josh had forbidden everyone to take pictures throughout the day for several reasons. One, they weren't there to take photos for social media. Two, they had an official photographer assigned to take pictures for their newsletter — Josh. Finally, they didn't want to go around the area showing off their expensive devices, making them a target for theft.

While Jeremy understood all those reasons and stood by them a hundred percent, he couldn't get rid of this sense of loss over all the great photos he could have taken. Of course, it wasn't like he could forget a lot of what had happened. The image of Rachel standing in the middle of that muddy clearing, with all those shanties surrounding her, would forever be ingrained in his mind. Just like the story of the gang leader he had met that afternoon. Uneasiness gripped Jeremy at the memory, so he pushed it aside and refocused on the pictures on his camera.

A light bump against the full-length window caught his attention. He creased his brows. It was past midnight. Was someone still awake? He stood up and slid the glass door leading to the balcony open. The humidity immediately hit him, and he would have backed out and gone back to the air-conditioned living room had Rachel not been there.

Curled up in one of the balcony seats — a shell-shaped rattan chair with a yellow cushion — her stare drifted from the distance in front of her to him.

"Still awake?" he asked.

"Can't sleep. You?"

"Same." He held on to the doorpost, his face aware of the humid tropical heat, while his back enjoyed the air conditioning indoors. "I was scrolling through the photos in my camera. I have so many pictures of you."

A small smile appeared on her face. "Oh?"

"You photograph well." He shrugged.

"I'll take that as a compliment."

"You should." Her smile eventually made him decide to brave the heat. "Do you mind some company?"

"Not at all." Rachel pushed the rattan chair next to hers toward him. "Join me."

He shut the door and welcomed a cool night breeze grazing his skin. Okay. He could bear this humidity for half an hour or so, if it meant hanging out with Rachel. A few minutes of comfortable silence followed, as they took in the view in front of them — not that special, because it really was just another row of townhouses with a backdrop of skyscrapers behind it. The peace and quiet was nice, though — not always easy to find in a city as bustling as Manila.

"What happened to you?" Rachel broke the silence. "You disappeared right after we got back here."

"You were looking for me?" Jeremy smirked.

There was no denial on her part. "Yeah. I wanted to find out how your day went, especially since that prayer time you had seemed intense. What happened?"

"You first," he said. "How was today for you?"

"It was an eye-opener." Rachel shifted in her seat so she could lift one leg to hug it against her chest.

"Care to expound?" he asked.

"It's hard," Rachel said. "It's a lot to unpack, but the gist of it is that this trip has shown me how blessed I am. What's happening back home suddenly seems so trivial when we put things into perspective. Like, we visited this one family, right? A single mom and her twin daughters. Lovely teenagers, so adorable and sweet. When we arrived, it was just the mom there. When she heard we were Christians, she was ecstatic. Apparently, she and her girls have only recently started attending church. She was telling us all about how they became Christians when her daughters arrived from school. It was a sweet time of prayer and fellowship. They even fed us cookies, which they called biscuits, for some reason."

Jeremy chuckled. "Yeah. I've heard that several times. They sometimes call cookies *bis-kwit*."

"It confused me, at first. Anyway, they were hospitable, even if it was easy to tell they didn't have much, you know? They still seemed so grateful and joyous and even generous with the little they had. So yeah, it was getting darker, and we needed to meet up with you guys. It was dark inside the house, even with the door and windows open. I was wondering why they wouldn't turn on the lights but feared it might be rude to ask. We said our goodbyes, and on our way back to our rendezvous point, the twins volunteered to walk with us. We loved their company, so why not, right? Vienna and I were a bit baffled, though, because they brought their school stuff with them. When we reached the end of their street, where a lamppost was, they hugged us goodbye." Rachel sighed. "Such a lovely pair, the two of them. Josh snapped a few photos of us with them, which I'm happy about."

Jeremy let out a huff, unable to hide his frustration about not having been able to capture memories from the trip. "So unfair that you guys got to take pictures."

"Perks of being on Josh's team." Rachel showed no signs of being sorry for him. "Glad I was with him and Vienna. I want to remember their faces. I'm afraid the comforts of home might make it too easy to forget."

"Those twins really made an impact on you, huh?" Jeremy shifted in his seat. Was that the end of her story? A bit underwhelming, in his opinion.

Her slow nod accompanied the quiver of her lips, almost as if she would break down in tears just thinking of them.

"If they made that much of an impact, which I hope and think they did, then even home wouldn't erase the memory."

"I'd like to believe that, but just in case comfort dulls my senses too much, it's nice to have pictures to awaken my heart for this place and its people."

Jeremy was about to respond, but Rachel lifted her forefinger in the air to stop him. "Story's not over, by the way."

"Oh okay." Jeremy chuckled. "Proceed then."

"We left them by the lamppost, and it was Vienna who eventually realized. The two girls were about to do their homework underneath the lamppost because they didn't have electricity back home. That was how determined they were to do well with their schoolwork." Rachel teared up as she spoke about them; in doing so, she revealed a tenderness to her that Jeremy hadn't quite seen in her before. "All three of us agreed to bless the family with electricity. You should have seen the look on the mother's face, Jeremy! It was like she had just witnessed a miracle, and we didn't even give them that much! I wanted to give them every cent I had in my pocket, and more, and I did! Even then, it didn't feel like it was enough."

"I would have felt the same," Jeremy said. "It's rare to find kids in that neighborhood who are determined to make a better life for themselves."

"Yeah, you told me earlier what a lot of the young ones are like in that community, so it made it all the more special to find those twins."

"That's inspiring. Thanks for sharing."

"Sure thing. Now, it's your turn to share. What happened?"

Jeremy sighed. "It's not as inspiring, unfortunately."

"Still eager to listen."

"It was intense. Phil actually joined our team because he wanted to take us to the house of a known gang leader in their community. He is about my age and already has a wife and two kids. There was something about him that stood out, like he had the ability to get you immediately at ease around him, even if you know in the back of your mind that you probably shouldn't trust him. When we shook hands, I noticed a scar in his hand — like a coin had been burned through it. Phil later explained to us it was a ten-peso coin. His gang is called *Sampu*, which means "ten" in Filipino, and their initiating ritual for new members is to burn the coin in the space between their thumb and forefinger."

"Ouch." Rachel winced.

"Yeah." He nodded. "Ouch is right. He brought the gang together as some sort of brotherhood. He has this leadership quality about him. Phil said he had the ability to gather up the youth in their neighborhood whenever he wanted. He calls, they show up. The sad part is he used to be a Christian."

"He's not anymore? What happened?"

"Let's just say someone who should have been taking care of him betrayed his trust in the worst possible way." Jeremy gritted his teeth. It angered him to even think of finishing the story, so much so that he clenched and unclenched his fists to release the tension.

Rachel caught wind of his motions and adjusted herself in her seat. She didn't say anything, a clear indication that it was up to him if he wanted to continue the story or not.

"I'll spare you the details." Jeremy hung his head as he recalled the grief and rage simmering within him when Phil first told him about the gang leader's story. "Suffice it to say that the church failed to be light, so he turned his back on Christianity — the gang leader, I mean. Now, it's almost impossible to get him to go anywhere near a church. Out of his relationship with Phil and Claire, he was still open to receive us as friends, but even when we prayed together, you can tell he was resisting. The Gospel was no longer good news to him. That's why we started praying when we got back. We were praying for him and all the kids in his gang. I didn't like not being able to do more, but I'm not the savior here. Jesus is. I have to believe God's not through with him yet. Phil and Claire certainly aren't giving up on him."

Rachel's tears reflected the way Jeremy felt inside. She opened her eyes and shifted in her seat. "I don't know how you stand it."

"Stand what?"

"The helplessness. Sometimes, I wonder if all we're doing is getting in the way of the Gospel. Just look at what's happening back home. We're bickering and fighting amongst each other for what? For position? Meanwhile, there are so many people in the world who have been broken by our own hands and so many others like us fighting just to stay in the light. It seems ridiculous how we're so wrapped up in who should and shouldn't pastor Connect. What would happen if we all just do what we're called to do, which is to bring actual good news — God's hope and love — to the world?"

Her words knocked the breath out of him. Was this Rachel Petersen talking? "Preach it." He let out a dry laugh. "I couldn't agree with you more."

"This is no laughing matter, Sinclair." She pouted and crossed her arms over her chest. "Even saying all that, I have this paralyzing sense of helplessness within me. Like, there's nothing I can do to change things. Here or back home, whatever I do, it's like it will never be enough. What have I done to be a light to anyone?"

At that, Jeremy had to scrunch his face at his friend — one whom he found ridiculously attractive, even more so now that she was all worked up about issues that mattered in God's kingdom. "Come on. You've done plenty to positively impact the lives of people around you."

"You haven't the slightest idea how broken I am." She sniffled. "I can't believe I'm crying again!" She wiped her face with the back of her hand, further spreading her tears across her face. "I'm a mess."

"A splotchy mess."

She playfully shoved him by the shoulder. "You're not helping."

"You're a beautiful, splotchy mess, Rachel, and it's okay. It's good to be broken, sometimes. God does love a broken and contrite heart, doesn't He? You've been Little Miss Perfect for too long, so maybe God brought you here for a little change of perspective."

"It's not very fun, is it?"

"What exactly do you mean by 'it'?"

"Being broken."

Jeremy snickered. "Well, God's discipline is rarely fun, but it always forms something beautiful in us and through us. From where I'm sitting, Rachel, in all your splotchy mess, I see beauty." He held his forefinger up. "Wait a minute. I want to get my camera, so I can take a picture." He rose from his seat to head inside.

"No!" Rachel grabbed his arm and pulled him back to his chair. "Stay here. You don't need to take a shot of everything, Jeremy. Some things, you can simply treasure in your heart. Let this moment be one of those."

"Fine." He gave in, mostly because her words resonated with him. He would always treasure this moment. Of that, he was sure. "For all it's worth, you have been a light in my life. You might find that hard to believe, considering what a wonderful relationship your mother and I have—" he rolled his eyes "—but it's true."

"You're just saying that to make me feel better." She collected her knees with her arms and pressed her thighs against her chest.

"What's with this version of you, huh? At the compliment I just gave, regular Rachel would flash that brilliant smile of hers, flip her hair back, and say she already knows all of that. Then she'll wave a hand in the air like a beauty queen and say hallelujah to the Lord for how awesome she is."

"First, it's hard to flip my hair back, because it's in a bun." She pointed at the mass of blonde hair over her head. To call it a bun was generous. "Second, nothing about me is regular. Please." She then waved like a princess, before lifting both her hands and saying, "Hallelujah to the Lord for how awesome I am!" She broke out in laughter, which he heartily joined.

"There it is. That's more like the Rachel I know." His laughter subsided as he fixed his stare on her. He took on a more pensive tone. "I'm serious, though. I don't think I ever gave you enough credit, but I am where I am, not only because of Max but also because of you. Not sure if you remember or even realize, but you're one reason I decided to return to the Lord and get clean."

"I am?"

"You are." He grinned. "Now, let me remind you." He told her the story of an evening encounter outside Connect Church between him and Rachel several years back, before concluding with, "When surrounded by darkness, we may struggle to find light, because we are the light, Rachel. We're the jars of clay, in whom God's glory shines through, and it is those whose lives are touched by His light within us who can see that radiance — God's glory manifested in all our brokenness. Remember that the next time you feel helpless. You may not see your own light, but others do. Remember that if God can get to me, if He can change me, He can do the same for the people we meet. It's all up to Him, not up to us. He is their Savior, not us."

As he spoke, her face lit up, and witnessing her radiance, Jeremy longed to remind her over and over again, lest she forget: she was light.

twenty—one

THE ONE WHO FELT LIGHT

Rachel couldn't keep the smile off her face as she listened to Jeremy talk. His recollection of his experience at rehab, the events that led him there, and the role Rachel played in all of it lightened her heart and soul. She would never tire of celebrating what God had done in Jeremy's life. It was a work of redemption, and as he sat there at that moment — handsome, young, and full of hope and life — he presented to her a living testament of what God was capable of doing for His prodigal children, if they would only return to Him. But what about people like Rachel? One who lived her entire life more like the other brother than the prodigal? What would Jeremy think if he found out she wasn't as pristine as the image she had been projecting? She wasn't actually as much of a straight arrow as she might have led them to believe.

Rachel leaned her head on top of her bent knee, her thigh pressed against her torso, her foot flat on the edge of her seat. She smiled at Jeremy, before expressing the opposing sentiment she was experiencing within. "You never found out what was actually going on with me the night you stole my phone, did you?" Of course, he never did! How could he? No one knew. No one but her mother.

"No, actually. What were you going through? Max made it sound like you were going through quite a rough time back then."

Could she really tell him the truth? Could she risk changing Jeremy's view of her irreversibly? Would he understand? She hoped he would. Of all the people close to her, it was he who had the greatest chance of giving her grace, because of all the grace he himself had received. Emboldened by that trust in Jeremy's ability to dispense grace, Rachel tested the waters.

"That summer, I was struggling with feelings for someone."

"Of course." Jeremy squinted an eye at her. "Max?"

She shook her head. "I had a huge crush on him before I went to college, but no, at that time, it wasn't him. It was someone else."

A slight flinch on his part made her bat an eyelash, but his quick smirk provided immediate comfort. "Anyone I've met?"

"It was Jenna." Rachel blurted the words out to strip off the Band-Aid and free Jeremy to process the implications. "She was my roommate, and though she never actually found out — and she never will — I developed feelings for her, this insane infatuation I still couldn't understand, over the course of our freshman year." Her words hung in the air. Rachel wanted to pry her gaze away from Jeremy, to hide from the shame of that confession, but the only thing that registered his surprise was the way his eyes grew for a moment, before he nodded slowly as she finished speaking.

"Is that why you were acting strange and sullen during their wedding? I assumed it was because of jealousy over Max, but it was over Jenna?" Jeremy shot her this confused, pointed look that made her squirm in her seat. "Rachel, what's happening here? Are you... coming out to me right now?"

Awkward laughter flowed out of her lips. "I wasn't aware I was acting strange during the wedding, but—" she set her jaw firm "—the answer to your question is yes and no. If I was acting strange, it was because something about that day triggered the residual guilt and shame I had for having harbored those feelings for her in the first place. It wasn't out of jealousy, more out of confusion over why I am the way I am sometimes." She set her head straight and leaned her chin on top of her knee, her eyes straight ahead. "As for coming out, no. That's not what I'm doing. God made me a woman, and someday, I will become the wife of the right man. It was just so confusing that I would be that obsessed with another girl."

"Why do you think that happened?"

She shrugged. "I was in college, missing home. Jenna was there, and she became sort of a lifeline to me — familiar enough to remind me of home, but different enough to help me embrace the unknown."

"Kind of like how Max was for me in college, only I didn't develop feelings for him."

Rachel squirmed. Jeremy had a point. She rubbed her palm up and down her leg as she processed what might have happened. "I guess part of me wanted to conform to my environment, to please the people around me. That was how I coped through the pressures and expectations at church. Same thing through high school. While I did encounter issues on gender identity and same-sex attraction in high school, I had my church community with me to keep me steady. Once in college, I was out on my own, and it was becoming more and more evident that the world embraced same-sex relationships as the acceptable norm, and not the strange exception. I wanted to believe that my own convictions were strong enough, but apparently, they weren't." Rachel let out a sigh, processing through her disappointment in herself. "It was the vulnerability coupled with the longing to please and belong, I guess. Also, Jenna is an amazing person, and she had so many characteristics that I wanted for myself, so it all fused together to form this attraction for her. Almost like an obsession, in fact. Does any of that make sense?"

"It does," Jeremy said. "I was never much of a people pleaser, so that's one big difference between you and me, I guess. Also, it's the spiritual and social climate we're in."

"Right." Rachel agreed. "It's a powerful spiritual and societal force nowadays. I guess I assumed that as Christians, we would be immune to it, but we're not. It didn't help that a lot of the girls in my dorm were in same-sex relationships, and seeing them made it tempting to start justifying the whole thing to myself. You know what college is like."

Jeremy squirmed. "Do I? I spent a year in college before dropping out, and I was drunk through most of it."

"Even in your drunken state, I'm sure you noticed the kind of influences we are exposed to in university. Your drunkenness was even proof of it, I think."

"I agree. It might have even gotten worse once you were in college, compared to how it was when I was there."

"You make it sound like we're a generation apart. You're what? Three or four years older than me?"

"Something like that." Jeremy shrugged. "That may seem like a short time, but how much has society changed in the past three or four years? Change has been gradual for decades, but it has progressively sped up over the past few years."

"That much is true," Rachel relented. "It was a confusing time for me, for sure, but as much as I love Jenna as a best friend, the flutters in my stomach are gone, and I don't see her that way anymore. Though I still would love to find someone who can make me feel the way she did. Like I'm home, but still stepping into the unknown."

A reserved smile crossed Jeremy's face.

Rachel could only guess what was going through his mind, but in so many ways, that characterization applied to him. Was the smile a sign that he was aware of that?

"How did you get over that season of your life?" he asked, diverting her attention back to the topic they were discussing.

"After you were released from rehab, I returned to our university and arranged for different housing, which was what Mom insisted I should do. If I wanted the feelings to go away, I had to distance myself from Jenna."

"Wait." He leaned forward. "Mrs. P knew?"

Rachel cringed. She hadn't meant to let that information slip out, but she couldn't take it back now. "She was the only person I told my secret to. I told her right after you tried to steal my phone at the parking lot."

"Hey. Let's be clear. I returned it."

"You did." She rolled her eyes before shooting him a smile of approval.

"How did your mom react to you telling her about your attraction to Jenna?"

A bittersweet smile appeared on her lips. "When the initial shock wore off, she entered battle mode. It was like she was willing to move heaven and earth to make sure I wouldn't walk that path. My mother can be overbearing and critical sometimes, but a lot of it stems out of a genuine passion for truth and righteousness. Unfortunately, a lot of people don't always see eye-to-eye with her when it comes to what they consider true and righteous."

"There's that and even if we do agree with her, it's her delivery that's kind of off. I'm sure you know what I mean."

Rachel nodded. "I do."

Jeremy lowered his gaze. "Look. As colorful as my history is with Mrs. P, I do believe she comes from a genuine, if not broken, place. I guess I just don't understand where that brokenness stems from. One thing I will never question, though, is how much she loves you."

Something about hearing those words from Jeremy shook Rachel. She was well aware of a lot of his negative experiences when it came to Rhoda Petersen. The fact that he would still be kind enough to see things through her mother's perspective made Rachel's heart smile.

"But back to your story. How did Jenna react to you moving out? She wasn't a Christian at that time, right?"

The light, fluffy feeling brought about by Jeremy's understanding of Mom lingered, even if the memory brought about by his inquiries left a bitter taste in Rachel's mouth. "She wasn't a Christian then, that's right. Jenna got upset about the whole thing, of course. She took it as me being judgmental and self-righteous, because she was being a bad influence on me or something. And in some ways, she kind of was a bad influence at that time, but the real reason was I needed to create space between us, because I refused to act on the attraction I had for her. That was difficult to do if we shared the same room."

Jeremy crossed his legs over his chair. "What happened next?"

"We drifted apart, stopped talking. My emotions for her faded. I believe it was our junior year when Max started visiting our campus to help with our college ministry. To cut the long story short, Max and I started dating. Jenna and I became friends again. Of course, you know what happened between me and Max. He broke up with me, I was devastated for a while. By the time I got over it and recognized it as wisdom, I already began noticing his chemistry with Jenna. Part of me still wonders if God allowed me to have that attraction toward Jenna just so I would be a way for Max and Jenna to find each other."

"Have your feelings for her ever returned after that?" he asked.

"Not really, no. Remnants of it, I guess. The guilt and the shame whenever I remember how fixated I was on her. The enemy tries to use it against me a lot, especially when I spend time with Jenna. He certainly was quick to send darts of accusation at me when I helped put together their wedding. Mom also sometimes insinuated that she was worried I might have those feelings for Jenna again, but I tried to assure her as best I could that it wasn't that way."

"Right. Anyhow, what if it's just a David and Jonathan situation? I mean, those dudes had strong feelings for each other. In the first book of Samuel, at Jonathan's funeral, David even stated that Jonathan's love for him was wonderful, surpassing the love of women. I don't believe for one second they had a romantic or sexual relationship, nor were they pining for one, but they certainly had a strong emotional — perhaps even spiritual — bond."

"How can I tell if that situation applies to me?

"Not to be crass, but do you want to kiss Jenna?

Rachel's eyes widened. "Of course not. It's not like I've ever wanted to have a romantic relationship with her. I'm happy when I'm around her, and I find myself looking forward to moments spent with her, that's all. The only thing that confused me was that it was very similar to what I felt for Max when we became a couple. If I was in love with Max, did that mean I was in love with Jenna?"

"Maybe you were in love with neither," Jeremy said. "Our current world's concept of being 'in love'—" Jeremy formed air quotes "—is so superficial, nowadays. It's all emotion and surface attraction, all of which fade once put to the test. Isn't that what happened to you and Max? Love, according to the Bible, is not that brittle. Remember what you said when I told you about my attraction to you? You said we don't have to act on every attraction. Your shame roots from the fact that you developed an attraction for another woman, but you rightfully never acted on it. If we let ourselves be ruled by our fleeting emotions and give in to everything that draws us, what kind of world would we live in?"

Rachel shuddered. "Don't even want to think about it."

"Right? But our world right now makes it seem like our fleeting attractions define our identity. I'm sorry for today's generation. It seems so much harder now to discover their identity in Christ, because the world teaches them to anchor their identity on their emotions, on the cravings of the flesh. As someone who has had my own seasons of trying to satisfy my worldly cravings, I know how punishing fleshly living can be. Those cravings are never satisfied." Jeremy dropped his crossed legs from the seat and set his feet flat on the floor. He angled himself to face Rachel. "I won't pretend to understand completely what you went through, but I pray today for God to continue to reveal His chosen identity and destiny for you. For all it's worth, I see you, Rachel. More than that, God sees you. You are steady and have always tried your best to walk the narrow road. The enemy will throw everything he can at you to derail you, but you have remained and you will continue to remain steadfast in your desire to serve God. He will honor that. Your faithfulness will not go unrewarded."

With every word Jeremy spoke, God's glory illuminated the shades of shame and doubt in her heart. By the time they both retreated to their bedrooms, Rachel embraced the brand new appreciation she had for Jeremy. She had just confessed to him the secret weighing heaviest in her heart, and somehow, he responded with enough grace to let her walk away from their conversation feeling light.

Author's Note: After the previous scene and before the next, Jeremy, Rachel, and Malaya attend a wedding in the mountains of the Philippines in the short story, Rachel & the Righteous Reckless. This read is optional and not necessary for you to continue, but if you'd like to read a fish-out-of-water story that adds a little layer to Jeremy and Rachel's romance, you can download the story for free by joining my mailing list at BookHip.com/ ZMMPHCC. You can also buy it via Amazon for 99¢.

- TEN DAYS LATER -

The number on his laptop's screen had to be some sort of error. How had a video Jeremy uploaded yesterday gone up to over a million views overnight? He refreshed the browser, expecting the number to go down and the error to self-correct. The number only grew several thousand more. Jeremy scratched his head. How had a video about him and Rachel going to a wedding in the mountains of the Philippines reached that many views? At this rate, it would even surpass the video he made of Cody and Lena, and that had gone viral and remained the most viewed video on his channel!

Stunned, he was about to refresh again when the notification of an incoming video call popped on his screen. Max. Jeremy put his earphones on for a private conversation with his best friend. The crowded coffee shop was a less than ideal place for an audio call, but he was curious about what Max had to say.

Max's and Jenna's faces showed up on screen. Their background revealed they were in the living room of the new house they had just moved into as a couple. Jenna waved at Jeremy, a huge beam on her face.

"Jeremy!" she exclaimed. "We just watched the video you uploaded. It was gorgeous. The editing, the shots you took, the princess herself. Rachel in that dress! Where did she get a dress like that while on a mission trip?"

"She's Rachel." Max shot his wife an amused look. "That's how."

"True. That's explanation enough." Jenna nodded. "But Jeremy! Let's not get side-tracked here. Your videos are going viral."

"Yeah. I saw the number of views for the first time right before you called, and I'm—" Jeremy grinned "—flummoxed. In a good way, of course."

"Flummoxed?" Max chuckled. "There's a word."

"An accurate word. I think."

"Are you alone?" Max asked. "You're in a coffee shop somewhere, yes?"

"Yeah. I'm waiting for Rachel, Vienna, and Josh to arrive. They are souvenir-shopping for their trip back home, and I don't really need souvenirs, so I figured I'd go to a coffee shop to check on my videos, so here we are now."

"How is Rachel doing?" Jenna asked. "I've never seen her as happy as she seemed in the video."

"Yeah. She's adjusting to everything faster than expected. It's like she was made for this. The wedding we attended was interesting, wasn't it?"

"Unique, for sure," Jenna said. "I wonder when yours will be."

"Don't pressure the man."

"Hon, you can't ignore the chemistry. We both saw it!"

"Guys, I'm right here." Jeremy waved at the camera. "Rachel and I are friends. Don't get it twisted. I admit, though, it feels kind of weird that this time next week, she won't be around anymore. I'm definitely not looking forward to sending her off."

Max and Jenna exchanged glances. She giggled. These two weren't even trying to be subtle.

"What are your plans after this trip?" Max asked.

"I'm returning to China," Jeremy said. "I have a team I'm leading there. Another two-week trip. After that, I'm not sure what's next for me."

"And me." Rachel plopped on the seat across the table from him. She was carrying nothing with her.

"Thought you went shopping for souvenirs to take back home." Jeremy raised a brow.

"No. I just wanted to accompany Vienna, but Malaya's there. They're all good. Who are you talking to?"

"Oh yeah. Sorry about that," Jeremy told Max and Jenna. "Someone just arrived." He turned his laptop so Rachel could see.

The delight that appeared on Rachel's face gave Jeremy a weird feeling. Was he starting to get jealous over how happy Rachel was when talking to Max and Jenna? He pushed the thought away. All that talk he and Rachel had been having over not acting on every attraction or craving was coming back to bite him.

Rachel waved at the screen before rushing over to his side, nudging him to move. Jeremy scooted over to give her space on the brown leather loveseat and handed her the other earphone, so she could join in on the conversation.

"How are you guys?" Rachel asked. "Are you back home? You both look amazing!"

"We're fine." Jenna said, before exchanging glances with Max. "It's been… challenging to be back, but we're grateful still. God has been good to us, and we're excited to live out this next stage of our lives. How about you? We were just talking about the video Jeremy made. It's gone viral, and you are gorgeous in it."

Rachel's mouth dropped open. "You've already uploaded it?"

Jeremy smirked. "I might have."

"I haven't seen it!" Rachel exclaimed. "How many people have already seen it before me?"

"Millions," Max and Jenna said in unison.

The color drained from her face, making Jeremy chuckle. What was she worried about? As Jenna said, she was gorgeous in the video. "They're exaggerating," he told her. "Don't worry."

A sigh of relief escaped her, but the relief was momentary, because Jeremy was quick to add, "It has only been a million views since I posted last night. We're not in the millions yet."

Rachel's lips slowly parted, her jaw dropping.

"You're so famous now," Max teased. "We'll have to roll out a red carpet for you once you get back home."

As quick as her shock came, it wore off, and Rachel shut her mouth. As if she had completely forgotten about the viral video, she made a face at Jeremy. "About home…"

His head tilted as he awaited her next words with bated breath. "Yes?"

"I had a talk with my dad last night." Rachel's gaze swept from Jeremy to their friends on screen. "I told him I wasn't ready to go home yet. The Lord is still leading me elsewhere. He wasn't happy about it at first, but when I told him how God has been leading me lately, he actually released his blessing, saying it might be for the best."

Jeremy's heart doubled its beat right then. She was staying!

"I was honestly not expecting that," Rachel said. "If he told me to go home, I would have, but not only did he give me his blessing, he even sent money to pay for my ticket to China."

"So, you're going with me to China?"

"Only if it's okay."

"Of course. How can it not be? Even if it'll be so much harder to convince Josh we're not a couple."

"Maybe you should be a couple." Max shrugged, amusement flickering in his eyes.

Rachel blushed. The hooded gaze beneath her long lashes sent somersaults within Jeremy. She shrugged before facing the screen again and changing the topic altogether. "So, what's happening over there? Candace mentioned something about all the youth gathering to pray about the situation?"

Max started talking in response to Rachel, but they had lost Jeremy to the blush on Rachel's cheeks and the breathlessness in her tone.

Was it possible she was starting to feel for him the way he did for her? His mental image of Rachel had always been with her back home, at their church. Never out here in the world with him. But here she was, in his element, thriving. What if Rachel Petersen could someday be Rachel Sinclair? Could something as impossible as that happen?

Yet again, Max was right. Maybe they should be a couple.

twenty-two

THE ONE WHO ATE CRISPY FRIED WORMS

Jeremy could not believe what he was seeing. Had Rachel really just popped a fried worm into her mouth?

With no sign of disgust or discomfort, Rachel chewed on the worm, like a food critic taste-testing a gourmet dish. The crunch between her teeth was audible to everyone at their table. All were silent as they awaited her verdict. "It's salty," she said. "Not at all slimy, like I thought it would be. Almost like a potato chip."

His eyes widened and his mouth hung open when she took another piece and put it in her mouth. "You did not just do that," he said.

"What?" Rachel smiled. "It's good. Have you tried these?" She pushed the bowl of fried worms to the center of the table. "Try one."

Jeremy scrunched his nose. He had been at this street-side *shāokǎo*[1] restaurant multiple times, and he had seen those worms served before, but he had never tried it. "Who ordered those?"

Malaya raised her hand, a sheepish grin on her face. "It looked like something memorable to try. It's not at all what one might think it's like in terms of texture. You should try one. Go ahead. Be brave."

---

1   shāokǎo : Chinese translation for barbecue.

As if to rub it in his face, Rachel took another half-an-inch piece of grub, placed it in her mouth, and chewed slowly. Her eyes twinkled with amusement as she waited for him to make his move. Who was this person? What had she done with the real Princess Rachel? This was more like something Jenna would do.

The rest of their team began chanting. "Try it! Try it! Try it!"

Unbelievable. They had only been in China for a few hours, and his team had already turned on him. Jeremy grimaced at the bowl Malaya was nudging toward him. Rachel pointed a camera at him. Why hadn't he thought of taking a video of her — or even just a picture — while she ate her crispy fried worms?

"Come on, Jeremy," Rachel coaxed. "You won't regret it, I promise."

"Fine, fine." Jeremy wouldn't be able to live this out should he back out of this dare. His lips curled as he picked a piece of grub. He threw it in his mouth and braced himself for an explosion of slimy worm innards on his tongue. The skin crunched between his teeth. The team applauded his adventurous palate. His brows lifted in surprise. Rachel was right. It was more like potato chips, given the saltiness and crispiness of the skin. "This isn't bad at all." He popped another one in his mouth. "This can be quite addictive. Who knew?"

"You should trust me next time." Rachel winked at him. "I won't feed you anything you'll regret eating."

"I'll take note of that." Jeremy's head spun with countless possibilities of food adventures with Rachel, but duty called. He checked the time on the wall. They had to get to the university in fifteen minutes. "We should pay now." He took another worm and bit into it. "Let's take this to go. We'll need to head out soon."

Rachel glanced at Malaya, who nodded at her.

"I'm on it," Rachel said, before bringing out a notebook and a pouch from her backpack. She headed for the counter, where she tried to communicate with the cashier through gestures and a translation app on her phone — an attempt to figure out how much she needed to pay for their meal.

"She volunteered for the challenge," Malaya explained, because she was the one Jeremy had been expecting to handle the team's budget.

Why was he surprised at Rachel's initiative? Of course, she would want to be of more help on this next leg of her first trip overseas. What would it be like to work with her on the field, long-term? With her organizational skills and ability to get along with people, what an asset she would be! Jeremy gulped and drew his thoughts back to the present before it could run off and paint a future with Rachel. *God, don't let me get ahead of myself.*

Malaya patted his shoulder and nudged him with her elbow. She nodded slowly, like she knew something he was also supposed to know.

"Malaya, what?"

"You have it bad for her, chief," she said in a low voice, so others won't hear. "We all see it. I'm surprised she doesn't."

Jeremy sighed. "Guess I have some praying to do."

Malaya tilted her head to the side. "No denial whatsoever?"

"Waste of time."

She grinned. "We're praying right with you, then."

"Please do." He wasn't about to waste his time denying what he recognized as true. He longed to be more intentional in pursuing Rachel, but he couldn't afford to take that step without a go-signal from the Lord, but what go-signal was he looking for, exactly? Did he want lightning to strike? The skies to open up and send a dove to descend upon Rachel as a sign of God's blessing? Was he over-spiritualizing this?

Rachel returned to their table, a smug smile of accomplishment on her face. "Shall we go?"

They left the little barbecue shop and stepped out into the night market, where several food stands lined the street. The night air was filled with conversations in Mandarin from students gathered in groups to enjoy a meal, while vendors hawked out their wares. The aroma of sizzling meat mixed with hints of garlic and this distinct, sharp smell of various concoctions of chili peppers made Jeremy smile, only because it reminded him of a time when the sights, sounds, and smells of China used to overwhelm him. Now, it was all normal to him, almost comforting, and from the wide-eyed wonder in Rachel's face, her smile genuine, and her expression curious, Jeremy believed this could be normal to her, too.

He sped up his steps to walk alongside Rachel. "Like what you're seeing?"

Her blonde hair — tied up in a high ponytail — bounced up and down as she nodded, the ends brushing against the base of her neck. "I can get used to this."

"Not missing home at all?"

She slowed down and took pause. "Are you?"

"Sometimes," he admitted. "In the back of my mind, I do worry about Dad, Serene, Max, and what they're going through, but I try to push it back, so I can be all here."

"I feel the same way about Dad, Mom, and Jenna."

"It's a feeling familiar to many who obey God's mandate to go, so we're in good company."

"Since you mention God's mandate to go, what are your plans after this trip?"

"Not sure, to be honest. I'm still praying. What are yours?"

"As much as this adventure has transformed me in ways I didn't quite expect, it's time for me to go home. I can't keep running. This peace I have, I need to bring it back with me there." She sighed. "But for now, I'm here. There's so much God wants to do through us, so I can't afford to keep second-guessing my choices. God has me exactly where He needs me to be right now."

"That's a good way to look at it."

"Hey, Rachel!" Malaya was at a clothing store, leaping up and down in excitement. "You have to see this! Come on, hurry!"

"Duty calls." Rachel grinned.

"Right." Jeremy rolled his eyes. "Duty."

Despite his reaction, he rejoiced in seeing Rachel get along with Malaya, whom Jeremy had already been on multiple trips with. It watered his hope that Rachel could be one among those sent to be on the field with him.

Was this attraction something he should act upon? Or was it one of those attractions he never had to do something about, other than to surrender it to the Lord? How though? Throughout this trip, his attraction toward Rachel had grown past the physical. She had a steadfastness about her that Jeremy admired. When she had confessed her struggle to him, even despite his shock that Princess Rachel — their Little Miss Perfect — would have such thoughts, she had earned his deepest respect, mainly because of her ability to still stand on her convictions. She had been vulnerable enough to bring all of it to the light to avoid being ruled by her emotions.

They reached the Chinese university, where a friend of Jeremy's was holding an English Corner for university students. It was a weekly gathering where students and young professionals could come to practice their English-speaking skills. They often joined whenever they visited China, because it was a great opportunity to get to know locals and build long-lasting relationships with them.

As they made new friends and split into different groups — women with women, men with men — Jeremy found himself stealing glances at Rachel throughout the night. The more he spent time with her, the more she grew in radiance and light in his eyes. Jeremy forced himself to snap his attention back to the task at hand, but it was getting more difficult to focus with Rachel around.

Mid-conversation with a Chinese student, Rachel's laughter distracted him yet again. The sight of her having a good time with her group lifted his spirits. Something about her both drew him in and challenged him. This was a woman who wouldn't be easily swayed by the ways and mindsets of the world, a woman who had lived a life genuinely trying to seek and please God. If Jeremy was to pursue her, he had to hear from the Lord Himself.

The four Chinese students in his group stared at him, waiting for his next question so they could continue with their discussion.

Jeremy tried to return his focus to them, but as the night wore on, his resolve strengthened. It was time to take a shot at pursuing Rachel Petersen. With that resolve came thrilling shots of adrenaline coursing through his veins, because he was convinced that a life with Rachel could be his greatest adventure yet.

twenty-three

THE ONE WHO EMERGED FROM A FAST

The day proved to be one of her most memorable, because of the risk their hosts took in getting them to the village south of China. At first, Rachel had been skeptical about the risk they had taken, but upon arrival, being able to spend time with the villagers and the children, being able to pray with them and their elders, made her feel like the risk had been worthwhile. As they distributed school bags, shoes, and various supplies to the village kids, Rachel's heart and perspective for the people of China expanded. She never should have questioned Jeremy's decision to send the team there.

What she could question, however, was why he wasn't there. It would have been amazing to talk to Jeremy about everything, but like he had been for the past two days, he was missing in action.

What happened to Jeremy Sinclair? Had he jumped ship and abandoned mission? Was he okay? What was he up to?

Rachel pushed back the ache in her heart, right when another big bump sent her butt flying inches above her seat before bouncing back down. Everyone else in the team slept soundly in an attempt to avoid getting dizzy from the bumpy, winding road leading them from the remote village back to the city. How they could sleep through this, Rachel had no clue. The combination of this roller coaster of a drive and the thoughts weighing on her mind foisted all her attempts to sleep, so she focused on the scenery they were passing by instead.

Malaya shifted in her seat. She lifted her head and blinked her eyes to check on Rachel. "You won't sleep at all? We still have at least two hours before we reach the city."

"Can't sleep."

"Still worried about Jeremy?" Malaya rested her head on Rachel's shoulder.

"He's our team leader. Why would he just stop showing up? You're a great leader, Malaya. You've been amazing at handling the team these past two days, don't get me wrong. It's just that I'm disappointed that he would shirk his responsibilities this way. Has he done anything like this before?"

Malaya patted the back of her hand. "Not at all. This is so unlike Jeremy. Through all our trips overseas, from what I can tell, he never takes his responsibilities lightly. He's gotten us out of a lot of tight spots because of his keenness when it comes to what's going on around him. I would trust him to lead a team anywhere in the world, any day. He has this intensity about him when it comes to the things he commits to out here on the field, so I have to believe he wouldn't hand the reins over to me and back away like this if he wasn't dealing with something important."

That didn't sound like the Jeremy she was used to, the Jeremy who risked being late for Max's wedding, just so he could take a video of strangers. Granted, Cody and Lena's story was priceless, but still... This version of a Jeremy who took his commitments seriously was a version of him Rachel had hoped to see more of on this trip, so his disappearance had only shattered her expectations. Then again, who was she to hold expectations over Jeremy?

Malaya's phone pinged. "Speaking of Jeremy."

"He sent a message?" Rachel fished her phone out of her jacket pocket. "We have data now?" She frowned when she found zero messages from him on her device.

"Yeah. There's data." Malaya peered out the window. "We're on the main highway already. We should be in the city soon."

"What did Jeremy say?"

"Hmm..." Malaya scrolled through the message on her phone. "Something about meeting with us before dinner the moment we get back."

"That's it?" Rachel frowned. It had looked like Malaya had read a longer message than that.

"That's the gist of it," she replied. She then shifted again, shut her eyes, and leaned her head on the leather lining the car window. She rubbed Rachel's knee. "Get some beauty sleep. It'll be an interesting night."

Rachel's ears perked up. Interesting night? Why? She was about to pry Malaya for answers, but her friend had already shut her eyes to go back to sleep, so Rachel backed off. Her phone started vibrating, and her heart leapt, hoping it would be Jeremy calling, only to have her heart drop when she saw her mother calling. Rachel threw her head back in surprise. It was almost five o'clock in the evening here; that meant it was almost four in the morning back home. Why was her mother calling at this time? Rachel placed her headset on and answered the call.

"Mom?"

Her mother sniffled on the other side of the line. "Hello, Rachel."

"Are you crying?"

"When are you coming home? How long will you keep doing this to your father and me? We need your support here. You don't know how much it will help to have you standing by us, but no. You're on the other side of the world, doing what, Rachel? What are you doing there?"

Rachel didn't have an immediate response. Her mother's voice was hoarse, a little broken, like she had been crying a lot. What was going on back home? Was it why Jeremy wanted to meet with everyone tonight? "Mom, what happened? Are you okay?"

"No, we're not okay. Everything is falling apart, and my own daughter has abandoned me." Sobs cut through the line.

Rachel was at a loss for words. Should she cut her trip short and go home? How would she comfort her mother? This was so unlike Rhoda Petersen. *Lord, what do I do? What do I say?* "Mom, I don't know what's going on, but have you and Dad considered striking some sort of compromise? What if changing churches isn't the way to go? It's too drastic and divisive."

"Are you calling us divisive?"

"No! Mom, I'm not calling you anything. You and Dad are doing what you believe the Lord is leading you to do, I'm sure. There's no questioning that, but have you paused to consider that Max may turn out to be a good pastor? He has so much room to learn and grow. What if Dad decides to mentor him instead of compete with him?"

"This isn't about any competition. It's like you don't know our hearts. It was never about position, or even about Max. This has always been about what is right. You don't know what's happening here, Rachel. The way this church has treated me throughout the years — even more so now — is not right. The things that have been said to your father and me these past weeks, it has all been so hurtful." Mom started sniffling again. "Rachel," she croaked out, "your father has been telling me about all the amazing experiences you've been having, and I'm happy for you, my daughter. I am. But please. After China, come home. Stop being so selfish. Enough of these adventures, when you should be back here. With your family."

Each word shattered Rachel's heart. She was being selfish for doing this. Her mother was right. "Okay, Mom. I hear you. After this trip, I'll go straight back home. I'm praying for you and Dad. Though I'm halfway across the world, you remain in my heart and prayers. I love you."

"I love you too, sweetheart. Forgive me if my words are harsh. It has been a hard time, and it would be a lot easier if you were here."

"I understand. I'll keep you updated, okay?"

"Okay. Bye, Rachel."

"Bye, Mom. And try to get some sleep."

"I will."

Once they hung up, Rachel's immediate impulse was to book a flight back home, right then and there, but one thing was keeping her from doing this: Jeremy. Now more than ever, she wanted to have a conversation with him, but where was he?

The quiet van gave Rachel space and time for her thoughts and emotions to simmer. When Malaya woke up, Rachel was staring straight at her.

"What?" Malaya grimaced at her. "Did you sleep at all? Aren't you tired?"

"I need to know where Jeremy is, Malaya. I need to talk to him. It's important. Trust me."

"Yeah." Malaya nodded, her eyes darting back and forth to acclimate to her surroundings. "I hear you, Rach." She sat up straight. "Jeremy is already waiting." She looked out the window. "We're in the city already. Good."

Fifteen minutes later, they arrived at the apartment a non-profit organization had allowed them to use during their stay in the country. When they stepped inside the apartment from the hallway, the first thing that greeted them was the dining table. On top of it was a generous spread of food. There were at least three dishes of meat — pork, chicken, and beef — plus at least five plates of vegetables, a big bowl of rice, and a pot of soup.

"Wow," one of the girls from their team said, "what's the occasion? And who made all these?"

Jeremy was standing at the head of the table, leaning his shoulder against the wall. "I asked a few friends to help me prepare. They'll be arriving after an hour, so dinner doesn't start until then. For now, I would like to make an announcement." He gestured toward the living room area.

When Rachel passed by him, she tugged at his shirt. "Where have you been? I need to talk to you about something important."

"We'll have time to talk, Rachel. I'll make sure of that." Jeremy brushed his thumb against her hair. "Sorry, I've been M.I.A.."

"You're okay?"

He beamed. "So much better than okay."

Rachel took pause. There was something different about him. The way his green eyes were glistening as they swept over her face alerted her senses and sped up her pulse. His smile had an exuberance about it that hadn't been there before. Something about his countenance was full of light — radiant. Whatever he was going to say, it had nothing to do with whatever was happening back home.

Jeremy held her elbow and led her to the living room before pulling up a chair for her. That was when Rachel noticed how all eyes were actually on them. Jeremy sat cross-legged on the floor next to her, as there were no longer any available seats in the crowded living room, with several already comfortable on the hardwood floor.

Malaya stood up and started introducing whatever this meeting was for. "You all have been asking these past three days where Jeremy was and why he hadn't been showing up. Some of you have your theories, guesses, and assumptions, and it has been interesting to witness how all of it has unfolded. Now, we all get to find out what our fearless leader has been up to, but I was asked to give a short introduction, so here we go. Three days ago, Jeremy approached me with a dilemma he was having, and because we've been through several trips together, he asked if I could take over for three days. When he told me why, I had to agree. I just had to!" Malaya clapped her hands together. "All I can say right now is Jeremy has been fasting for the past three days. What he has been fasting for and the results of the fast, he is about to reveal to us, so Jeremy—" she stepped aside and took a seat on the couch, where the women made space for her.

Jeremy stood up and made a sweeping gaze of the entire team before setting his eyes directly at Rachel. A huge smile spread across his face, and for some reason, despite how clueless she was about whatever was happening, Rachel's heart skipped more than a few beats. She had always seen Jeremy as handsome, but not the way he was right now. At that very moment, it was as if a veil had been lifted from him, and Rachel was able to see him through a different perspective, see him as he was and as he could be.

"I won't draw this out," Jeremy said. "I've been fasting for direction, especially when it comes to a certain special someone." Jeremy's smile widened as their eyes locked. "Rachel, I've been praying, and I would like to respectfully request everyone to pray with me. Especially you."

She swallowed hard. What was going on?

"I've been praying whether or not I should pursue you, Rachel, especially with everything that's going on back home."

"And?" Malaya asked. She was doing a poor job at suppressing her giddiness. She was on the edge of her seat, just a fraction of an inch close to falling.

Jeremy smirked and, in the most nonchalant way a man could say a sentence that had life-altering consequences, he declared, "I believe Rachel Petersen will someday become my wife."

twenty-four

THE ONE WHO WAS NOT NERVOUS AT ALL

Jeremy had taken his shot, and the ball was now in Rachel's court. What he hadn't expected, however, was that she would give him a taste of his own medicine and take her own three days to isolate herself and fast. On the morning of the third day of not having seen Rachel since he had made his announcement, Jeremy slipped out of the room he was sharing with the men and laid his laptop on top of the dining table. He had two important calls to make before hearing out how God had led Rachel to respond to his declaration.

Six in the morning in China was five in the afternoon back home. Hopefully, Serene would already be at Dad's place. Jeremy made the call. Within seconds, the faces of his father and sister appeared on his laptop screen.

"Hey there!" Jeremy waved. "Good evening to you guys."

Dad waved back. "What time is it there, Son?"

"Close to six o'clock. Have you had dinner yet?"

"No," Serene replied. "Still too early. We'll have it after this call. Nolan and Lily Red went out for a daddy-daughter date. They're bringing dinner after. Good morning to you. Everyone still asleep?"

He nodded. "Yes. It's one of our free days. Everyone can explore the city or meet up with local friends they've made. Most of them will likely sleep in, because there's no fixed schedule or activity for the day."

"Has the trip gone well so far?" Dad asked.

"Amazing. We've had a lot of breakthroughs, and I did something pretty huge which I want to discuss with you guys, but first, how are things over there?"

Dad and Serene exchanged glances. Dad took a deep breath, his shoulders sagging, his eyes tilting downwards. "It's been challenging. Robert and Rhoda, along with four other families who have been a part of the church for years, have stopped attending church since Max and Jenna returned from their honeymoon."

Jeremy cringed. Part of him wanted to ask which families followed the Petersens, but that wasn't important at the moment. The more pressing concern was how all of this would impact Rachel.

"Roughly a third of the church is gone, Jeremy," Serene said. "Not all of those followed the Petersens. Some just left because they don't like the controversy. They find it unbecoming of a Christian church to be this divided. Can't say I disagree."

Despite his determination to make Rachel a priority, Jeremy's heart broke for his church and for his father. Even if he had already known this could happen, part of him had still dared to hope they could prevent it. "I'm sorry to hear that. I was hoping it wouldn't get to this. How are you dealing with all this, Dad?"

"It weighs heavy on my heart, I won't lie. I'm just grateful your mother didn't live to see this happen. It would have devastated her, though in hindsight, I wonder if she had seen this coming all along."

"Oh?" Jeremy's brows shot up. "Why do you say that?"

"I often heard Aida praying for the unity of our church, and she mentioned to me several times that she was surprised Robert and Rhoda haven't tried to separate themselves, because they always seem to be disappointed with the direction we are taking the church."

"Why is that, anyway?" Jeremy asked.

"Well, there were three of us — Aida, Rhoda, and me. We started Connect Church when we were in our university years. I wasn't much younger than you were at that time, Jeremy. We were all in love with Jesus, and it all started just as a place to connect with one another, because we were all struggling with a sense of belonging and connection, and if there was one connection we wanted, it was with God. The gatherings weren't that large, but we were seeing fruit and true fellowship. As we continued in ministry, excited over what God was doing, I fell in love with your mother. When Aida and I became a couple, that's when Rhoda started to drift away. She became a lot more critical of us and the things we did. Eventually, the leadership of the campus group fell on Aida and me. Our small group turned into a church. We've always worried about Rhoda and whether she felt like we undermined her or pushed her away, but whenever we spoke to her about it, she always denied having any feelings of the sort. For a while, we thought she would change when she got married to Robert, but through the years, there was always something she was upset about, something that didn't please her. We never seemed to be doing enough."

Serene and Jeremy locked gazes through the screen. This was the first time Jeremy had heard of his mother suspecting Mrs. P might pull something like this. His chest still ached at the mention of Mama Aida. She would have been so happy with the announcement he was about to make, but it felt kind of off to tell his dad and sister about it now that they had just told him what was going on back home.

"There's not much we can do about it right now," Serene said. "All we can do is pray."

Dad nodded in agreement. "How is all of this affecting you and Rachel?"

"Yeah," Serene seconded their father. "You're both so cocooned from all the chaos, I'm sometimes jealous I didn't go on the trip with you, but all things work together for good, right? How are you both dealing with everything?"

"We don't talk about it much. We've pretty much embraced Jim Elliot's mindset when he said, 'wherever you are, be all there'. Rachel and I have tried our best to 'be all here', but I do think we should start talking about it, especially since we'll both be going home right after this."

His father's eyes lit up. "Really? Do you plan to stay home for a while? Or is this another short stop on the way to your next assignment?"

"I'm staying for a while." Jeremy nodded. "That's what the Lord is leading me to do for a season. Get settled until it's time to go again."

Serene narrowed her eyes at him. "What do you mean, get settled?"

Jeremy hesitated. He still didn't have Rachel's answer. Also, he had no way of knowing how the people back home would receive what he was about to say. Would his relationship with Rachel change anything at all? Would it somehow help make peace between their divided church? Or would the situation back home only make it impossible for him to be with Rachel?

There was no way to know, but Jeremy was sure about the direction he had received from the Lord. Of that, he was confident, so it was time to put the word to the test. He had to tell his family what he had told Rachel.

He scratched his head. "I did something," he said. "I'm not sure how it will impact what's going on, if it will have any impact at all, but it's pretty huge."

"Jeremy, are you and Rachel together?"

His jaw dropped. He couldn't believe it was his father who had asked the question. It would have been a lot less shocking had it been Serene. A wry laugh escaped his lips. "No, we're not," he said. "But I did tell her in front of the entire team that I believe she's my future wife."

It was their mouths' turn to gape open.

"You did what?" Serene asked.

"I fasted for three days to seek the Lord about it, and I just had this uncanny confidence that this is what the Lord wants me to do. I can't explain it to you. There was this moment of clarity and peace, and I'm sure of it. God is leading me to Rachel."

"Jeremy, this is crazy." Serene shook her head. "Rachel's parents have been asking about whether the two of you are a couple, and we've been backing you up, saying you're not. Even Josh and Vienna clarified, and now, you're coming back here possibly engaged? You really are something, you know that? Don't you ever do anything the normal way?"

At that, Jeremy had to laugh. "No one is more surprised than I am, Serene — well, maybe Rachel — but at some point along the trip, I saw a possible future with her, and now, I can't shake the idea that we're meant to be together. Every vision I have of my future now includes her." He took a deep breath before addressing his father's silence. "Dad? What do you think?"

"Does it matter what I think?" Dad shrugged. "What does she think? Has Rachel said yes?"

Jeremy grinned. "Not yet. After I told her, she asked for her turn to fast for three days to seek God's thoughts on this."

"First, Max and Jenna; now, the two of you." Serene chuckled. "Meanwhile, it took Nolan and I years to get engaged and years to get married because of our careers."

Jeremy scratched his head. "It's not like I thought it would work out this way. Maybe it's just the difference in generations. You're more from the generation of Caleb and Nova. They waited a long time, as well. Then again, don't we discourage long engagements?"

"That's true." Dad nodded and gave Serene a pointed look.

"Nolan and I have been happily married for almost a decade now. Spare us the teaching on love, courtship, and marriage."

Dad shrugged it off and looked at Jeremy. "Son, I want to make sure you know what you're getting into. Your time on the field has taught you to count the cost. This isn't going to be an easy relationship, especially given the less than perfect timing."

"I'm aware of that, Dad." Jeremy swallowed hard. "This is not something I'm taking lightly, even if it might seem that way."

Serene scoffed. "Most of the time, it looks like you take everything way too lightly."

"That's because it's hard to circle the world when you don't know how to travel light, gingerbrain."

Dad cleared his throat.

The siblings gave him their full attention.

"For all it's worth, Jeremy, I trust God speaks to you, so if you believe Rachel is the woman for you, then I will support you fully. Especially since the way the Lord assured me that Aida was the woman for me was very similar to the way He assured you. It was just this rest. This confidence that this was what He wanted. No voice from above, no visions, no dreams. Just peace."

Jeremy swallowed hard. "It means a lot to hear you say that, Dad. Especially after all the ways I've disappointed you and Mama, it would mean a lot to be able to make it up to you and make you proud the way I was never able to with Mama. I broke her heart so much, it led to her final breath."

Dad's eyes twitched before he narrowed them at Jeremy. "I don't understand why you would say something like that. We have always been proud of you. Sure. You were quite a handful at times, but we were always proud of the leadership and bravery we saw in you. You also had such a love for people and a depth of understanding for them. Aida always gushed about how powerful you would eventually become the moment you realized how unfulfilling the world is and started walking in the light. She always believed you would follow God with all your heart someday, and that once you did, there would be no going back. Look at you now. You have become exactly the kind of man she always said you would be. Your mother was already weak from a lot of ailments before the aneurysm took her. We didn't tell you, because we didn't want to worry you. Her death had nothing to do with you, Son. All these years, have you been blaming yourself for her death?"

Jeremy tried to hold it back, but the tears rushed down his cheeks as he nodded slowly. "I was stressing her out so much, and—" he choked up and bowed his head to wipe away his tears. "Thanks for saying all of that, Dad. It means the world to me." His cheeks tingled from the tears that had just fallen from his eyes.

"Your mother would be so happy to find out that you're pursuing Rachel," Dad added. "She always thought you two would make a good pair."

"Oh, Jeremy." Serene gave him a soft smile. "I wish I could jump across this screen to hug you. Mom would be so proud of you. We're all proud of you. Don't I say that to you enough?"

"Not at all," Jeremy teased. "You should make more of an effort to remind me how awesome I am."

Serene rolled her eyes and shook her head. "Whatever. Look. As insane as it is that you two would decide to get engaged—"

"We're not engaged yet. She hasn't said yes, remember?"

"Okay, fine, but my point stands. I believe she is blessed to have someone like you. You two will balance each other out and be strong where the other is weak. Now that I think about it, I'm not sure why we never realized how perfect a match this is!"

Jeremy gulped several times to fully recover from his tears. "Probably because we were too distracted by how much Mrs. P disliked us."

Serene's face blanked. "That is so true."

"Well, as lovely as this has been—" Jeremy sighed "—I have to go. Before that, other than to tell you that I told Rachel she's going to be my wife, I also wanted to ask for prayer. Right after this, I have another call."

"Why? Who are you talking to?" Serene asked.

"Rachel's dad." Jeremy grinned. "I wanted to talk to both her parents, but her father said it would be best if it's just him and me for now. No explanation given."

"Oh, we'll be praying for you." Serene deepened her voice to make it sound more serious.

They said their goodbyes. The clock ticked six-thirty. Jeremy braced himself for the next call. He had just found Robert Petersen's name on the contact list and was about to press the call button when someone pulled up a chair next to him. Despite the unexpected surprise, Jeremy's first impulse upon seeing Rachel beside him was to smile. "Hey there, beautiful."

Rachel stared at him as she leaned her elbow on the table to prop her chin up with her palm. "Are you nervous at all?" she asked.

"About what?"

"That I might say God didn't give me a go-signal to be with you. That I might say no."

Jeremy tapped his forefinger on his chin to make it look like he was thinking it through before saying, "No. Not at all."

"Interesting." Rachel grinned.

"Does that mean you are done with your fast? Are you going to make the announcement I'm expecting you to make?"

"Let's just say I've heard from the Lord already, and I'm pretty confident I heard right, but there's one thing that needs to happen before I can tell you what God said to me."

Jeremy narrowed his eyes at her. "Yeah? What's that?"

Rachel peeked at his screen. "You're about to call my dad?"

Jeremy nodded. "I was about to tell him what I told you."

"Gutsy." Rachel said. "Let's find out what he says. Do you mind if I join the call?"

Suddenly, Jeremy's heartbeat and pulse raced. It was one thing to have confidence about what the Lord was saying to him and Rachel, but Robert and Rhoda? There was no way these two would give Jeremy their blessing. It would take a miracle. Still, this was necessary, so he gave Rachel a curt nod. "Not at all." Even to him, he didn't sound as confident as he had earlier. Jeremy shared his earphone with Rachel and made the call.

Robert Petersen's face appeared on the screen. The moment he saw Rachel on the call with Jeremy, his face fell. Not a good sign.

"Jeremy." Mr. P nodded at him and then at his daughter. "Rachel."

"Hi, Dad." Rachel waved.

"I wasn't expecting you to be a part of the call."

"It was a last-minute thing."

"Shall we get straight to the point, then? What is this call about, Mr. Sinclair?"

Jeremy gave Rachel a nudge before addressing her father. "Sir, I am aware of everything that has been going on back there, and I hope you don't think I'm taking all of it lightly. I understand the weight of the situation, and how this might be affecting you and Mrs. P. However, over the month I have spent with your daughter, I have begun to see her in a new light. I've been praying for her."

Mr. P's countenance darkened. "Go on."

Jeremy gulped. "Last week, I started a three-day fast to ask God if I ought to pursue her. I finished my fast, believing she would be the woman I would eventually marry."

Mr. P shot his daughter a look, his jaw tightening.

When he said nothing, Jeremy continued. "After I told her and our team about what direction the Lord is giving me, she decided to spend time in prayer and fasting, as well. Since then, I have been gathering the guts to finally speak to you about this, which is why I've been trying to schedule a call with you." He looked at Rachel. "I still don't know what God told Rachel, if we're on the same page, but either way, I wanted you and Mrs. P to know what has been going on."

Mr. P stared at them through the screen for the longest time, as if he was trying to figure out if they were joking. He cleared his throat. "Have you two ever had a relationship before this trip? Be honest with me."

Jeremy and Rachel exchanged glances before both shook their heads.

"No, Dad. Never," Rachel said. "We've never been in a relationship. I never even saw Jeremy that way until a couple of weeks into this trip."

"Is that true of you as well, Jeremy? Have you never seen my daughter as a future partner before this trip?"

Jeremy gulped before shaking his head. "I'm not sure how to answer that, Sir. The truth is I've always held deep admiration for your daughter. There's something about her and the way she cares about people that has always drawn me to her. I've also always found her quite beautiful. All that to say that, Mr. P, I've always been attracted to Rachel, but it's this trip that made me realize I could have a future with her. I didn't want to do or say anything until I've heard from the Lord, so here we are now."

"What do you think about all of this, Rachel?"

The radiant smile that appeared on her face was enough of an answer. When she reached out to clasp hands with him, Jeremy had no doubt what her answer was going to be. "Dad, I can confirm what Jeremy heard from the Lord. It's interesting actually, because when I stepped out of my bedroom this morning, I was planning to call you to tell you and Mom about all this. The first thing I saw was Jeremy right here, about to make the call to you."

Jeremy couldn't believe what he was hearing. Even if he had been confident about what he had heard from the Lord, he still hadn't expected everything to turn out this way. Still, there was no way to be sure about how Mr. P would respond.

Mr. P closed his eyes and shook his head slowly, before finally, he started nodding. "This has been a tough time for all of us. It has been a humbling season for me and Rhoda. A lot has happened in your absence, and I honestly don't know how things could work out between the two of you once you get back home, but—" he sighed "—before Rachel went there, I gave her an ultimatum. I asked her to spend time with us, to seek the Lord with us, before she made her final decision about going on this trip with you. During that time, we secluded ourselves as a family and, for the first time, sought the Lord together. I was fully expecting the Lord to tell Rachel to stay here, but for the first time in her life, I saw my daughter be so sure about what God was asking her to do. She still went ahead and joined you on this trip. Mr. Sinclair, I won't lie. You are not the kind of man I dreamed my Rachel would end up with."

Jeremy's breath hitched. "I can understand why you would—"

"I'm not done, Mr. Sinclair."

"Oh. I'm sorry. Please go on, Sir."

"As I was saying, you are not the kind of man I imagined Rachel would choose, but I can also see why God would choose you for her. Rachel has never been more sure of where God is leading her until this trip — so much so that she would stand up to her mother in the most respectful way she knows how. My Rhoda has been struggling with this, and I don't know how I'll be able to tell her about this news, but for all it's worth, if you both are sure about what God is asking you to do, you have my blessing."

An audible sigh of relief escaped both their lips. Jeremy hadn't even noticed how hard Rachel was gripping his arm while her father was speaking. Her nails were already digging into his skin. He didn't care. God had just performed a miracle. They had actually gotten the blessing of Rachel's father!

Jeremy pressed his palms together and actually bowed. "Thank you, Mr. P."

"Now, let me make myself clear, Mr. Sinclair. You don't have my permission to marry her halfway across the world from here. Take my daughter home, face what is happening here together, and then we can discuss a wedding. The last thing I want to encourage is for you two to start a family, thinking you can run every time things get hard."

"Of course. I wouldn't dream of anything less for her," Jeremy assured. "We'll be home a week from now, Sir."

"I'll hold you to that." Robert smiled. "I know you and my wife haven't always seen eye-to-eye, Mr. Sinclair, and I am not at all happy about the prodigal seasons of your life, but I've heard many times of Aida's wish that someday, you and Rachel would end up together. It seemed like that could never happen as you both grew into adults, but God does have a way of surprising us. I'm sure if Aida was still here, she would be most pleased by this news."

"That, we can agree on, Sir." Jeremy choked up at the well of emotion springing up within him.

When they ended the call, Rachel confirmed a lifetime of adventure with him, when she traced her fingers against the tattoo on his arm, smiled, and whispered, "Together, we will be light."

TWENTY-FOUR: THE ONE WHO WAS NOT NERVOUS AT ALL

twenty-five

THE ONE
WHOSE LIGHT
WILL SHINE

Rachel had gone to her first flight away from home as a single sojourner, trusting God to lead her on an adventure and give her direction through her first trip out of the country. A month and a half later, she was lining up for her flight back home, with her fingers intertwined with a man whose very presence now made her heart rush with anticipation and excitement about the future. Still, even in his company, a sense of dread came over her over the trouble waiting for them back home.

"Nervous?" Jeremy asked as they waited to board their flight.

"A little," she admitted. "I don't know what we're going back home to."

"We did our best to make ourselves as ready as possible. The rest is beyond our control. It's all up to God now."

She grimaced. "I don't like not being in control."

"Too bad for you, because now that you're stuck with me, you'll realize more and more how little control we have." Jeremy grinned. "But that's okay, because God will carry us through." He lifted his camera. "Come on. How about a smile?"

"Really? You want to take a shot now?"

"Any time is the best time to capture memories. We can tell our future kids about that one time we went back home from China, only to discover our church had exploded into smithereens."

"That's not funny." Rachel rolled her eyes, but then smiled anyway, so he could take a photo.

"Beautiful!" he exclaimed.

They reached the boarding gate and handed over their passports and boarding passes.

Rachel linked arms with him as they made their way through the connecting tube leading them inside the plane. "Can you imagine planning a wedding while all the drama in church is going on? It'll be almost impossible."

"If there's anyone who can do it, it'll be us."

"You're not nervous at all?"

"Rachel, I'm about to marry you." He strode a few steps ahead of her to get to the airplane first before turning to face her. "One, I'm thrilled about that, but also, you're you. I have to step up to be the husband God meant for you. That's a lot of pressure, so yeah, Rachel. Of course, I'm nervous."

For some reason, that sounded like the sweetest thing she had ever heard. Rachel took his hand in hers again before they both got inside the plane and took their seats, with Rachel by the window. Once they were settled, she took another deep breath.

"Want to pray?" Jeremy asked.

Relief washed over her. Why hadn't she even thought of that? "Yes, please."

They held hands over the arm of the chair between them. Rachel closed her eyes while Jeremy started the prayer.

"God," Jeremy said, "we don't know all the details about what's happening back home. I'm not sure if we're ready for what's waiting for us there, but You said in Your Word that the battle is Yours. Whatever we come home to, it is You we are putting our trust in. The same way we trusted You to be with us when we flew halfway across the world, we trust You to walk with us as we return home. God, You are the One who goes before us, the One who is behind us, the One who surrounds us, the One who is within us. It is because of You that we are confident. It is because of You that we can be light. You make things light. Prepare us for what is ahead, and whatever happens, let us continue to be light."

"Amen," Rachel said. When she opened her eyes, she found Jeremy's eyes fixed on her. He smiled as he held her gaze. He leaned forward and Rachel gasped, sure that Jeremy was about to kiss her, but he stopped and brushed his thumb against her cheekbone.

"I'm pretty sure you have never been kissed," Jeremy said.

Rachel blushed. "Max never even tried."

He grinned. "I told you I need to step up. Not until our wedding day?"

Part of her wanted to say no, but Rachel gave in, anyway, because she was sure it would be worth the wait.

They relaxed in their seats as the airplane took flight, and throughout the fourteen-hour trip, anticipation began to build within Rachel as she imagined what her wedding would be like. Jeremy was right. There was no reason she shouldn't be excited about her own wedding just because of everything going on.

By the time the plane landed, Rachel had an electronic tablet full of notes about things she wanted for her wedding and a fiancé whose gait was confident and whose trust was anchored in God. Full of faith and falling in love, the couple walked out of the baggage area with hopeful hearts, and then there it was — a vision of what had been waiting for them. Rachel's parents were standing in the arrival area, while Pastor Sam, Serene, and Nolan were standing right next to them along with Max and Jenna.

A momentary truce that would hopefully turn into a long-lasting peace. Rachel flashed her usual smile — only this time, it was no longer a mask meant to appease people. It was a genuine one that only grew when her future husband lifted his camera and said, "This I need to take a picture of! Can everyone just squeeze together so I can take a few shots?"

Posing for the camera, Rachel looked forward to the day when they would show the photos to their future children and tell them about how their parents had gone back home and brought with them God's peace.

Now that they were light, it was time to let their light shine.

- THE END -

PRODIGALS ONCE
To find out what happens to the couples of Connect Church after Jeremy and Rachel return home, read *Prodigals Once*, sequel to the entire Prodigal Ones Collection.

THE ONE WHO WROTE YOU A NOTE

Thank you for reading *The One Who Shot Away*!

As I've already mentioned on the note in the beginning of this book, I'd like to share a little of my testimony regarding same-sex attraction.

It was a few years ago when I volunteered at a non-profit and found myself attracted to a woman I met there. She was talented and beautiful, and something about her made me feel like she "got" me. It was confusing to me, because what I felt for her was exactly what I felt for men I had been attracted to before.

The same signs were there. The inability to stop thinking about her, the longing to be around her, all the hallmarks of infatuation.

I had never experienced anything like it before, so I didn't immediately jump on the "I might be a lesbian or bisexual!" bandwagon. I was already in my thirties and had a more secure identity in Christ.

To cut the long story short, I didn't do anything about the attraction. She was my friend, and I treated her just as I would any other friend. The infatuation, I laid before the Lord daily, seeking His wisdom on how to handle it.

At some point, God revealed to me an area of bitterness I had regarding the country she's from. Once I surrendered that bitterness to Him and released forgiveness, the infatuation disappeared overnight.

264

I realized then how easily we mistake infatuation or attraction for something romantic, something deeper. To the point where we stake our identities — the very core of who we are — on it.

Thus, the traces of this experience with Rachel's attraction to Jenna, though I could argue her struggle in this book was more intense. I can only imagine what it is like for those who have a deeper, more physical and emotional, struggle in this area of their lives. My heart and prayers go to them.

I know this is a controversial topic in this day and age, and one of my readers mentioned that a lot of Christians have already made up their own minds regarding this issue, so I can get in trouble for even brushing upon this topic, but as I said, I felt it was necessary.

I believe God made us to be man and woman. Our identities and destinies are intrinsically woven into that original creation, and I can only pray for this generation and the generations that follow to discover who they are in God's eyes. Not who they are according to the world.

This is the last book in this collection, apart from a sequel that wraps the entire story line up, and I write this feeling like I've accomplished what I set out to do in writing these books.

I hope you were somehow blessed — perhaps even challenged — by the story of Jeremy and Rachel, as well as the rest of the couples in this collection.

I hope to hear from you, but for now, God bless you!

joanna alonzo

THE **O**NE
WHO WROTE
THIS BOOK

Joanna Alonzo is an author of Christian fiction novels with grit, grace, and wonder. She has a Bachelor's Degree in Information Technology from St. Louis University, but her creative leanings drew her away from software development to a career in faith and uncertainty. Her homebase is La Trinidad Valley in the Philippines, but she wanders around too much to have a permanent residence. She is a fascinated apprentice to the Greatest Storyteller of all and loves to highlight His supernatural grace in her stories. She loves having coffee chats with people, but isn't a fan of them hugging her too much.